JONAH'S WAR

Endorsements

Renalds tugs on the heartstrings once again in *Jonah's War*, a tale of a young man grappling with God's will. She seamlessly combines romance, action, and drama while addressing the subjects of abortion and racial discrimination. Both classic and timely, this page-turner will grip you to the very end.

—Audra Sanlyn, blogger and author of *Impact* and *Through the Eyes of a Veteran: A History of Winchester*.

Claudette Renalds's novels have all been page turners and *Jonah's War* is no exception. The moment I began reading the manuscript, I couldn't pull myself away2wwww until I finished it. Without a doubt, this third offering is her best work yet. I wasn't aware until I was halfway through this book, but *Jonah's War* is actually a follow-up to her first book, *By the Sea*. One hallmark of good writing is producing an engaging sequel that effortlessly reintroduces a story arc from the previous book without compromising the reader's emotional connection with the present characters and plot. The relationship between Jonah Abbott, an undercover narcotics officer who rediscovers his faith and Katy Wilson, a feminist social worker with a soft heart and a feisty spirit, is a testament to how God can restore the brokenhearted and unite two seemingly incompatible people in the bonds of true love. A relative newcomer to the world of Christian romance, Ms. Renalds's storytelling is on par with longstanding luminaries in the genre such as Karen Kingsbury and Sara Mitchell.

—Robert Christopher Brown, Licensed Professional Counselor and Author of *Coming Terms with The Potter*.

Jonah's War by Claudette Renalds, which shows how faith transcends politics, presents a much-needed message of hope and unity in diversity during this challenging, polarizing time. Through a compelling story, Claudette explores many issues that can divide people politically. She challenges readers to view those issues from a greater perspective than politics—through the lenses of personal holiness and social justice. *Jonah's War* shows that what counts is not whether we're liberal or conservative, but whether we're on God's side. Even better, it celebrates the reality that God is on everyone's side because of His great love for us all.

—Whitney Hopler, *Waking Up to Wonder* author, www.whitneyhopler.com.

Claudette Renalds has done it again. Not only has she created a sweet love story in *Jonah's War*, but has boldly addressed real life issues. Facing the devastation of a drug-related tragedy, Jonah Abbott abandons his college pursuits, training as a police officer to join the war against drugs. Deep undercover, Jonah clashes with newly minted social worker Katy Wilson when he arrests her on a tip about a female drug source selling out of the renovated home in his assigned neighborhood. With her upscale fashion and residence in the renovated house, Katy is not a typical to the urban community she traverses. She counsels and offers classes and friendship to the at-risk teens in her neighborhood.

We see Jonah and Katy working through serious life issues with integrity and grace—matters of faith, poverty, racial tensions, family conflicts, and at-risk teens. Not only do they fall in love, but they form community friendships and join with their urban neighbors and their colleagues and families to bring justice and equity to their sphere of influence and concern.

Renalds has created delightful characters and a plot which captures our attention. You will be entertained and challenged by her story.

—Johnese Burtram, Capital Christian Writers' Fellowship—Board of Directors, writer, speaker, teacher, supporter of Christian writers.

After reading Claudette Renalds, *Journey to Hope: The Legacy of a Mail Order Bride*, which I loved, I was so excited to read another book by this talented author. I was definitely not disappointed. *Jonah's War* is an even deeper look into making choices according to the plan of God. The answers to the relationship and social challenges presented in the book are a refreshing change of pace to what is currently acceptable in today's world. Choosing God's way to live will never steer you wrong. I'm so thankful for an author that offers biblical solutions to worldly dilemmas. Great job, Claudette.

—Wendy Wallace, blogger at www.OneExceptionalLife. com and author of *Victory Over Affliction:30 Mindset Challenges to Motivate You*

JONAH'S WAR

CLAUDETTE RENALDS

PUBLISHING THE POSITIVE
Plymouth, Massachusetts

COPYRIGHT NOTICE

Cover and Interior Design: Derinda Babcock

Editor(s): Judy Hagey, Deb Haggerty

PUBLISHED BY: Elk Lake Publishing, Inc., 35 Dogwood Drive, Plymouth, MA 02360, 2021

Library Cataloging Data

Names: Renalds, Claudette (Claudette Renalds)

Jonah's War / Claudette Renalds

304 p. 23cm × 15cm (9in × 6 in.)

ISBN-13: 978-1-64949-317-0 (paperback) | 978-1-64949-318-7 (trade paperback) | 978-1-64949-319-4 (e-book)

Key Words: drugs; gangs; redemption; romance; family; police; social work

Library of Congress Control Number: 2021942272 Fiction

DEDICATION

I dedicate this story of courageous faith to my three grandsons, Andrew Ryan Davis, Paul Mark Renalds, and George Charles Renalds. Amid a chaotic world, they are becoming mighty men of God. May they continue to grow in God's love and to stand with Him in love for truth, justice, and forgiveness.

ACKNOWLEDGMENTS

The older I grow the more I have learned to depend upon the work of the Holy Spirit in my life. Without His guidance, inspiration, and anointing, my writing would be just another story. Along with God's generous gifts come a host of others who have contributed to the publication of this book.

My heart overflows with gratitude to Deb Haggerty and her team at Elk Lake Publishing, Inc., including Derinda Babcock and Cristel Phelps. To my talented editor Judy Hagey who continues to make my writing better than ever.

Special thanks to those who agreed to read my work in progress and provide valuable feedback and encouragement: JoAnn Brown, Robert Brown, Johnese Burtram, Judy Cole, Kaycee Emilienburg, Gia Gray, Whitney Hopler, Joni Isaac of CareNet Pregnancy Centers, Johnnie Mikel, Pat Ogden, Audra Sanlyn, Wendy Wallace, Adria Wilkins and my sister, Paulette Zawadzki. Along with members of the Capital Christian Writer's Fellowship, they provide honest critiques and suggestions.

In addition, I am blessed with supportive friends including the BK Brunch Bunch, the Juliet's led by Jean Furman, and the Gainesville Life Group, led by Barbara and Earl Stinson. I depend on the prayers and encouragement of these faithful committed friends.

I am thankful for you, the readers, who have given excellent reviews, warm wishes and encouraging comments. You inspire me to keep writing.

Lastly, I am thankful for a supportive family: My husband, Charlie—my faithful friend and companion.

Our children, Sherry and Ray Davis and Steve and Sophia Renalds who are generous with their unconditional love. support, and prayers. As for my grandchildren, Megan, Elizabeth, Andrew, Paul, Anna-Maria, and George—they continue to make us proud.

CHAPTER ONE

Jonah Abbott crouched behind a weathered fence across from a targeted house on Fifth Street. He removed his sunglasses to wipe the perspiration from his forehead. A warm breeze stirred the weeds at his feet—the only movement for over an hour. Stretching his neck, he eyed the cool shade in the back of the house and wondered how much longer he'd have to endure the scorching heat.

When his legs cramped, Jonah sat on the rough ground and massaged his tight muscles. Relieved, he slumped against a fence post and closed his eyes. The buzz of his telephone jerked him from his stupor. "Hey, Joe. Anything on your end?"

His partner issued a frustrated sigh. "Nothing so far. We've either been set up or our suspect was tipped off."

Jonah stood and shook the numbness from his legs. He stretched his back and looked toward the deserted street. "Could be, but I'm not quitting until I have that low-life behind bars. Shutting down this one operation would put a huge dent in the area's drug trafficking."

Jonah wiped each hand down the front of his T-shirt, then tightened his grip on the phone. According to their informants, the storybook house had become a hub for illegal activity. They claimed people came and went openly—often picking up packages at the door. The woman lured young people into her home, many staying through the night. According to one source, she sold her body along with the drugs. In anger, Jonah aimed a discarded can at the disgusting house and kicked. The container hit the fence with a bam.

Jonah heard Joe Riley clearing his throat. "What was that?"

"Sorry, just releasing a bit of frustration. This heat messes with my head. Have you heard anything from the rest of the team?"

"Not since Chip checked in an hour ago. He says there's a vehicle in the garage. If our suspect fled, she left behind a brand-new Volkswagen. I'm beginning to think we're wasting our time."

"Just another reason to doubt those snitches. If the woman doesn't return within the hour, we'll move in with the search warrant. Arresting her for possession would be better than nothing."

The call ended, Jonah thought of the residents living in the nearby homes. They represented a mixture of cultures and behaviors. From his first day working the area, he noticed small children playing unsupervised on the street corners. Young people congregating near the 7-Eleven kept time to the beat of rap music. To escape their unairconditioned homes, senior citizens rocked away the afternoons on their front porches, welcoming anyone willing to join them.

The neighborhood to his left represented an entirely different culture. From the open windows, arguments in Spanish could be heard above the beat of salsa music. Young people wandered aimlessly, often finding acceptance through membership in gangs. Early each morning, day laborers gathered on the street corner waiting for someone to offer them a job.

Unemployment had reached an all-time high, with many dependent on welfare. Those who did have money often received it from nefarious means. While the gangs marked out their territories, drug pushers moved freely across invisible lines, luring the unsupervised young people into addictive traps.

Jonah tightened his fist at the injustice—the very reason he quit college to join the Trenton police force. He had vowed to do everything possible to arrest the dealers responsible for the rise in drug abuse and tragic overdose deaths.

With another look toward the street, Jonah willed his mind to focus. For the past few weeks, his undercover team had divided their time between the two neighborhoods, making contacts and seeking information that might lead to arrests.

Early that morning Jonah did a double take when he glimpsed the targeted house. Casual drive-bys had not prepared his team for what they encountered. The well-maintained house didn't fit the image of a typical crack house.

Jonah admired the attractive home with its fresh coat of white paint and shiny black shutters. Window boxes filled with colorful, cascading flowers complemented the potted ferns hanging on the wrap-around porch. Wicker furniture with bright-colored cushions beckoned guests to relax in the peaceful setting.

The Victorian two-story was surrounded by a white picket fence enclosing a lush garden with magnolias, crepe myrtle, and azaleas. A huge live oak tree dripping with Spanish moss shaded much of the backyard. The rope swing hanging from one of the high branches danced in the breeze. What child wouldn't love to play in such a setting?

Jonah scratched his scruffy beard and released a breath filled with longing. One day he wanted to own such a house. He let his mind wander as he imagined a beautiful woman dressed in white, pushing a miniature of herself on the swing and laughing playfully. The daydream reminded him of the girlfriend he'd lost to a drug overdose.

After three years, Jonah still grieved Monica's mysterious death. He had met the energetic young woman during his first semester at the university. Forced to share a table at the crowded student center, they became fast friends. Only weeks into their friendship, they acknowledged their mutual attraction. By spring, Jonah had visions of marriage and a family. The beautiful, talented freshman met every requirement for the kind of woman he had hoped to marry one day.

But something changed over the last summer before their senior year. Monica became a different person. She had been the one who kept him grounded—the one who preferred the library over social activities—the girl who didn't attend wild off-campus parties. Though she spoke openly against drug and alcohol abuse, she died of an overdose at the kind of party she abhorred. The circumstances surrounding her death continued to haunt Jonah.

With the toe of his sneaker, Jonah pushed at a rock lodged below the surface of the dry ground. Monica had begged him to go with her to the party, but he had brushed her off, citing a meeting with his study group. Never thinking she would go without him, he began to worry when she didn't answer her phone. His life took a decisive turn the next morning when his numerous calls were returned by a police detective. If he had gone with her, his friend would still be alive.

In his peripheral vision, Jonah spotted movement to his left. Shaking off the painful memories, a rush of adrenaline alerted his senses. A young woman came down the street toward him carrying a plastic grocery bag in each hand. She wore an expensive silk blouse, designer jeans, and top of the line athletic shoes. She appeared as misplaced as Lucy in Narnia.

Jonah blinked a few times at the unexpected sight. Preoccupied by the sounds coming from her earbuds, the woman bounced along to the beat, even skipping a time or two. Her dance drew his attention to her long, slender legs. As his eyes moved upward along her perfectly formed body, warmth flooded his insides. He hadn't been attracted to a woman since Monica. That one experience had been more than enough heartache to keep him single. Though he missed the way a woman made him feel, he didn't need the distraction.

Jonah rubbed at the stress building in the back of his neck and berated himself for allowing a pedestrian to mess with his head. She definitely didn't fit the suspect's profile. "Get your mind back in the game," he chastised. Taking one last look, Jonah's heart skipped a beat when the object of his interest opened the gate to the targeted house. She walked up the flag stone path as if she belonged, took a key from her pocket, and opened the door. What the ...

Jonah released a heavy sigh as he hit redial and jogged toward the gate. "Heads up, Joe. The owner just came home, but she's far from what we expected."

"Should we wait for her to make a move?"

Jonah stopped inside the gate and swallowed hard. "I don't think so. No need to drag out the inevitable. I'll take her in for questioning while you guys use the warrant to search the house."

As he walked up the flagstone path, Jonah wondered if he hadn't made a mistake. He gritted his teeth at the conflicting facts flashing through his head. His sources insisted on her guilt. Still, Jonah couldn't picture the carefree woman selling drugs to minors. But if she were innocent, why had they targeted her?

While waiting for Joe Riley, Jonah gazed at the welcoming porch. He'd rather crash on the comfortable furniture and pretend the day never happened than make an arrest that might prove controversial.

"You okay?"

Jonah shrugged. "Sorry, just daydreaming. Besides, I'm exhausted, and I have a bad feeling about this whole thing. Maybe she …" He nodded toward the door. "… can shed some light on this messy business. Let's get on with it."

Jonah knocked and waited next to his partner. The door opened with a rush. He stepped back, mesmerized by the woman's bright smile, then took one step toward the opening. Her smile vanished, and the door slammed in his face. Before she engaged the lock, Jonah pushed his way into the foyer. The force of his weight against the door sent her crashing into a table. He cringed at her high-pitched scream.

The woman stared at the remains of a porcelain vase scattered about the marble floor. Her hands curled into tight fists at her sides. She turned angry eyes toward him. "Look what you did. Get out of my house before I call the police."

Jonah ignored her angry scowl. "I'm Officer Jonah Abbott, an undercover police officer. Are you the resident of this home?"

The suspect mumbled a reply while navigating over broken glass to distance herself from him. "Yes, this is my home. What's going on?"

"You're wanted for questioning in regard to drug trafficking and prostitution."

The young woman narrowed her eyes into a cold stare. "What? Say that again."

As Jonah repeated the charges, the color rushed back into her face. She stiffened and glared at him. "You jerk! Who do you think you are? Look at you! You couldn't be a police officer!"

No longer willing to give her the benefit of doubt, Jonah yanked his identification badge out of his jeans pocket and shoved it in her face. She pushed his hand away. "Get away from me. You could have stolen that."

As he read her the Miranda rights, something shifted in her attitude. She watched him out of emerald-green eyes with a hint of mischief tilting the corner of her mouth. Or was she scheming something in that pretty head? Whatever her intent, she rattled Jonah. He watched warily as she straightened her blouse and folded her arms across her chest, as if daring him to touch her.

When Jonah slid his hands quickly down her sides to check for weapons, she jerked away. "What are you, some officer in charge of manhandling women? I should have you arrested."

Jonah threw his head back and laughed. He waved a piece of paper in her face. "Excuse me? But this warrant says you are the one under arrest."

Still chuckling, he jerked her around to handcuff her. She lowered her head and sniffled. "This is not funny. You ... you," she stammered.

As he grabbed her arm to escort her out of the house, she kicked him in the shin. "Ouch! What'd you do that for? Are you asking for additional charges?"

"You deserve more than a kick in the shin—I told you to take your hands off me."

Jonah again grabbed her by the arm and yanked her toward the door. He regretted the rough treatment, but the woman infuriated him. "The house is all yours, Joe. Find those drugs and while you're at it, add resisting arrest to the charges."

Jonah ignored the elbow aimed at his ribs. When he placed his hand on her head to guide her into the back of his Mustang, she jerked away. She bent over and stared at the interior of the car. With a look of disgust, she wrinkled her nose at him.

Viewing the mess from her perspective, Jonah winced. Take-out bags covered almost every inch of the back seat and floor.

"What is this? Your dumpster?" The woman didn't move.

Jonah spoke through clinched teeth. "We don't have all day. If you don't get into the car, I will be forced to help you. Believe me, you won't appreciate my method of assistance."

Her scathing look could have melted an ice cube, but she complied. With the inside of his elbow, Jonah caught the perspiration dripping from his forehead. He wanted to kick himself for allowing her to get to him. How had she managed to turn the tables and make him out to be the criminal?

CHAPTER TWO

Despite his manhandling of her and his trashed car, Katy felt a rush of adrenaline. She braced herself against the seat back while the officer sped to the station. Why would anyone consider arresting her for drugs and prostitution? Wait till Daddy hears about this.

At the thought of her father, her adrenaline dwindled. The man had a temper that would scatter even the bravest of souls. He'd be furious. She'd have to temper her explanation with sufficient humor to defuse his anger.

At the station, Katy kept her head down, hoping no one recognized her. The arresting officer took her into a conference room and removed her handcuffs. She winced at the red marks on her wrist. Everything in her wanted to tackle him, but she clasped her hands together and considered her situation.

Although she'd never been arrested, Katy had watched enough Law and Order reruns to know her rights. She patted her pocket for her cell phone before she remembered the frisking. Amid their mutual embarrassment, her phone had conveniently disappeared into his pocket.

"Before you harass me further, I need to make a phone call."

Katy stuck out her hand. The arresting officer fumbled in his pocket. He frowned when he pulled out a gray Android. "Try again," she teased. "Mine's a pink iPhone."

Perspiration dotted the officer's brow as he patted another pocket. When the bright pink device finally materialized, his nervous smile did something strange to her insides. She took the phone from his shaky hands but didn't take her eyes off him. Worried lines creased his forehead as he ran his hand across his beard. The man had been so distracted he hadn't even asked her name and address. Katy almost felt sorry for him.

Officer Abbott cleared his throat and motioned toward the unused phone in her hand. "You were calling someone?"

Katy smiled and punched speed dial. "Daddy, you'll never guess where I am. This nice police officer arrested me and took me to the precinct."

She held the phone at a distance to protect her ear drums from her father's roar. "Arrested you? What are you talking about?"

When she noticed the officer leaning her way, she puckered her face and moved to the other side of the room. "I thought you might find that amusing."

"Katy girl, I see nothing amusing about your predicament. That neighborhood has been nothing but trouble since you moved there. Just what are these so-called charges?"

Katy fished for a laugh. "Can you believe this? Someone told them I sold drugs out of my house, and the officer even mentioned prostitution."

Wrong choice of words. Her father sputtered. "What? If the press gets word of your little misadventure, we're all doomed."

"Calm down, Daddy." Katy batted her eyes at the stern face across the room. "The officer and I just had a little misunderstanding. I'm sure we'll come to an agreement soon."

Officer Abbott—the name she remembered from his identification—sat at the conference table and drummed his fingers against a yellow pad. Katy wondered what thoughts were flying through his head.

After another brief look, Katy returned her attention to her father. He huffed out an angry growl. "You bet we'll come to an agreement. I'll be right there to straighten out this mess that you've made."

Skipping formalities, her father ended the call. Katy should not have called him. Her fun would be over the minute he walked through the door.

Of course, her father would be upset. The man was obsessed with pleasing his constituents and generating positive news feeds. The way she used her degree had always been a sore spot with her parents. Her arrest would be just another argument against her position.

Officer Abbott wasted no time getting down to business. He motioned for her to sit, calmly reached across the table, and reclaimed her cell phone. "Name, address, and telephone number, please."

"Since you seem to know so much about my private life, why don't you tell me?"

The officer released a frustrated sigh. "That's not how we do things, and you know it. Just answer the questions."

Katy held her breath while he wrote her name on a yellow legal pad. When she saw no reaction, she took a long breath and sat back in her chair. She didn't know how long she had before her father popped everyone's bubble, but she planned to enjoy every delightful minute with the ruggedly attractive officer.

As the man made notes on his tablet, she studied him from across the table. Even the streaks of dirt and shabby beard didn't hide his handsome face. His long blond hair was tied back with a frayed leather thong while his well-defined abs bulged under his perspiration-soaked T-shirt.

Warmth spread over her forcing her to reign in her wayward thoughts. How could she be so attracted to such an uncouth individual? Katy shook her head at the absurdity. Had swearing off men turned her into some pathetic, obsessed woman?

Katy took a few calming breaths. "Aren't you going to take my fingerprints, Officer Abbott?"

With no grounds to formally book her, Katy knew she'd be released, especially after her father arrived. But what if the officer's team had found evidence against her? Had someone planted drugs on her property without her knowledge?

The thought of being framed had Katy's stomach twisted into knots. She caught herself before she chewed her fingernails to the quick. She wouldn't put anything past those drug pushers. They wanted her out of their neighborhood.

Only a few weeks before, the drug lords had tried to discredit her work. They were furious when she refuted their lies and stood up to them. Every time she rescued one of their victims and sent them to counseling or rehab, she threatened their livelihood. In the past, she hadn't cared how many people hated her, and she refused to give in to fear now. She would not let them destroy the very people she tried to help.

Katy lifted her head when she realized the officer had asked her a question. "Excuse me?"

"Ms. Wilson, you don't seem to understand the seriousness of your situation. Where did you get the money for all those expensive clothes and furniture?"

Katy stared at him. She had grown weary of the man's ridiculous assumptions. "That's none of your business. Let me ask you a question. What did your men find in my house besides, food, mouse traps, diapers, and formula?"

The officer scooted his chair forward. "Since you brought it up, what are you doing with those baby items you mentioned? Are you selling babies?"

Katy's mouth dropped open. "How absurd! Of course, I'm not selling babies."

She balled her hand into a fist. If he'd been closer, she might have hit him. "Such stupid questions do not deserve an answer."

Crossing her arms over her chest, Katy looked the opposite direction. The officer ignored her defiance and continued in his authoritative voice. "Did you ever turn tricks for money?"

"How dare you?"

Each question wound Katy's stomach into a tighter knot. "Since you refuse to reveal your source of income, I need to know where you are hiding the drugs."

She'd had enough. Katy jumped from her seat, leaned over the table, and glared at the aggravating man. "There are no drugs. I fight against the lowlifes who bring illegal substances into my neighborhood. In fact, I discourage drug abuse and provide resources to help the victims beat their addictions."

Katy slapped her hands down with such force her palms burned in pain and the table shook. "Furthermore, haven't you ever heard of using mouse traps to control the rat population? Rodents spread disease in case you didn't know. The food and baby items are for the mothers who do not have enough money to buy even the basics for their children."

The officer's mouth dropped open and his eyes expanded with each bit of information that flew from her mouth. "My father helped me buy the house, because he knows I want to live near the people I work with. Why do you suppose I went to college for four years studying to be a social worker? If you did the least bit of research, you would have found the answers to all these questions without badgering me.

"Is there anything else you want to know? If not, I need to go. I've already missed my afternoon class with unwed mothers and have to prepare for another group coming at five."

Katy headed for the door. When Officer Abbott didn't respond, she turned around. Without moving, he stared at her with his mouth slightly open. His muscles popped as he arched his back and looked toward the ceiling. A deep sigh escaped her lips. Poor guy. If it hadn't been so satisfying to see how he'd botched her "arrest," she'd offer him a sympathetic hug.

When Ms. Wilson finally started talking, Jonah struggled to keep up. He stopped taking notes and stared like a fool. She barely took a breath during her improbable story. Was she telling the truth? Jonah shook his head at the discrepancy. She certainly sounded more like a social worker than a drug dealer or prostitute. Well, she would have little trouble playing that last role with her shapely figure and good looks.

"So, Ms. Kathryn Wilson, before you make your escape, what exactly are you about?"

Before she could respond, the door burst open and the mayor made a grand entrance. Jonah rose so fast his chair tipped backward and crashed to the floor. "What in heaven's name are you doing to my daughter?"

Jonah almost choked when he saw the pleased expression on Katy's face—a look she might give a boyfriend before introducing him to her father. He wished.

"It's okay, Daddy. Officer Abbott is just doing his job—trying to rid your fair city of the druggies. He must be an excellent policeman to be suspicious of your daughter. Don't you think?"

The mayor came toe to toe with Jonah. "You imbecile!" He jabbed his finger in Jonah's chest for emphasis. "You are wasting my time and the city's money if you think my daughter capable of passing out drugs. And where on earth did you get the idea that she engages in prostitution?"

The irate man rubbed the back of his neck as he paced the front of the room. "Next time, I suggest you do a bit more investigating and less time believing those pimps you hang with. Do you get my drift? If this ends up on the front page of the paper, I'll have your hide."

Jonah's posture slumped along with his confidence. The man intimidated him like no other. From day one, he'd been warned to steer clear of the "bulldozer." Even the chief had cited the mayor as someone to avoid. Yet, he'd fallen headfirst into a pile of muck. Of all the people to falsely accuse, he had chosen the mayor's daughter.

Why had he not followed his initial instincts? Katy Wilson hadn't come close to the person described by their informants. In fact, her spunk and concern were clues enough, but in his rush to make an arrest, he'd ignored every warning. There was no one to blame but himself.

Jonah pulled back his shoulders and looked the mayor in the eye. "I read you loud and clear, sir."

Mayor Wilson checked his watch and frowned. "I have a meeting in twenty minutes. Since you brought my daughter here, you can take her home. On the way, I suggest you apologize for your incompetence. Make sure you treat her like the fine southern lady her mother and I raised her to be. You hear?"

"I may not meet your expectations as a police officer, sir, but I do know how to treat a lady."

Jonah and Katy both jumped when the door banged against the wall. Jonah stared at his unlikely suspect and lowered his voice. "Why didn't you tell me?"

Katy studied the carpet and gnawed on her lower lip a moment before she looked into his eyes. "I'm sorry. At first, I thought you were trying to molest me. Then, you made me so angry I couldn't think straight."

Eyes twinkling, she shrugged. "Even though I didn't understand why you were accusing me, I rather enjoyed the process. Not long after my kick to your shin, I realized that we were both working toward the same goals. Forgive me?"

Jonah moaned under his breath and raked his fingers through his hair. Something didn't add up. "Yes, I forgive you, but I find nothing about this day amusing. If you are so innocent, why would my sources name you as a drug dealer and even worse?" Jonah picked up his yellow pad and led the way to the door. "During this apology ride, I expect you to enlighten me."

Jonah still had a job to do. If eating crow helped him get to the bottom of this fiasco, he'd choke down a whole black-feathered meal. Speaking of food, neither of them would have eaten since breakfast. Perhaps they could put their heads together over dinner and find some answers.

Ms. Wilson grimaced. "I'll do what I can, but I'm confused. Do you think someone wants to frame me?"

"That's a possibility." Jonah followed Katy Wilson into the corridor and got another look at her legs. He rubbed down his T-shirt to dry his sweaty hands. The woman was more outspoken than he preferred, but he couldn't ignore the emotions she stirred—desires he thought he'd buried along with his former girlfriend. In the hallway, he licked his lips when he got a whiff of her floral fragrance.

Jonah slammed his fist into his other palm. What had gotten into him? He'd been a mess all day. He hadn't made a rational decision since Katy Wilson came sashaying down the street. How would he ever do his job when he allowed one attractive woman to distract him?

"Okay, Ms. Kathryn Wilson, daughter of the mayor of Trenton, North Carolina. Since you are no longer a suspect by the police department, would you do me the honor of having dinner with me?"

"You're kidding, right?"

Jonah pointed to himself. "No, I don't think so."

Katy shook her head and frowned.

"Why not?" Jonah rubbed his chin. "I thought we might talk about this very strange day."

The woman looked at him over her turned up nose. "I'm not sure I want to be seen with you. You not only look like a homeless person, but you also reek. Just take me home. We'll talk on the way."

Jonah examined his dirty tee and sniffed at his armpits. He realized he needed a shower, but he resented her pointing out the obvious. Her dictatorial complaint only frustrated him more.

"I'm anxious to see the damage done to my house under this ridiculous search. As far as eating out, I prefer to eat at home where I know what I'm putting into my mouth."

Ms. Wilson paused and put her finger to the side of her nose. "Why don't you just drop me off and go wherever you go to take a shower? I'll make us both dinner and we can talk over a nice home-cooked meal. I'm interested in your ideas for cleaning up this neighborhood—I happen to like living here."

She stopped again as if confronting a problem. "Oh, I forgot. In your haste to arrest me, I didn't have time to put away my groceries. The chicken breasts would be spoiled by now. May we make a quick stop by the store?"

Jonah scrubbed his hand over his face. "I'm sorry about that ... and many other aspects of this day. Perhaps if I make the purchase from my own wallet, I might compensate for some of my discrepancies." He paused in search of the right words. "Please forgive me for frightening you, accusing you falsely and not believing you when you tried to explain. Although you did give me a surprisingly good bruise on my shin."

Jonah stooped over and massaged his nonexistent injury. He clicked his tongue and shook his head. "With such violence, I figure we're more even than you'll probably admit. Just make sure you tell your father that I apologized and treated you like—what was that phrase? A fine southern lady?"

The woman hit him playfully on the shoulder and smiled. Her whole face lit up as she casually slowed her pace to walk next to him. Darts of mischief shot from her eyes while heat rushed up Jonah's neck and warmed his face. Was she flirting with him? From the moment he saw her strolling down the street, he had fought the attraction. But if she harbored similar feelings, he was in big trouble.

Jonah pushed back his hair and looked away in hopes of hiding his interest. No one had offered to make him dinner in a long time. He hardly remembered the feeling. Even her suggestion of a shower didn't deter him. He'd never met a woman who affected him so much, so fast. Jonah felt as if he'd been caught in a magnetic field.

"In that case, you must call me Katy, but I suppose I must continue calling you Officer Abbott. Do you have a given name?"

"I will gladly call you Katy, but only if you call me Jonah when we're alone or with mutual friends. Okay?"

Katy tilted her head to the side. "Are we going to have mutual friends?"

"Of course. We'll begin by the two of us becoming the best of friends. What do you think?"

She puckered her face. "I don't know. Just a few hours ago, you were putting handcuffs on me."

Katy drew him in with her cheeky smile and sparkling eyes. He placed a hand over his heart. "But you will forgive me, won't you?"

Jonah grabbed them each a water bottle as they skirted the break room. They teased and bumped shoulders as close friends tend to do. She stirred emotions he hadn't had since Monica.

The pain returned full force, reminding him of why

he'd avoided close relationships with women. Katy had awakened a place in him he'd thought long buried. Jonah shook himself against the conflicting emotions. What difference did it make? Although he saw her as a woman worth pursuing, he would never be able to maneuver past her overprotective father.

As they headed toward the exit, Jonah's boss caught him by the arm. "Tell me, Jonah, how did the surveillance go? I heard you made an arrest."

Jonah caught the smirk on Katy's face out of the corner of his eye. Pulling his chief aside, he had little time to consider how to pose the fiasco to his boss. "Unfortunately, we received identical, yet false tips from two different sources. Our major suspect … uh … didn't match the description of the person of interest. I'll explain tomorrow morning after Joe and I have a chance to check out our sources."

Chief Morrison frowned when he noticed Katy waiting near the exit. Had the chief recognized her? "Why do I think you're leaving out some important details? Is there something you're not telling me?"

"Trust me, sir. Everything will be okay. First thing in the morning, I promise a full report."

Jonah grabbed Katy by the arm and maneuvered her through the door before the chief had time to question him further. He almost choked when he thought of Katy's father. What if the mayor got to his chief first?

Nah. Jonah brushed off the possibility. He would just have to make sure that didn't happen. Donning his most engaging smile, he placed his hand in the center of Katy's back and guided her toward the parking lot. The nagging guilt lifted in anticipation of an enjoyable evening.

Katy glanced at him with a raised eyebrow. "I guess you didn't tell your boss what happened, huh?"

Jonah laughed. "That's pretty obvious since you didn't hear screaming or see foaming at the mouth. The absence of a murder threat should have clued you in."

Jonah opened the door to his beat-up Mustang and offered Katy his hand. When she didn't respond, he looked back at her pursed lips. "This is what you drive when you're not in a patrol car?"

He glanced at his trashy car and shrugged his shoulders. "This is what I drive most of the time. I live in the middle of the worst part of town. Working undercover, I've got to look the part—from the way I dress, to the car I drive. Otherwise, no one would confide in me."

Katy rubbed her hand across the top of the car. "Your Mustang is a classic. Why do you treat your car like a piece of junk? With a good paint job and a thorough cleaning, the car could be the envy of every guy in the neighborhood."

"That sounds incredible, but do you know how long before I'd be reporting my classy car stolen?"

Katy thought a moment before her face relaxed with understanding. "Touché"

"Who knows? Perhaps one day I'll splurge on a facelift for the two of us. We both need a little tender loving care. Don't you think?"

Katy tilted her head to the side and smiled mischievously. He wouldn't mind a little tender loving care from such an intriguing woman. That smile, however, might be the death of him.

CHAPTER THREE

After a quick stop at the neighborhood market, Jonah parked near the gate of the house he and his team had mistaken for a drug house. Katy waited until he opened the car door, and he gave her his hand. He reached for the bag of groceries and followed her up the flagstone walkway.

The tranquil setting contrasted with Jonah's unease as scenes from the botched stakeout scrolled through his mind. Rubbing a hand across his whiskers, shame and regret threatened to destroy his high expectations for the evening. What a mess he'd made.

When he didn't join her, Katy turned around. He shifted uncomfortably until she reached for his hand. "Tell me, officer, what disturbing thoughts are responsible for that sour look?"

"Will you please forgive me? Coming back here reminded me of the way I treated you. You did not deserve such harsh treatment."

"Don't worry about it. I told you I enjoyed the adventure. Now give me a smile before you leave." With a finger from each hand, Katy touched the corners of his mouth and gently pushed upward.

"There. That's better."

Warmth and desire spread over Jonah. With his free hand, he grabbed one of her fingers and returned it to his mouth. He caressed the fingertip with his lips before releasing it and handing her the bag of groceries.

Jonah bounced toward his car with the tune of a rap song playing in his head. His energy surged like a teenager with out-of-control hormones.

A tug on his shirt stopped him. He turned to find Katy frowning at her watch. She tapped the face and turned her disapproval on him. He wondered if his vision of an exciting evening wasn't about to go south.

"I have a class starting at five. Don't come back until eight. The girls should be gone by then."

Jonah's stomach growled. "Aren't you hungry now? I don't know about you, but I haven't eaten since that donut bright and early this morning."

Katy twisted her palm toward him. "Well, that's your problem. Sugar only makes you hungry later. Have a healthy snack before you take a shower. Try a few carrot sticks and a handful of almonds. That should hold you 'til dinner. I would fix you a little something here, but I want to make sure there are no signs of your men trashing my house. I've had enough questions for one day."

Katy paused and gave him such an endearing smile he didn't want to leave. "What if I come in and help you? It's my fault if they left your house a mess."

"No, you go on home. I don't want you around when the girls show up."

Jonah kicked a rock near the gate and grumbled under his breath. The woman acts like a dictator. She might control when he returned and what she served, but she couldn't dictate what he ate. His refrigerator hadn't seen a carrot stick in years. He'd stop at his favorite fast-food restaurant and purchase their largest burger. Just the thought of the juicy sandwich made him salivate. His favorite high carb meal would be the perfect comfort food to soothe his disappointment and fill his empty belly.

Jonah groaned when he turned the corner and saw the long line of cars at the drive-through. His thumbs beat to the rhythm of a popular song playing on the radio while revving the engine in frustration.

When he finally placed his order and drove forward, the teenage girl smiled at him with mischief shining through her dark eyes. "The woman in the car ahead of you paid for your food, sir. She said to tell you that in case you've forgotten, Jesus loves you. Enjoy your meal."

Perplexed, Jonah watched his donor's car disappear around the bend. After he drove forward and retrieved his free food, he found a shady parking space perfect for wolfing down the supersized meal in peace. Grease oozed between his fingers and dripped onto his jeans. He licked his fingers before reaching for the paper napkin. As a last display of independence, he wadded up the trash and tossed the wrapper over his head. One more item for the perfect woman to complain about.

Jonah issued a loud burp and patted his stomach before he backed out of his parking place. He rubbed his hands against his jeans to keep them from slipping on the steering wheel. Would everything remind him of Katy Wilson?

Jonah checked in with Joe, who agreed to a meeting later that evening. He unlocked the door to the shabby apartment he shared with his partner and tossed his phone on the kitchen counter. He stripped off the grungy T-shirt, stepped out of his jeans, and left a trail of dirty laundry all the way to his bedroom and adjoining shower.

Putting aside the weird encounter at the fast-food restaurant and his frustration with Katy, he relished the flow of hot water running over his tired body. The soothing cascade cleared his mind and relaxed his muscles. When he felt himself slipping into oblivion and feared he'd fall asleep standing up, he toweled off and looked with longing at his unmade bed. His sleep-deprived body yearned for a power nap. After a quick wink, he would wake up refreshed and ready to take on the lovely Ms. Wilson.

Jonah stretched his relaxed muscles as his inner alarm clock awakened him around five a.m. For once, he had slept through the night without the disturbing nightmares. Jonah looked at his watch and panicked when he remembered his meeting with the chief. He'd have to hurry to make it on time, and he had no idea what he would say. Had he even talked with Joe or Katy?

Katy. A heart-stopping thought hit him like a brick wall—he had slept through Katy's dinner.

"Blast it." He pounded his head with his fist. "I am the world's biggest loser. How could I be so stupid?" He continued berating himself while searching the house for his cell phone. "She'll never collaborate with me now that she thinks I've stood her up."

Jonah checked the time again and scrolled through about a dozen messages from Joe. Another person he'd stood up. Why hadn't Joe awakened him?

If he left immediately, he'd have time to swing by Katy's house. At least he could apologize for the botched evening. Normally, he would call, but his sappy brain had failed to get her number.

Not until he rang the doorbell repeatedly did he consider that she might not be up at the crack of dawn. Instead of sneaking away like a whipped puppy, he leaned against the door and groaned. How could I be so thoughtless? Behind him, the door flew open without warning and he fell into something soft and warm. When he came to, he stared into a pair of angry, green eyes.

"Are you trying to kill me? Get off me before I'm permanently stamped into the tile." Jonah couldn't move. He was nose to nose with Katy, and all he wanted to do was push back that mass of curly hair and kiss away her angry frown.

"What is wrong with you? First you arrest me. Now you flatten me on the floor."

Jonah did a push up to free her from his weight. But first, he let his eyes drift downward. Her oversized nightshirt did little to cover the shapely legs entangled with his. She wrestled to free herself.

Jonah rolled to his side, jumped to his feet, and pulled Katy up in one swift motion. He patted down her arms and examined the back of her head. "Get your hands off me. What are you doing, frisking me again?"

"I'm only checking to see if you broke anything when you fell. You surprised me when you opened the door without warning. I didn't mean to hurt you. Please forgive me."

"Forgive you? How many times must I forgive?"

"I know. I ..."

Katy ignored him and continued. "What happened to you last night? Did you not have a dinner invitation? I waited hours for you, then threw a perfectly good meal into the trash. I can't wait to hear your excuse."

Jonah stared at the fireball with her hands on her hips. How did she do that? Before he could answer, she poked her finger in his chest. "Did someone die? Were you called into work? At the very least, you could have picked up a telephone."

Jonah held up his hand. "Hold on. If you'd pause for a minute, I'll try to explain. You won't like my excuse, but I grabbed a quick sandwich on the way home. After my shower, I was so exhausted I fell asleep and forgot to set an alarm. I didn't wake up until about an hour ago. I know I don't deserve your mercy, but please try to understand."

Katy stood stiff and unyielding, glaring at him for what seemed like forever. Instead of staring back, he leaned against the doorframe and let his eyes feast on the appealing woman. "For the record, you are kind of cute when you're mad, but I prefer the smiling Katy. Let me fix it."

He put his fingers to the side of her mouth, but before he could pull her lips into a smile, she slapped them away. Even his levity didn't move the stubborn woman. Her silence nearly killed him. "Please, say something."

"I should never speak to you again. You must have filled up on carbs if you were that tired. I told you to eat a little something healthy. I worked hard on that meal, and you threw the whole evening back in my face. Don't you ever think of anyone but yourself?"

As Katy rambled on with her complaints, her anger turned to tears. Watching a tear trail down her cheek, Jonah's chest tightened. He hated seeing a woman cry, especially when he was the reason. While his arms ached to hold her, her single tear turned into a flood. Jonah's compassionate heart took over, he pulled her into his arms and gently rubbed her back.

"Shhh. I left here counting the minutes until I could return to you, but I messed up big time. I know I deserve your wrath, but I'm begging for understanding."

Jonah knew the moment Katy realized she was in his arms. She moved closer and molded her body against his. As her arms came around his neck, his mind drifted to a short T-shirt and long, long legs. Get a grip, Jonah.

Jonah pulled her hands from behind his head. After placing a kiss on her forehead, he released her and stepped away. "I'm late for work. I have a meeting in about thirty minutes on the other side of town, but I can't leave until I'm certain you've forgiven me. You have, haven't you?"

Katy stared at him in confusion while twisting the tail of her nightshirt. The skimpy garment shortened with every turn. Jonah averted his eyes and headed for the door. Before the lock completely engaged, he heard her whispered goodbye. Halfway to the car, he realized she hadn't said a word about forgiveness.

On his way to the precinct, he tried to make sense of their brief encounter. Every time they were close, his body heated to a slow boil. His pastor father taught him to never base a relationship on outward beauty or physical attraction. Jonah laughed when he remembered the sex talk with his Dad.

"Let's take a walk on the beach. Since you're at the age when boys start fantasizing about girls, we need to talk."

"If this is about sex, I'm afraid you're a little late. Charles and Chad filled me in a couple of years ago."

"You're kidding."

His father grinned and waved his hand. "Well, humor your slow-moving father and pretend you are hearing the information for the first time."

After the first talk, Jonah realized his father's version covered more than the brief talks with his brothers. The strong reaction between a man and a woman came up more than once. Though he'd felt desire with other women, nothing came close to the overpowering chemistry that sizzled between him and Katy Wilson.

Jonah admired Katy's concern for those living in poverty, but he'd be interested in her take on family values. Something told him they'd be worlds apart in a discussion over such controversial subjects. If he knew what was good for him, he'd keep their relationship platonic and stick to finding the person or persons who wanted her to disappear. Finding her enemies might also lead to those supplying drugs to the kids.

With so much at stake, Jonah couldn't allow himself to become sidetracked. He vowed to keep future meetings professional. Anything else threatened to cross into dangerous territory.

Obviously, Katy kept a low profile in the community. Though his team had been a few blocks away for weeks, no one had mentioned her. Perhaps she thought working behind the scenes would be more effective. Incognito certainly worked for him. Whatever her reason, he appreciated her involvement and hoped she would cooperate for the good of all.

Jonah shifted to mentally preparing for the meeting with his chief. How would he defend this fiasco? He would be in deep trouble if the mayor got to his boss first. He accelerated, pushing the Mustang over the speed limit.

The tires squealed as he made a sharp turn into the precinct parking lot. Grabbing his laptop from under the seat, he rushed into the building panting for breath. If he didn't hit the weight room soon, he'd never catch the next fleeing suspect. He arrived out of breath and self-confidence.

Refraining from his usual fist bumps and back slaps, he breezed past his befuddled coworkers and headed for the chief's office. The receptionist rolled her eyes as he rushed past her desk and stopped at the chief's closed door. Leaning against the door jamb to catch his breath, he heard his name coming from a voice he recognized—the mayor's.

"I don't care how efficient you say this boy Abbott is, he wasted a whole day for several officers and a lot of the city's money on a tip that had my daughter in handcuffs. In my book, that's plain incompetence. I want to know what you plan to do about that young hoodlum."

Between the spew of words, Jonah heard the distinct sound of wheezing. For a moment, Jonah's concern for Mayor Wilson trumped his reaction to the man's angry words. If the man didn't calm down, Katy would be without a father and he'd be without a job. Jonah strained to hear the chief's response, reluctant to open the door. He hoped the chief's soft-spoken answer represented a voice of reason.

As Jonah stood on the threshold of indecision, he heard the same message he'd received from the person who had paid for his supersized meal. *Jesus loves you.* Warmth spread over him and he felt the urge to pray—a habit he'd developed long ago but had neglected in recent years. His disillusionment over Monica's death had nearly uprooted his faith. Church attendance, along with daily Bible reading, journaling, and prayer were long neglected.

If he were honest with himself, he had missed the close fellowship with God, his parents, and his friends within the Christian community. Now would be the perfect time to renew some of those relationships. He'd start with God—the only One who might have the answers he needed. God, help me, he breathed before he knocked on the chief's door.

He took a few deep breaths, straightened his spine, and prayed for courage. Since he'd initiated the investigation, Jonah knew he must accept the responsibility for its failure. Chief Morrison had been patient with him the last three years and had seen him through some difficult times. He couldn't allow the man to take the flack for his mistake.

When the chief motioned for him to enter, he ignored the accusing look coming from Katy's father. "Sir, do you want the report on yesterday now or would you prefer I come back later."

Mayor Wilson stood and pointed his finger at Jonah. "I want a full report, young man. As far as I'm concern, you botched that whole deal."

Jonah's eyes widened at the realization—Katy was just like her father. "Where on earth did you get the idea to arrest my Katy? Did it ever occur to you to check out the suspect? She's no criminal. I'm not happy with her working in the slums, but she wasn't satisfied until I bought her that house in a rundown neighborhood. Now it appears someone doesn't want her around, and I want to know who."

The man paced the small area before stopping in front of Jonah. "They're probably laughing their heads off at your stupidity. I'm giving you one week to get some answers, or you're both out of here. Got it?"

So much for the full report. Jonah felt the angry blow to his self-confidence as the mayor breezed past him. The mayor slammed the door so hard the furniture rattled. Jonah cringed. Chief Morrison just shook his head and offered Jonah the seat the mayor had abandoned.

"I know you thought you'd received accurate information, but Mayor Wilson is right. You should have done a background check on the suspect before rushing into a raid. I understand the need to move fast when you get these tips, but this is one surprise I could live without. A mistake like this could haunt us for months—a major setback to our efforts in that neighborhood. Do you have any leads as to who might have targeted Katy Wilson?"

Jonah tapped the arm of the chair. "I had hoped to have information from Ms. Wilson before this morning, but we haven't been able to discuss the situation at length. I hope to see her later today when I leave work."

"Since the mayor has made this a priority, I suggest you see her now rather than later."

"Before I see her, I need to double check my sources. The same tip came from two different individuals, including Alfonzo, who has yet to steer me wrong. Their insistence led me to believe we had a breakthrough. Also, I trusted my instincts. Everything made sense until I met the suspect. Now, I'm baffled. What happened yesterday seems important even though the sting didn't bring about the results I'd imagined. Regardless of yesterday's failure, I can't dismiss Katy's ..."

Jonah paused and watched the chief write something on his notepad. Clearing his throat, he shifted uneasily. "I mean Ms. Wilson's involvement. Her presence in that neighborhood has ticked somebody off, and I'm determined to find out who. I refuse to consider the day wasted."

Chief Morrison raised his eyebrows but didn't react to Jonah's familiarity with Ms. Wilson. As if in deep thought, he played a staccato beat on his desk with a pencil. "I have to say I like your attitude, and I hope you're right for the sake of both our jobs. Check in with me again tomorrow, and let me know what you uncover."

When Jonah left the chief, he skirted past his cubbyhole with its stack of neglected paperwork. He couldn't begin to describe what went down the day before. Maybe he could talk Joe into a little paper pushing. Right now, he had an appointment with someone he'd neglected for a long time.

In his three years with the force, Jonah had never found himself so helpless. If he expected to find the culprits out to get Katy, he had to look beyond himself. Instead of pushing ahead with his own plans, Jonah pulled his car into a community park. Looking out at the green foliage, he waited for his mind to clear. When he sensed the familiar presence from the past, he knew he wasn't alone. He bowed his head over the steering wheel and prayed for the first time in months.

"God, forgive me for blaming you for Monica's death. Free me from the anger and bitterness that has consumed me. Restore my faith and confidence in you and heal my damaged soul. Please bring clarity to the confusion surrounding Katy Wilson. Direct me as I move forward with the investigation. In the name of your Son, Jesus."

Feeling refreshed and more confident than he'd felt for some time, he left the park with a plan to meet Joe at the diner near Katy's house. If they were lucky, they might run into Alfonzo, who often hung out there.

CHAPTER FOUR

As Katy focused on her daily routine, she tried to erase Jonah from her mind. From the moment he had burst into her house, she'd sensed a physical attraction that drew them together—a force stronger than she'd ever experienced. If she looked past the untrimmed beard, long hair, and tattoos, she saw a handsome, appealing man. Though they had nothing in common, and she should know better, she couldn't stop thinking of him. Why did she long for a man she did not need?

Sucking in her breath, she made a mental list of reasons why a relationship with Jonah would not work. Her parents would think her crazy to date such an uncouth individual. Despite ignoring her dinner invitation, she couldn't free him from her mind. The ill-mannered brute had caused her to waste her entire day. Angry and frustrated with herself, she determined never to set eyes on Jonah Abbott again.

She closed the door on the last of her afternoon tutoring groups, returned the books to the shelf, and straightened the living room. Her thoughts of Jonah and the day before were interrupted by the front doorbell. Since most of her clients entered through the rear, she wondered what or who she might find on the front porch.

Katy moved quietly into the foyer and peeked out the window. She startled when a pair of sad eyes stared at her. Jonah. Since he had seen her, she had no choice but to open the door. No way would she let him cross the threshold. She would tell him up front that he wasn't welcome no matter how sad the eyes or how hot and sexy he looked leaning against her doorframe. She yanked the door open intending to send him packing, but before she could utter a word, Jonah's apology melted her resolve.

"Katy, I realize I made a mess of things yesterday, but we still have some unfinished business. Can I come in so we can talk?"

The sex appeal beneath Jonah's freshly trimmed beard and his clean shirt was undeniable, but he still looked more like one of the neighborhood druggies. "I should never see you again. I still can't believe I made you dinner after the way you treated me earlier, and then you had the nerve to ignore the invitation. That was inexcusable."

"I know. But if you forgive me, I promise to make it up to you and never treat you that way again. I'm not sure why, but I feel we were thrown together for a reason, perhaps even for a higher purpose. You can't deny the strong feelings between us."

Katy crossed her arms. "I don't know about this higher purpose, but there is definitely a chemistry between us. It makes no sense though, because you are not my type, and I would never consider a relationship with someone who can't keep his life organized enough to show up for dinner."

A crooked grin accompanied Jonah's sincere apology. "You are never going to let me forget that are you? I'll just have to prove to you that I'm not usually so unreliable."

He looked down at his feet. "I'd had a long, stressful day. I was exhausted and hungry."

"Don't tell me. Let me guess. You ate fast food and crashed for the night."

Jonah rubbed the back of his neck and grinned sheepishly. "Busted."

"Just as I thought."

"But I'll make it up to you." Jonah looked at her with a hopeful smile. "Let me buy you dinner tonight. We don't have to go out … I'll have a meal delivered from a healthy place, your choice."

Katy didn't want to let him off the hook so easily, but she had to admit his appeal had weakened her resolve. In the past, she'd avoided men who made her feel weak and helpless, yet she felt powerless against Jonah's charming personality.

"Come on, Katy. You must forgive me. I couldn't even focus on my assignment today for worrying about how I treated you. I don't know how it's possible, but after only knowing you a few hours, you have completely destroyed my ability to function."

"If you are so mesmerized, how did all thoughts of me escape your subconscious while you slept through our dinner engagement?"

The crooked grin reappeared. "I've no doubt that you showed up in my dreams. Just not in time for dinner. Could I please have a second chance?"

Katy could resist him no longer. She opened the door and stepped back, keeping her distance lest she succumb to his charm. Whenever she found herself slipping, she vowed to remind herself how different they were and how totally unacceptable Jonah Abbott would be to her parents.

"Do you want to order dinner first or just tackle the problems that surfaced yesterday?"

"I don't want you to order dinner at all. I have something in the Crockpot. When we are hungry, I will throw together a salad."

Jonah cocked his head. "Are you always this efficient and prepared? Don't you ever make mistakes or find yourself in a situation you can't handle?"

Katy wrinkled her forehead. "I don't know what you mean. I like things well organized and on schedule."

Making lists and following them had become second nature for Katy. The only mistakes she remembered making concerned past relationships with the opposite sex and they had all ended in disappointment. Was she about to make another major mistake?

Jonah looked confused as she continued. "Don't you believe in planning ahead? My day is full, and if I had your attitude I would never accomplish a thing. Besides, I'd be big as a cow, grabbing fast food instead of making healthy, nutritious meals. My organizational skills keep me focused."

Jonah raised his hands in surrender and stepped back. "Whatever works for you."

Katy huffed at his condescending attitude, but Jonah shifted to work mode. "Since we aren't hungry this early, can we get right to work? I now understand you have good intentions toward the people in your neighborhood, but that doesn't explain why someone tried to frame you. I had hoped we might work together to determine who would go to such trouble."

Jonah peered into the room. "Could we use your dining room table for a workspace?"

Without waiting for an answer, he took a laptop from his briefcase along with a spiral notebook and looked around for an outlet. The beeps from his computer pulled Katy from her wide-eyed stare. The man was full of surprises. Katy nodded her agreement while hiding her approval behind a shaky hand.

The man wasted no time getting down to business. "One question has bugged me since yesterday. Why were you fingered as a drug distributor? Earlier today, I talked with one of the guys who gave me the false information. He sounded pretty vague—I suspect he knows more than he's willing to share. My gut instinct suggests he was paid off, but after yesterday's blunder, I hesitate to make a judgment."

Jonah moved to the chair next to Katy. As he turned the computer around and leaned over to scroll the screen, she smelled the fragrance of a fresh shower. She gnawed on her lower lip and tried to focus on Jonah's instructions. "Here's a list of names for you to look over. Let me know if any look familiar. Some have pictures.

"Chief Morrison and I, and your father"—Jonah emphasized—"want to know why you were targeted as a person of interest."

Katy looked at Jonah. "You talked to my father?"

"I wouldn't say we talked." Jonah made air quotes. "Our conversation was more like him barking orders while the chief and I listened."

"Welcome to the world of my controlling but loving father."

Jonah raised an eyebrow and mumbled under his breath. "Controlling, yes. Love? Not so sure."

Katy turned back to the computer and scrolled through the names. Not far into the list she realized how few of the people used their given names. "None of these names look familiar. They obviously prefer street names; I wish your records had more pictures."

Even after scrolling through the list several times, she only identified five names that looked familiar. Katy wrote them on a yellow tablet and handed the pad to Jonah. She had underlined two for emphasis. "I'm not certain about most of these." She tapped the paper, "But these two I will never forget."

Jonah drew his eyebrows together. "What happened?"

"When a mother brought me her son half-dead from an overdose, I kept him alive until the paramedics arrived. In the hospital, he confessed he not only took the illegal substance, but he also earned a lot of money selling drugs for the dealers. Since he was just a kid, I negotiated with the district attorney for six months of rehab instead of juvenile detention."

As Katy told the story, Jonah pulled the computer in front of him. "Let me check how the police and ER handled the case."

Jonah sat back in his chair and motioned for Katy to continue. "A few days after the incident, these two ruffians stopped me on the street and threatened me bodily harm if I didn't leave their neighborhood. They didn't physically touch me, but they cursed in my face and told me I didn't belong."

He covered her hand with his own. "Why didn't you report the incident to the police?"

"What good would that have done? Yes, they frightened me, but I wasn't about to let them destroy my work in this community."

Jonah squeezed her hand before releasing it. "You are a very brave woman, Katy Wilson, but you've made a few enemies here. I worry your life might be in danger."

"I doubt they would physically harm me. They're just trying to bully me into leaving."

Jonah shook his head. "I hope you're right, but you should be careful regardless."

Jonah and Katy worked for over an hour before she stopped to prepare the salad.

"What can I do to help?"

Jonah washed his hands and waited for her instructions. "While I put the salad together, you may cut the bread, set the table, and fill our water glasses."

She suspected Jonah rarely cooked for himself, yet he moved about the kitchen with ease. "You seem to know your way around the kitchen. Why do you eat carryout all the time?"

"No time. Takes too long to prepare a good meal. Unfortunately, the refrigerator I share with my partner only contains leftover carryout containers. I haven't taken a day off in three years."

Katy blinked and raised her eyebrows. "What about your family? Don't you have someone you'd want to cook for?"

"I have family, but they're out of town."

Jonah turned away, anxious to change the subject. "Who's this?" A yellow tabby rubbed against his legs.

"That's Missy. I'm surprised to see her warming up to you like that. She rarely comes downstairs when strangers are in the house."

Jonah picked up the cat and stroked her soft fur. "I'd say she's nothing more than a spoiled pussy cat. Instead of this affectionate feline, you need a guard dog."

"My father says the same thing. What is it with men and their dogs? Missy doesn't bother me unless she's hungry. Yet, she's ready for my attention when I need her."

Jonah rubbed Missy behind her ears and snuggled her under his neck. "She might enjoy your company but look how she relishes the affection of a stranger. You think this sweet little thing would protect you from a burglar?"

Katy watched Jonah put his face into Missy's golden coat. "Well, I can see she has no trouble capturing at least one intruder."

Steam along with a spicy aroma rose from the bowls Katy had filled with stew. Her spoon was halfway to her mouth when Jonah grabbed her left hand. "May I ask a blessing over our meal?"

Katy coughed to clear her throat, dropped her spoon into the bowl, and bowed her head. "Sure, go ahead."

When Jonah released her hand, she opened her eyes a slit to see what she might have missed. He rubbed both hands down the legs of his jeans before retaking her hand. Instead of bowing his head, he looked toward the ceiling. "Father, we thank you for this time because we know you have brought us together. May we honor you in all we say and do. Thank you for this delicious smelling meal Katy has so thoughtfully prepared. Bless her in every way possible and most of all, keep her safe from those who wish her harm. In the name of your Son, Jesus. Amen."

Jonah looked her way and caught her staring. When she shifted uncomfortably, his eyes softened, and he squeezed her hand. "I guess your family doesn't say grace before meals?"

"Just on special occasions. Do you always pray over your food, even when you're alone?"

"Yes, I usually offer a silent thank you before I eat, but other than that, I haven't prayed much lately. After what happened yesterday, I'm trying to do better in the prayer department."

Katy wondered about the man she'd allowed into her home. Though he didn't look religious, something bothered her about his prayer. If he turned out to be another of those weirdos who thought the Bible contained the only answer to life's problems, they would never agree on anything.

Since Katy had been old enough to understand, she'd despised religious bigots who opposed everything she believed. Most of them were close-minded and refused to listen to anyone's views but their own. As a young adult, she had shouted them down at abortion clinics and had even gone to Washington to march for a woman's right to choose.

Katy went to church every Sunday with her parents and worked hard to improve the lives of others. She didn't need some screaming, self-righteous preacher pointing out her sins and telling her what she could or could not do.

Despite her unease, Jonah's prayer had touched her. No one had ever prayed for her like that. She wasn't used to praying over her food, much less having someone pray for her safety or that she be blessed. Surely a simple prayer didn't mean Jonah adhered to all that strict ridiculous nonsense.

Over the last couple of hours, she realized how wrong she'd been to accuse him of incompetence. He was thorough, efficient, and intelligent as he examined each topic from different angles. Jonah's eye for detail impressed her, but he had a major problem if he tried to push his brand of religion down her throat.

Katy brushed off her fears and turned back to the meal Jonah tackled with enthusiasm. "This is delicious. I haven't tasted anything this good since I left home. Now, I feel even worse about the meal I ruined last night."

"Don't worry; I shouldn't have reacted out of anger. The day had been difficult for both of us."

Jonah reached across the table and reclaimed her hand. "Thank you." After rubbing his thumb across her knuckles a few times, he released her and went back to the food.

Following the meal, Jonah helped her clear the table. He rinsed the dishes and handed them to Katy to stack in the dishwasher. As he reached for the hand towel she had draped over her shoulder, his eyes locked with hers. A sense of connection surged through her.

When he made his way into the dining room, gathered his papers, and unplugged his laptop, she realized his intention. She panicked at the thought of him leaving so soon. Their conversation over dinner had been pleasant with him asking questions about her family and college years. He questioned her with enthusiasm regarding her work in the community. Although the conversation had little depth and avoided anything about his own past, she enjoyed being with him and longed to delay his departure.

"Do you have to go? We haven't even had dessert."

His wide grin told her she'd found the answer. "Well, I've never been one to turn down something sweet."

Katy bumped his shoulder and batted her eyes. "Does that teasing smile mean you think I'm sweet? How would you know, Mr. Praying Officer?"

"Just because I bless my food doesn't mean I'm immune to pretty girls with an offer of dinner and dessert."

Katy felt her resistance weakening as their eyes met, and he followed her into the kitchen. She pulled a cheesecake from the refrigerator. Despite her anger when she made it that morning, Katy knew the dessert would not disappoint.

Jonah stared with wide-eyed approval when she placed the confection before him. The cherries and chocolate shavings on top more resembled a dessert on display at a gourmet bakery. His response set her heart to galloping as she cut two generous pieces.

At his first bite, a look of sheer pleasure spread across his face. "Surely you didn't make this from scratch?"

"Of course I did. You think I'm a spoiled little girl, don't you? Since my third year in college, I have lived alone and been forced to cook for myself. I appreciate the taste of a well-prepared, healthy meal. In fact, I've been teaching the residents to cook and eat healthy."

Katy remembered his capable help. "I don't see you being lost around the kitchen."

"My no-nonsense mother raised three boys and felt obligated to her future daughters-in-law to make sure we knew how to cook. No one could accuse her of spoiling her boys."

Curious about Jonah's family, Katy took her time savoring another bite. "Did your mother have a career?"

"Not in the literal sense, but she always helped my father at the church office. Right now, she directs their preschool program—her first opportunity to use her degree in school administration. Until the church opened the school, her children and husband had been her main priority."

"Is your father a minister?"

"He is. Dad has pastored Community Church on Shell Island since he graduated from seminary. Our house on the intracoastal waterway was the only home I knew until I left for college."

With a look of longing, Jonah stared out the bay window. "My brothers and I thrived on the relaxed atmosphere of the island. We enjoyed a freedom few children have today. In clear weather, my dad took us out on the boat at least twice a week. With our early ambitions leaning toward sea captains, we loved anything to do with the ocean and sea life. Dad taught us to fish, dive, water ski, surf, and swim."

Jonah's eyes sparkled with pleasure. "Water sports wasn't all Dad taught us. Every late afternoon excursion, we were fed small doses of character-building lessons from a man we admired. I miss those times with my dad."

"Sounds as if you and your brothers had an idyllic life."

"Come to think of it, I was probably a little spoiled as well."

Jonah laughed at his revelation as he stood to leave. Katy watched him pick up the empty dessert plates and rinse them in the sink—such a contrast to the way he trashed his car. The man kept her confused. Regardless, she liked everything about him but that prayer. A blessing over the meal seemed completely foreign to the bad boy look he otherwise projected. Neither of them could deny the physical attraction, and she wasn't about to ignore the passion he generated. She wanted him like she'd never wanted another man. With that resolve, she made her move.

When Jonah turned to express his thanks, she put her arms around his neck and matched his lips to hers. His stiff response prompted Katy to pull back and question him with her eyes. Seeing the hint of a smile on his lips, she knew she had him. The briefcase dropped, along with his resistance. Moments later, he molded her into his body and deepened the kiss.

Katy shuddered with passion. Jonah might have conservative ideas, but his kisses were off the charts. Fire burned in her abdomen. She was so turned on she lowered her hands from his neck and pulled his shirt from his jeans. The warmth of his bare back weakened her knees.

Jonah stiffened and pulled away. He reached behind him and captured her exploring hands. He placed his forehead against hers. Katy waited for the rejection. His passion-filled eyes squeezed together as if in pain. Without releasing her hands, he gave a frustrated groan and took a step backward. "I'm sorry, Katy, but this is not who I am. I need to go."

In frustration, Katy swore under her breath and tried to pull away. "What? Explain to me what just happened?"

Jonah tightened his hold on her hand. "I know you don't understand, but I can't do this. This kind of lust will lead to something I don't want to happen. I took a pledge when I turned fourteen to refrain from sex until I married."

In a fit of anger, Katy jerked her hands from his and tried to swallow the lump forming in her throat. "You're joking, right? Of course, you are."

"I realize you find my reaction unusual, but I wouldn't lie to you. I've never been with a woman like that, and I don't plan to dishonor you by making you my first."

Katy rolled her eyes, unable to stomach such nonsense. "You must be gay then, because no man as good-looking and sexy as you would tolerate years of celibacy."

Jonah shook his head. "I'm not gay. How could you think that after such a passionate kiss? Of course, I'm attracted to you, but I believe marriage is a sacred covenant between a man and a woman. A night of passion based on physical attraction falls short of what God wants for us."

Katy remembered Jonah's devout prayer over their meal. "Are you one of those radical Christians?"

CHAPTER FIVE

Jonah knew he needed to get away from Katy and her tempting kisses. He didn't want to leave her confused. "What are you talking about?"

Earlier, after he'd prayed over their meal, he'd caught Katy glaring at him—a troubled frown marring her pretty features. Since his decision to renew his relationship with God, he was determined to live his faith instead of hiding it. He wanted her to see the real Jonah Abbott instead of some impersonator.

After an unladylike snort, Katy's words stumbled over each other in a rush to make her point. "You know, those people who claim they're always right. They don't care if the whole world disagrees with them—they're determined to push their religious ideas on everyone else. They refuse to even consider another point of view."

Katy tossed her head as if flipping off those who dared to disagree. "I've met plenty of them spreading their propaganda outside family planning centers. They accuse the clients of murder and make them feel like criminals when all they are doing is exercising their right to choose what happens in their own bodies. Not only that, but they hate people who are born with a different sexual orientation, refusing to let them marry."

Jonah rubbed at the pressure building in his chest. The harsh words spewed from Katy's mouth as if she'd recited them many times. "One ultra-self-righteous woman told me God made men stronger than women so they could rule over them. Some won't even use birth control. If you're that kind of fanatic, we have nothing in common, and I don't want you in my house."

The fire in Katy's eyes had changed from sensual desire to angry suspicion. No doubt she suffered from past hurts at the hands of a few overzealous pro-life advocates. Now would not be the time to tell her he had participated in Right to Life marches and even held protest signs at abortion clinics.

Jonah shook his head at the contradiction. Katy sounded as close-minded as those she criticized. Any attempts to discuss his pro-life views would be futile.

When they'd kissed, he imagined marriage, kids, and years of happiness. For that scenario to happen, one of them would have to change. That wasn't an option for him. How could he have been so wrong about a person?

Jonah touched her arm. "Please, I don't always agree with others' behavior, but I don't hate anyone. Are you telling me you refuse to listen to anything that might challenge your own ideas? That sounds a bit like your accusation against sincere Christians. Have you ever sat down and discussed these issues with someone who disagrees with you? Perhaps you need to be more open to what others have to say."

Katy huffed and pushed his hand away. "I've listened to the rhetoric from those fanatics enough to know how ridiculous their claims are. I suppose you think you can change my mind?"

"I'd like the opportunity to at least share with you what I believe. Though I'm not a right-winger, I am a Christian." Jonah leaned forward. "I know some find Christ's teachings difficult, but the more we study God's Word, the more we understand his heart for us."

With hands firmly on her hips, Katy stared at him. "I do believe you missed your calling. How did a judgmental preacher end up as an undercover cop? And, who gives you the right to judge me? I go to church every Sunday and from what I know of the Bible, you people skipped right over the verse that tells us to love one another."

Katy fumed. Jonah had awakened long-dormant feelings in her. Yet, part of her wanted to boot him out of her house. The man had her so confused, she couldn't think. Dr. Jekyll and Mr. Hyde were not as different as the two faces of Jonah Abbott. But was he right? Were these passionate feelings only lust? What a thing to say? Did he consider her loose? If he did, she would remind him that he acted as hungry for her as she did for him.

"I'm sorry if I came across judgmental. I can't deny the chemistry between us, and that's the reason I want to discuss our differences. If we are to help the people in this neighborhood, we need to find common ground and have a reasonable conversation."

Katy bit her tongue to keep from lashing out. She would show the self-righteous charmer how well she listened to the ideas of others, and she'd do so without showing the least bit of interest in him. Neither his sexy smile nor his tender touches would change her position on women's rights or any other social issues.

"Okay, officer, or is it Preacher Abbott? I know you need to leave for now, but the next time we're together, I'll show you how good I am at listening to other viewpoints. But listening works both ways—you must hear what I have to say as well. I've run into your kind before, and I bet you are as closed-minded and self-righteous as they come."

Katy paced the floor fuming at Jonah's arrogance. She stopped in front of him and jabbed his chest. "You think you have all the answers, but you're nothing but a male chauvinist pig. In case you didn't know, I've studied social issues since before I left high school, and my debating skills are at an all-time high. When we finish this discussion, you will have wished you'd never crossed me."

The gleam in Jonah's eye infuriated Katy. She rubbed her hands together to keep from slapping the confident smirk off his face.

Moving closer, Jonah took her finger and kissed the tip before asking in a low sultry voice, "So, what topic do you want to debate first?"

Katy jerked her finger away and raised her chin in defiance. "The one that's certain to provide strong opposing views—a woman's right to choose."

Confident with her subject, Katy lifted her head and marched to the door. She waved her hand for Jonah to leave, then scolded herself. Why had she reacted in such anger? And why had she agreed to see him again?

Jonah had not left in anger, as other guys with whom she'd had such strong words might have. No, he cradled her head in his hands and gazed into her eyes. She melted at his touch. With a quick kiss to her mouth, he'd grabbed his briefcase and rushed out the door.

Conflicting emotions swirled around Katy as she watched him hurry down the sidewalk. As she stared after him like a love-sick fool, Jonah turned around with a wide smile. "Katy, my love, you don't know with whom you have tangled. I'll call you to set up our little debate."

Before turning to leave, he winked and gave an exaggerated bow. Katy's heart thundered in her chest. She slammed the door and cried against the barrier between them. Why do I have such strong feelings for such an infuriating man?

Katy kicked at the closed door. Jonah was crazy if he thought he could challenge the ideas and beliefs that had motivated her to serve others. She twirled a strand of hair while remembering the other Jonah—the tender man who cared what happened to her and the people in her neighborhood—the man who would never hurt her.

She shivered at such conflicting thoughts. Her only hope lay in her ability to change him from the staunch, straight-laced man she feared into a broad-minded individual who respected the ideas and actions of others.

When Jonah called two days later, Katy rubbed her hands together, hyped for operation reprogram. She made a mouth-watering pork roast with apple crisp for dessert. Though the cold, dreary Wednesday would have been perfect for lovers to snuggle by the fire, there would be no romance.

Katy released a loud sigh as she tried to justify her attraction to this otherwise unacceptable man. His parents had to be responsible for such skewed ideas. To the contrary, her parents had raised her to be a progressive thinker. While still a preteen, her mother gave her the sex talk. "Listen, Katy, this is important. When you start dating, you must never engage in sex without your partner wearing a condom. We don't want an unplanned pregnancy or for you to come down with some disease." Her mother even suggested birth control pills when she found someone special.

Katy never forgot that wise counsel and had generally followed her mother's advice. The few times she had slipped ended in disaster. Now when the perfect man arrived— someone she'd consider for a long-term relationship—birth control wasn't necessary. She moaned as the doorbell interrupted her thoughts.

After she took his jacket, Jonah greeted her with an affectionate hug. Katy wanted to melt into his arms and never let go. But he'd made himself perfectly clear—nothing would come from such actions. Keeping his mandate in mind, she would resist him no matter how difficult. In fact, giving him a cold shoulder might keep her from folding under the emotional pressure.

Katy watched him take a book from his briefcase. "What do you have there, officer? Your textbook?"

Jonah tossed her a resolve-melting smile while handing her the book. The fine, black leather felt soft and pliable as she traced the spelling of his name etched in gold calligraphy on the front. The book's worn edges indicated years of use.

"Just my Bible. I base all my thinking on God's Word. Do you have a Bible?"

"Of course, I take one to church every Sunday. I've also seen religious freaks flashing Bibles in college and at protest rallies. I'm not immune to your resource."

"That's good to know. Since you're already familiar with the Good Book, I won't have to establish it as a viable resource."

Katy handed the book back to Jonah and headed toward the kitchen. "No more religious talk. Let's have tea and cookies and relax by the fire a few minutes. I don't enjoy this damp cool weather, but it's inevitable with winter around the corner."

Weather talk? Katy cringed. At least they wouldn't be arguing from the get-go. "How are things going with the investigation?"

Jonah leaned against the counter and traced a dark vein running through the granite countertop. "I've been snooping around for information on the names you gave me. I don't want to frighten you, but something's up regarding your presence in this neighborhood. Someone wants you out of here, and they don't care how they do it."

Katy's lips trembled and her legs weakened. She grabbed the edge of the counter to regain control. Gritting her teeth, she refused to surrender to unscrupulous men threatening to destroy her.

Jonah went to the kitchen window and checked the lock. "Make sure you keep your doors locked—even in the daytime. I asked for more police presence. That might discourage the person or persons with a vendetta against you. You need to be diligent too." Jonah shifted his weight and hesitated before asking, "Is there someone who might stay with you at night? I'm concerned that you are here alone." His tone brightened. "Maybe I should camp out on your front porch."

Katy dismissed his concerns with a wave of her hand. "You're the only one I would invite to spend the night, and I don't mean camping on the porch."

She touched the tip of his nose. "And we already know your opinion on sleepovers."

Jonah flinched at her touch. Katy drew back, uneasy with his silence. "I understand your concerns for my safety, but I refuse to cave to their threats. People are in and out of my house all day long. Three evenings a week, I have classes until nine o'clock. That's enough invasion of privacy."

Breaking the silence, Katy handed Jonah a platter of cookies. She picked up a tray containing her grandmother's tea set with a pot of chai spice tea and followed him into the living room.

After they were seated on the sofa, Katy watched Jonah examine the tiny roses surrounding the brim of the teacup.

"These are beautiful. Are you sure you want to waste them on me?"

Jonah sniffed the rich aroma before touching his cup to hers. "A toast to a beautiful hostess!"

He smiled over the edge of the cup before taking a sip. "The tea tastes delicious. Do you prefer tea over coffee?"

"No, I like both, but chai tea is my favorite for an evening by the fire."

Jonah took a cookie from the platter. Instead of taking a bite, he stared at the gas logs in the fireplace. When he looked back at her, the flames dancing in his eyes melted her resolve. Her body seemed to have a mind of its own as she scooted closer and felt the heat from his thigh against hers. She ached for him to pull her into his arms. Jonah coughed and readjusted his position.

Katy released a frustrated breath—no sense wishing for someone miles away.

CHAPTER SIX

Jonah shifted his leg away from Katy's. Was she trying to mess with his head? A quiet by the fire—even the Victorian tea set screamed romance. Regardless of her attempts to seduce him, he refused to take the bait. Perhaps returning to the subject of her safety would cool her jets.

"Do you happen to own a gun and know how to use it?"

Katy rolled her eyes. "Of course not. I'm for gun control, not spreading more violence. Do you know how many people are killed every year with guns kept in their homes for so-called protection? Haven't you ever heard the phrase, 'Violence breeds violence?' Don't tell me you're a member of the NRA, too?"

Jonah swiped his hand across his face. Did Katy not see the danger of living here alone? Even a dog would help, but knowing her, she'd pick the small cuddly version, or the mutt destined for extermination. Despite her liberal views, he admired her nonviolent stance and her regard for justice. If she only cared as much for the thousands of unborn children murdered daily.

Taking her hand, Jonah examined each of her fingers. "I care about you, and until we find who wants to harm you, please stay safe. Let's pray before we begin our debate."

Katy removed her hands from his and shoved them under her thighs. "I know what you're doing. You think having God on your side will make two against one."

Jonah laughed. "I like to think I'm on God's side."

"That's doubtful, but I can pray too. If he really is a

God of love, he will agree with me. Unlike you and your unreasonable rules, I love everyone—even those who don't look or act like me."

Still chuckling, Jonah doubted his ability to find the first serious thought, much less pray. "When I finish, you may add your own prayers."

Katy frowned. "I'm not comfortable praying aloud."

"Fair enough. Praying in your heart counts also. Maybe we can at least agree in prayer."

She flipped her hand. "Go for it. If I don't agree, I'll let you know."

Jonah shook his head. "I'm sure you will."

After a few moments of quiet, Jonah looked toward the ceiling. "Father, we ask you to be with us today. Invade this place with your presence and guide the direction of our words and thoughts. We want to understand your ways. Thank you for Katy and her heart to help those who suffer. She sees them as you do—and you love all people. Help us to listen and learn from one another. Instead of conflict, we pray for unity through your Holy Spirit. Please help my team while we search for those determined to hurt Katy. May the God of heaven's armies surround her with protection and care. In the precious name of your Son, Jesus, who died so we might live for him. Amen."

Jonah opened his eyes, lifted an eyebrow, and gave her a snarky smile. "Did that meet with your approval?"

With her mouth slightly ajar, Katy stared at him through teary eyes. "That was beautiful. Thank you for praying for me. Do you really believe God protects people? People are killed every day. What about them?"

"I don't have all the answers, but I do know he wants us to ask. We have been given free will and violence occurs when evil people refuse to obey godly principles. No matter what happens, God has promised to be with us."

Katy grew quiet as if in deep thought. "It sounds good, but I'm not sure I understand why God would choose to protect some and let others fall into the hands of murderers or rapists." A slow smile spread across her face. "That was some prayer though. Where did you learn to pray like that?

You sounded as if God sat here with us."

"God promised he'd never leave us nor forsake us. So, yes. He is definitely here."

Katy tucked in her lower lip and looked around the room. She remained quiet as Jonah turned the pages of his Bible. "May I read a couple of Scriptures before we begin?"

She motioned for him to continue. "What can we bring to the Lord? Should we bring him burnt offerings? Should we bow before God Most High with offerings of yearling calves? Should we offer him thousands of rams and ten thousand rivers of olive oil? Should we sacrifice our firstborn children to pay for our sins? No, O people, the LORD has told you what is good, and this is what he requires of you: to do what is right, to love mercy, and to walk humbly with your God" (Micah 6:6–8).

Jonah flipped back a few pages to the Psalms. "You made all the delicate, inner parts of my body and knit me together in my mother's womb. Thank you for making me so wonderfully complex! Your workmanship is marvelous— how well I know it. You watched me as I was being formed in utter seclusion, as I was woven together in the dark of the womb. You saw me before I was born. Every day of my life was recorded in your book. Every moment was laid out before a single day had passed" (Psalm 139:13–16).

Katy scooted to the edge of the couch. "I'm not sure where you're going with this unless you're trying to convince me that a fetus has rights over that of the woman."

Comfortable with the subject, Jonah sat back on the couch. "Okay, let's start there. If you and I were married and decided to have a baby …"

Katy interrupted with a chortle. "In my wildest imagination, I don't see that happening. Just think. We would constantly be at odds, and every election one would cancel the vote of the other."

Jonah laughed at Katy's scenario which didn't veer far from the truth. But, despite their differences, he refused to suppress the feeling that God had brought them together.

"At this point, I realize a marriage between us might

be a stretch, but just pretend for a few minutes. So, we get married and are expecting our first baby. At what point would we start calling him or her a child? When you first started feeling a little nauseated as your body reacted to the hormone changes? How about the first time we saw him moving around on the sonogram? When he puts his finger in his mouth, and the doctor tells us he is a little boy? Or perhaps when we felt the baby move for the first time? When he kicked you in the ribs, and we laid in bed talking and singing to him? Or would we have to wait until the day you gave birth?"

Jonah prayed under his breath as he passed her a brochure. "Here. Look at these pamphlets I picked up at a pregnancy care center. It shows the pictures of the baby at different stages of development. At twenty weeks, this tiny baby is sucking his thumb. Cute, huh? Can you honestly tell me he's not a baby?"

He scooted closer and turned the brochure over. "I once attended a fundraiser for this organization. The speaker was a young woman who'd survived a late-term abortion. The doctor had left her for dead in a cold back room, but a sympathetic nurse saved her life. The nurse quietly sneaked the baby out a back door and took her to the ER.

"When the nurse who adopted her was told that her daughter would never talk or walk, she didn't give up. Instead, she worked tirelessly with the child to help her overcome her handicaps. Her loving hands spent many hours giving her child physical therapy while praying for strength and wholeness."

Jonah sat back and watched Katy's body slump over a cushion she cradled in her arms. Instead of offering her comfort, he continued his story. "God definitely had a plan for that 'fetus.' There wasn't a dry eye when she finished her speech. The young woman's face glowed as she sang a beautiful song of praise and worship to the one who had given her life.

"After that night, I never again questioned the abortion issue. The right to life belongs to God alone."

"Stop!" That's all Katy said, before she bent double and

wailed into the soft pillow. Jonah knew his suspicions were true—her defense of a woman's right to choose had been fueled by guilt.

No longer interested in pressing his point, Jonah reached for Katy. He held her in his arms and prayed. "Oh, Father, you see Katy's broken heart. You promised to be near the brokenhearted and to save those who are crushed in spirit. You care about every part of her life. Let your Holy Spirit comfort her as she grieves the loss of her child."

Katy sat upright and searched his eyes. "How do you know why I'm upset?"

Sympathy welled in Jonah's chest as he thought of his own broken heart—the guilt he still carried over Monica's death. "I suspected as much when you wanted pro-choice to be our first topic of debate. You were too defensive. I watched your expression when I talked about our future child."

Katy began to cry again. "You must hate me. I've heard all the arguments about the difference between a fetus and a baby, but when you're talking about your own child, the pain becomes real. That's why I've been so faithful to pass out birth control to the young people in this neighborhood. I don't want them to have to go through what I did."

"If you're so adamant about not wanting them to get pregnant, why won't you consider teaching a class on abstinence?"

Katy rolled her eyes. "How can you be so naïve? Young people will have sex no matter what anyone says. They might as well be equipped to prevent disease and pregnancy."

"But you are expecting them to fail when you make their sexual promiscuity easy. Wouldn't some listen if they understood the consequences? If you taught them to have a relationship with God and to consider his thoughts on premarital sex, they would have a reason for self-control."

Leaning away from him, Katy stared. "Is that what you do? Did you think about God in the middle of our knee-weakening kisses? If you think I'm going to buy that, you're a little dense, and I don't need another screwed up person around here."

Jonah chuckled at Katy's description of the chemistry

between them. "I know my claim seems strange, but when I'm about to displease God, his Spirit gently reminds me of who I am in him. That might be difficult for the average person, but I have always depended on a conscience submitted to God. I wasn't in close fellowship with him the first time I kissed you. And yes, I was tempted to ignore the voice of reason screaming at me. That moment frightened me enough to waste no time getting alone and having a serious talk with God.

"Unless I'm putting God first, everything else becomes skewed. After I read a few Scriptures on sexual sins, I asked God to forgive me. Now, I must ask your forgiveness as well. I dishonored you by my actions and the thoughts running through my mind."

Katy waved her hand, dismissing his concerns. "Does the Bible really talk about sex?"

"Actually, the Bible has a lot to say on the subject of sex and marriage. Jesus compared the way a husband loves his wife to the way God loves the body of Christ. God created sex as a special bond within marriage and to propagate the earth. I'm motivated to obey God not only because of the possible consequences, but because I love him and want to please him. Let me show you a few verses."

After Jonah read a passage from 1 Thessalonians, Katy took his Bible and silently reread the verses. She finally looked up. "You believe this?"

"Yes, I do. God cares how we treat our bodies and the bodies of others. He wants us to avoid sexual immorality. In fact, Paul called the people heathen if they were unable to control their lustful actions."

Jonah took the Bible from her and turned to a verse in 1 Corinthians where Paul called our bodies temples of the Holy Spirit. He continued reading verse after verse to make his point.

Katy stood and paced the area before him. "According to this, I can never hope to be with someone like you. You have saved yourself for your wife while I'm considered unclean."

Jonah quoted from memory 1 John 1:9 to refute her claim.

"If we confess our sins, he is faithful and just to forgive us our sins, and to cleanse us from all unrighteousness" (KJV).

Next, he read 2 Corinthians 5:17. "This means that anyone who belongs to Christ has become a new person. The old life is gone; a new life has begun!"

Jonah grabbed her hand and eased her back to her seat. "You don't have to worry about being accepted by God or me. We all sin. Some of our sins bear more consequence than others, but we are imperfect people attempting to live as close to God as possible. Instead of debating social issues, why don't we just study the Bible together?"

Katy rubbed her hands down her jeans. "I guess so. Are you sure the Bible isn't just a bunch of rules somebody made up to keep us from enjoying life?"

Jonah chuckled. "Of course not. God loves us, but love involves sacrifice, forgiveness, and reconciliation. His plan of salvation through his Son, Jesus, allows us to live in his perfect love. When we see the truth of our own sinfulness, we are free to extend love and forgiveness to others."

Katy withdrew her hands and leaned away. "Who are you? You scare me. You kiss me as if you want to make love to me; then you act like some fundamentalist preacher. I'm pretty confused right now, and I'm not totally convinced that God cares about all this. You should leave."

"What about the Bible study?"

"I don't know. Right now, I'm in information overload. I'll have to let you know later."

Jonah took Katy's face in his hands and looked into her eyes. "You are precious to me and to God. I love the way you sacrifice your time and resources for others. God loves you very much. Give us both a chance."

When Katy leaned into his touch, Jonah sighed in frustration. *Why did you put this tempting woman in my path? Her body stirs me to the core, and I am falling for her despite the huge mountain separating us.*

When he pulled her into an embrace, Katy stiffened and pushed him off. She jumped to her feet and marched to the door. "One last question before you go. Since you are so adamant that abortion is wrong, have you ever protested at an abortion clinic?"

Jonah couldn't lie to her, yet his honest answer might end all hope of seeing her again. From her reaction he suspected she had been hurt by overzealous protesters trying to stop her from making a terrible mistake. *Please help her to understand.*

"I want you to consider what you would do if one of your students lay dying of an overdose of drugs. Wouldn't you do all you could to save her? Yes, I have carried signs and even begged young women to reconsider what they planned to do."

At his answer, Katy's face turned an angry red. She pressed her lips together in a tight pout. Jonah had lost her as surely as the night is dark. "Katy." He reached for her. "Don't be like this. Try to understand."

Katy batted at his hands. "Don't you ever touch me again, Officer Abbott. Get out of my house and don't ever return. I do not need your help or your promise of love and forgiveness. I've done nothing wrong."

Jonah's shoulders slumped in defeat. "I'll be praying for you, Katy."

"Don't bother. I got along fine without your prayers. Besides, we aren't praying for the same things."

Realizing he couldn't agree with the angry woman, Jonah picked up his briefcase and left. She slammed and locked the door behind him. He paused on the porch, reining in his emotions. As he moved toward the steps, he heard Katy's wail on the other side of the door. He had to stop himself from banging on the door and demanding entrance. She didn't want him or his religion, and she wouldn't want the comfort of his arms. Jonah prayed for strength as he willed his feet to leave Katy's porch for what might be the last time.

CHAPTER SEVEN

Katy slumped against the door until her legs collapsed beneath her. Between sobs and wails, she berated herself for her actions. The man both confused and annoyed her at the same time. He wasn't the typical conservative. He loved and cared for everyone without an ounce of prejudice—even those who disagreed with him.

But his strict interpretation of the Bible bothered her. She enjoyed reading the Scriptures in church. Katy believed the authors were influenced by the traditions and cultures of their times.

Jonah claimed the Bible revealed God's love for his people. He probably said mankind, but to her, even that sounded sexist. Most of what she read in the Old Testament contained violence, murder, and abuse—men ruling over women and mistreating them. She failed to see the love thread.

Katy plopped on the couch with a deep sigh. The differences between the two of them were too great. No matter how handsome or how much she longed for Jonah, they could never be together.

Katy wiped the tears from her face and adjusted the cushions on the couch. Her hand hit something solid—Jonah's Bible tucked under one of the pillows. She wanted to throw the book into the fire, but the soft leather felt good in her hands. Curious, she flipped through the thin pages. Nearly every page contained highlighted sections and handwritten notes in the margins. Katy felt like an intruder on Jonah's private thoughts.

When she came to the note, praying this for Chad, she had to read the verse to discover what he meant. "I pray that from (God's) glorious, unlimited resources he will empower (Chad) with inner strength through his spirit. Then Christ will make his home in (Chad's) heart as (he) trusts in him" (Ephesians 3:16–17).

Jonah had inserted the name Chad into the verses with a pen. Why would he mark up the Bible he considered so sacred? Katy wondered. Despite her confusion, curiosity kept her reading to the end of the chapter.

Just as she decided to close the book, her eye caught a note near the bottom of that same page. For Katy and me to be made new in the attitude of our minds. What did he mean by that? There was absolutely nothing wrong with her attitude or her mind, and she didn't like to be included in his weirdness. Katy closed the book with a decisive thwack, hoping to dismiss thoughts of Jonah and his abandoned book with the same resolve.

Finding Jonah's Bible wasn't the problem. She suspected he had left the book as an excuse to see her again, and Katy hadn't changed her mind. She didn't need Jonah Abbott or anything he had to say.

Katy tightened her grip on the book. "Finders keepers," she mumbled as she thrust the Bible on a high shelf. At least the book would be out of sight.

Unfortunately, out of sight didn't guarantee out of mind. Often when she entered the living room, her curiosity trumped her resolve. Katy retrieved the Bible from its high perch and hungrily searched for her name. She'd only known Jonah a few days, yet she found numerous verses he'd underlined and marked, for Katy. Most were in the Psalms and related to healing and comfort.

She sat for hours flipping through the thin pages, intrigued by the words. Sometimes she read several chapters before returning the book to its lofty perch. Katy flinched. Fascination with his book did not mean that she would allow Jonah back into her life.

With tidbits of Jonah's notes scrolling through her head, Katy paced the living room. The preacher man and his

Bible kept her in a state of uncertainty. She questioned the validity of facts that had formerly motivated and inspired her. Lips pursed, she wondered what she longed for more— Jonah or his knowledge of God.

For the next two weeks, Katy wavered between two conflicting emotions. She blamed Jonah for the self-doubt he'd initiated, and she never wanted to see him again. At the same time, she didn't see herself living another day without him.

Despite her emotional turmoil, Katy continued to read from Jonah's Bible each morning. The book now occupied a prominent place on the round table in her sunroom—her spot for meditating.

Not a day went by that she didn't pick up the phone to call Jonah. He would have the answer to questions tormenting her. But before the call went through, Katy remembered why she avoided him. She pressed the off button and slumped back in the comfortable chair.

After two weeks of hanging up before the call connected, Katy dialed the number again. While remembering the warmth of Jonah's arms and his comforting words she'd read in his Bible, she heard a familiar voice calling her name.

What had she done? Katy pressed the off button and threw the phone into a nearby chair. Her only reason for calling was to ask questions of the biblical scholar, not be distracted by his soft, sexy voice.

Katy bit her lip when the phone rang. Jonah's picture identified the caller—the picture she'd taken before she knew anything about him. Just before the answering machine picked up, Katy accepted the call, but remained silent.

"Katy? You called?"

"Don't do this to me. I don't know why I'm calling you."

"Is it possible you have something that belongs to me and have decided to return it?"

Katy frowned at the phone. "Don't give me that song and dance. You are the one who left your Bible here. If this book is as precious as you say, I would think you'd have tried to retrieve it by now."

"Oh, I knew where I left the book. In fact, I left my Bible for you in case you couldn't find your own. I have another."

"Are you trying to convert me to your right-wing philosophy?"

"I'm neither right nor left. I'm on God's side and that's the safest place to be. Have you thought any more about us getting together to study the Bible?"

"Oh, yeah. That must be the reason I called. Since you seem to be the expert on reading God's mind, maybe you could help me understand."

Jonah laughed while Katy clenched her teeth. What was wrong with the man? He never seemed rattled or upset. The only time she saw him confused was the day he had placed her under arrest. She had been drawn to his vulnerability, but, unfortunately, she hadn't seen that look since.

"I would love to explore any questions you might have. Would you consider inviting some of the young people from the neighborhood to join us?"

Katy frowned at the idea of an audience while discussing personal issues with Jonah. But the excitement in his voice was hard to refuse. Jonah acted more like a minister than a police officer.

Regardless, she thought back to that day he had prayed for her. A weight had lifted from her shoulders, and she breathed freely for the first time in years. She wanted to know what made him tick—where his strength came from.

Katy tapped her foot against the tile floor. How would she resist the chemistry between them? Perhaps the young people would serve as a buffer to keep them focused on the Bible. Jonah cleared his throat, breaking the silence. He barreled ahead. "Why don't we meet every Wednesday evening. Is that good for you?"

Resigned, Katy rested her chin on her knees. "That's one evening I don't have a night class, but I don't want you pushing your extreme ideas on the young people. You can talk about abstinence, but that's all."

"My plan is to study the Bible. Why don't we just see what God reveals through his Word?"

Katy clenched her stretchy jeans at the knees. Did he have something devious up his sleeve? Like brainwashing her with his weird ideas? Jonah interrupted her thoughts. "Don't worry about the details. We'll just take it one day at a time and if something makes you uncomfortable, we'll reevaluate the whole thing."

Katy caught her breath. Could he read her mind? They hadn't even had their first meeting and she was yanking at her hair. "If you're sure."

"Good. We'll begin the study in the Gospel of John, one of the clearest pictures of Christ's love. The young people need to know what God thinks about them. How about you read the book before next Wednesday and help me lead the discussion?"

Katy wasn't even certain where to find the book of John, but she refused to acknowledge that to her walking Bible. She worried about his ideas rubbing off on her. If she'd been wrong about one issue, could she be wrong about others? Despite her reservations, she needed answers and a Bible study with Jonah would be a good place to start.

"So, it's okay if I keep the Bible you left at my house?"

"Sure. If you need it."

Katy didn't need his Bible. She had one somewhere, but she didn't want to give up his notations. She hungered for more of the treasures she found every time she opened Jonah's book.

Monday evening Katy sat down with Jonah's Bible searching for the book of John. Since she recognized the name as one of Jesus's disciples, she opened to the middle and flipped to the right. While on her hunt, she stopped when she came across a familiar name—Jonah. She traced the title of the short book with her finger. Tempted to investigate further, the fear of facing Jonah unprepared trumped her curiosity.

Katy searched to the end and found more than one book attributed to John. Releasing a breath of frustration, she turned back to the first book and began to read. The words jumped off the page and pricked her interest. John called Jesus the Word and claimed he was with God from the beginning.

She covered her heart with the open Bible and pondered her discovery. How could she have spent years in church without seeing Jesus as more than the babe in a manger? Her curiosity pricked, Katy continued reading. She had read several chapters before taking the first note. Never had she expected to find a page-turner within a religious book. Excitement built at the thought of lengthy discussions with Jonah.

At Jonah's suggestion, Katy posted a flyer advertising the study. The big draw would be free pizza purchased at Jonah's expense. She smiled as she thought of Jonah and food—his answer to almost everything. When she had accused him of bribery, he brushed her off with one of his uncanny quips. "Anything for the kingdom."

Whatever did that mean? Although Katy wanted to discover more about the Bible, Jonah's strange talk worried her. She feared he would change her program into something she didn't recognize or want. Her work in the neighborhood had become her life. She would not allow one overzealous man to destroy her mission. If he did, she'd never forgive him.

CHAPTER EIGHT

By seven Wednesday night, Katy's home was filled with teenagers. After they wolfed down ten pizzas, Jonah debated ordering more. But Katy stopped him and invited the kids into the living room.

Jonah cringed at the raucous laughter coming from the overcrowded room. What had he been thinking? Massaging the back of his neck, Jonah paced back and forth in the kitchen. He should be out beating the pavements in search of the persons determined to discredit Katy. But so far, his team had struck out.

Jonah paused in his trek across the tile floor. Perhaps God had a different idea. Some of the kids recognized him, but he didn't think they were aware of his occupation. He groaned in frustration at the inconsistent turn of events. The idea of playing bad boy had lost its appeal. Besides, his actions contradicted the positive message he wanted to convey. Still, Jonah couldn't disappoint Katy.

Moments after he thought of her, Katy came into the room. Her gentle touch to his arm stopped his pacing. "Calm down, Jonah. You make me nervous. You were right about the food—free pizza and an opportunity to mingle with friends brought them here. Now you need to get a grip before they have the place rocking with their own entertainment. My house cannot take much more. Pull yourself together and do what you think is so important."

At Katy's nudge, Jonah walked into the foyer and surveyed the crowded room. Kids had filled the couches and chairs and were sprawled over every inch of the floor. His heart skipped a beat when he thought of the battles the teens faced every day—battles he never had to face. Tears stung his eyes. *God show me how to help them.*

He breathed a prayer of thanksgiving when a familiar story came to mind. Jonah opened his Bible to one of his favorites—the woman at the well. Some of the young people might relate to her dysfunctional life. He hoped her story would lead to a discussion about prejudice, sexual promiscuity, and forgiveness.

Jonah put two fingers to his mouth and produced a loud whistle, then cleared his throat. "Let me have your attention. I know you're enjoying your friends, but we came here to study the Bible. Let's begin with prayer."

After prayer, Jonah thanked Katy for opening her home. He needed a question to break the ice. "What do you know about God and the Bible?" His question generated only silence and blank stares until a girl sitting on the couch raised her hand.

"You want to know why I came tonight? My Grandma made me. She said you were serving pizza, and she didn't want to cook. So, she sent me and my brother here for dinner. She said a little Bible study wouldn't hurt me either."

Everyone laughed, and the girl he remembered as Sierra stood and bowed while her admirers applauded and whistled loudly. Jonah grinned when he remembered Katy's prediction. "They'll come for free food." The woman knew her clients.

Jonah coughed to stem his own laughter. "Moving right along. How many of you read the book of John before coming tonight?"

Only a few hands went up before Jaylen stood. "Listen, man, I don't have a Bible, and I don't have money to get one. How you expect me to read—go to the library?" Again, everyone laughed and nodded their agreement with the over-dramatic comedian.

Katy stepped forward and interrupted the melee with her hand. "If you don't have a Bible and want one, see me after the meeting. I'll purchase some before next week. I don't know about you, but I'm anxious to get to the study. I read the Gospel of John for the first time and found the stories fascinating."

Jonah looked at the woman standing beside him. He wanted to hug her. She may not agree with him on everything, but she had made herself vulnerable—willing to listen and stand with him to help others. And he loved her the more for it.

"Since you didn't get a chance to read the book for yourselves, I'll pick one of the stories for us."

After Jonah read the story of the Samaritan woman, he looked around the room, praying for the right words. "When we study the Bible, we look for examples to help us live better lives—to avoid the mistakes of the characters. The woman who met Jesus at the well has at least two strikes against her. First, she was a woman in a culture that did not value women. Second, she lived in the area called Samaria. In Jesus's day, men generally didn't speak to unescorted women, and the Jews hated the Samaritans. Did either of those two circumstances keep Jesus from addressing her? No, he saw her as a person and treated her with respect. What do you think he noticed about her?"

The kids were determined to keep the comedy act going with outrageous answers—some too raw to repeat or even acknowledge. To regain control, Jonah returned to his own take on the story and held his questions for the end.

"Jesus saw her hungry, thirsty heart. She longed for someone to really love and care for her. When he pointed out that she lived with someone without the benefit of marriage, she changed the subject, and talked about worship. From what happened next, we know she didn't forget what he told her. When she went back into the village, she told everyone, 'Come see a man who knew all about the things I did, who knows me inside and out' (John 4:29 MSG).

"Not once did Jesus condemn her, but his kindness led her to desire the gift he offered. He invited her to drink of the living water that only he could provide—the water of eternal life. When she wondered if he were a prophet, he revealed himself as the Messiah she'd been waiting for all her life. Jesus replied, 'Anyone who drinks this water will soon become thirsty again. But those who drink the water I give will never be thirsty again. It becomes a fresh, bubbling spring within them, giving them eternal life'" (John 4:13).

Jonah hadn't taught a Bible study in years. He'd forgotten the satisfaction of watching the responses on the faces. Though a few of the teens whispered or checked their phones, most were attentive. "Three things stand out to me in this story. Number one: She was needy, thirsty for something that none of her lovers had been able to give her. Number two: She had been ostracized and persecuted because of her race, her religion, and her lifestyle. Number three: Although Jesus pointed out her sin, he loved and accepted her without prejudice or judgment. The Bible has much to say about sexual sins and how they not only affect us but others as well. Next week we will search the Scriptures to find out what God has to say about sex—something he created at the very beginning of time."

Some of the guys were punching each other and making rude remarks, but Jonah halted their bantering when he reached behind the couch and pulled out a guitar.

"Before we dismiss, I would like to sing a song I remember from youth group a few years ago. When we finish singing, you may leave or stay behind if you want to talk with Miss Katy or myself. Thank you all for coming."

While tuning his guitar, Jonah breathed a prayer for the young people. He played the song taken from Psalm 51, "Create in Me a Clean Heart," and sang the words as a prayer.

When he finished, no one spoke or moved for a couple of minutes. Then one of the older boys stood and started clapping. "You know anything besides church stuff. How about a little rap?"

Jonah laughed and began playing one of the popular Christian rap songs with lots of string play. Some kids gathered around while others left. Katy entertained a few of the girls in the kitchen with leftover cookies and soda.

After a couple more songs, Jonah put down his guitar and encouraged the kids to leave. "You guys be careful on the way home. You never know what might be lurking in the shadows. Whatever you do, don't walk home alone."

Jonah chuckled and shook his head at his lecture. When had he become his father? Walking into the kitchen, he stood at a distance and watched Katy standing at the sink. A wayward strand of light brown hair hid her face as she rinsed the cookie platter. When she turned off the water and noticed him, she pushed back her hair to reveal eyes glistening with welcome. A surge of warmth spread over his body. Every moment spent in Katy's presence drew him closer.

"Thank you for hosting the Bible study. I'm not certain how God will use this time, but I think we're doing the right thing."

She gave him a shy smile. "I agree. Thank you for the suggestion."

Jonah glanced at the overflowing trash can. "I'm sorry about the mess. Since the weather is warm, do you suppose we might confine the food and drink to the patio? Let me help you clean up."

"The patio isn't a bad idea. We could build a fire in the pit and have a little music outside before we come in for the study. That might work better."

Katy handed him a stack of pizza boxes. "Here, take these to the trash and come back for the recyclables. I could kick myself for filling the kids with fat and chemicals. You're a bad influence on me."

Jonah chuckled as he gathered the trash. He knew unhealthy food went against Katy's grain. "If you can come up with an acceptable alternative, I'd be happy to oblige. The fire pit might work too. Let's try that."

"I'll see what I can do before next week about the food and the outdoor idea. Speaking of next week, I didn't know you played the guitar. You amaze me with your numerous talents—police officer, preacher, teacher, counselor and now, musician. You have any more surprises you want to reveal?"

Jonah found Katy's sweet, teasing smile hard to resist. He pulled her toward him and whispered huskily in her ear,

"I think I'm falling in love with you. How will I endure such temptation?"

Katy planted a quick kiss on his lips before pushing him away. "Since you have no intentions other than driving me crazy, get back to cleanup. I'd appreciate a decent night's sleep, for a change." With that little quip, she pulled him toward the closet and reached for an upright vacuum.

Jonah sang a contemporary Christian song as the vacuum sucked up cookie crumbs and bits of pizza crust. Music had not spoken to him like this in a long time. Growing up with his older brothers in a preacher's home, they hadn't listened to secular music. But after Monica died, he wanted nothing to remind him of his failures and disappointments.

To fit in, he embraced loud rap or heavy metal. While cruising the neighborhoods, his car rocked with the blaring music. If he ever left the force, he'd need hearing aids to compensate for his damaged ear drums.

Jonah stuck a finger in his ear and turned off the vacuum. He noticed Katy on her knees, tackling a stubborn stain on the carpet. When he saw tears dripping from her chin, he did a double take. Kneeling beside her, he took the cleaning supplies from her hands and set them aside. He captured her hands and whispered a prayer while massaging her knuckles.

Jonah handed her a tissue. "What's wrong?"

She wiped her nose and looked into his eyes. "I'm not sure. The story you told about the woman keeps replaying in my head. She reminded me of myself—so empty inside and thirsty for something she didn't understand. Your song touched me. Remind me where I can find that verse in the Bible. The words described my feelings perfectly."

"I'll write down the reference for you, but you can find a video performed by Keith Green on YouTube. The original words are from Psalm 51. King David prayed this prayer after he committed adultery with Bathsheba. He had her husband killed to hide his sin. David asked God to forgive him and restore the joy of salvation to his spirit."

Katy drew her eyebrows together. "Are you sure? I've heard about King David, but I never knew he committed such crimes."

"Like I've told you, none of us are perfect. God saw David's humility when Nathan, the prophet, told him how his sin grieved God. Even with such violence in David's life, God called him a 'man after his own heart' because he was willing to confess his sin and seek God."

Katy sniffed and looked up at Jonah. "I guess that means there's hope for me then."

"Absolutely! God is faithful to forgive. We only need to ask."

"How do you happen to know the Bible so well? You not only quote verses but know exactly where they're found. Did you study to be a minister? I thought you said you were majoring in business and finance."

Jonah chuckled at Katy's question. "When you grow up with a family of ministers, some of their influence is bound to rub off. Even my mother had a verse for every occasion. My brothers did everything together—same college, same major and same profession. Since I wanted my own identity, I went a different direction. Believe me, a policeman wasn't my first choice. Although I studied accounting, I still maintained a close relationship with God. All through high school and college, I attended Bible studies."

At the thought of Monica, Jonah lowered his voice and grew solemn. "In my senior year, something terrible happened. I left the university and almost dropped out of life. Perhaps one day I'll be able to share the details."

Katy cocked her head. "Were your parents okay with your change of professions?"

"They thought I'd jumped off the deep end, and sometimes I think I did."

Jonah pulled Katy to her feet and held her close. "Let me pray for you before I go. In Jeremiah 29:13 we are told, 'If you look for me wholeheartedly, you will find me.' Just do what the Bible says."

As Jonah prayed, he'd never felt so close to another person. He'd misjudged her. Her physical beauty belied her depth of character. She possessed courage, strength, and a heart of love and compassion. How could he have been so wrong?

CHAPTER NINE

Following the success of Wednesday evening, Jonah called Katy every morning. Instead of repeating his crack of dawn performance, he waited until after ten. His excuse to call was legitimate—to talk about the Bible study. But, more than anything, he wanted to hear her voice.

In his occasional telephone calls to his parents, he avoided any mention of Katy. So far, he'd escaped the dreaded, "Are you seeing anyone?" They would not understand his obsession with someone so different. Their connection didn't make sense to him either, but he couldn't escape the hold she had on him. Eventually he'd have to tell them, but for now, they didn't need another reason to doubt his judgment.

Dealing with Katy's father was a different matter. Almost every day, the mayor called the police chief demanding answers. Chief Morrison passed along the mayor's threats to dismiss Jonah if the persons responsible for endangering his daughter weren't arrested soon.

Jonah chased one dead-end lead after the next. The villains taunted him—throwing out bait, then mocking his failed efforts. If not for Katy, he would have abandoned the chase. But every day, he uncovered further proof that someone wanted her dead. When he suggested she return to her parents' home, she almost threw him out of the house. Her independence frightened him, while her personality tempted him to the limit. He struggled to keep his mind and his hands off her.

They met on Friday afternoon, Jonah's first day off, to plan future Bible studies and pray for the young people. After the planning meeting, they decided to go out for dinner. Katy wanted to try a trendy new place specializing in fresh organic and natural foods. Jonah would have preferred pizza, but he'd eat anything to be with Katy.

On the drive to the restaurant, they passed one of the kids running toward Katy's house. The teen kept looking behind him as if he were being followed.

"Turn around. That was Antonio. He looks upset." Katy turned to watch Antonio. "He's headed for my place."

When the boy again looked behind him, he recognized Jonah's car and ran toward them. Tears streamed down his face. Out of breath, Antonio held onto the side of the car to keep from falling. "You've got to help me, Mr. A. My brother—I can't wake him up."

"Get in, Antonio. Tell us where you found him. What's your brother's name?"

Antonio hesitated as if afraid to answer. Fear for his brother's life proved greater. "His name is Montel, and I think he's on heroin. Does God love him like you said Wednesday night?"

"Yes, Antonio. He loves both of you. This would be a good time to pray."

Jonah prayed under his breath as the frightened youth directed them to an abandoned warehouse a few blocks south. From the outside the place looked deserted. Jonah held Katy and Antonio back while he slipped inside. When he didn't find anyone, he motioned for them to join him. The young man led them past storage crates, cardboard boxes, and trash bins until they reached a far corner of the warehouse.

Antonio rushed forward and knelt beside the body of a young man. Curled into a fetal position, the boy looked to be no more than fifteen or sixteen.

Jonah touched the teen's face and checked his nose for signs of breathing. "Montel, can you hear me?"

Despite the shallow breaths, a weak pulse alarmed Jonah. "Call 911, Katy. Antonio, run outside and check the address for the EMTs."

As Katy and Antonio followed orders, Jonah pulled a packet from inside his jean jacket. His hand shook as he reviewed the directions and tore open the packaging. The emergency treatment for drug overdose, Naloxone, had been introduced that very morning in staff meeting. The drug just might save the young man's life.

Jonah sprayed the medicine in the teen's nostrils, then turned him back to his side. While waiting for the ambulance, his mind wandered over the chain of events. Even the slightest detail didn't escape God's attention. Meeting Katy, his renewed relationship with God, the Bible study, even the life-saving drug he'd given the boy—all part of God's grand plan.

Jonah put his hand on Montel's chest and prayed. Despite the temptation to look around, he stayed with the boy. A heroin overdose could send Montel into convulsions. With the recent influx of the dangerous drug, Jonah suspected a connection between the main supplier and whoever threatened Katy.

Not long after Jonah heard the wail of sirens, he looked up and saw Katy directing the emergency personnel toward him. She had her arm around Antonio and whispered in his ear. The woman amazed him. She loved all people regardless of their behavior, color, culture, or creed. And he didn't mind that her unconditional love spilled over on him.

A wave of conviction swept over him when he remembered an incident not long after he had joined the force. He'd been on the lookout for a suspect who had robbed a convenience store. When he stopped the first suspicious person he saw, intense anger looked him in the eye. "Tell me, Mr. Policeman, would you have stopped me if I wasn't Black?"

That question haunted Jonah for days. To be honest, he had no other reason for suspecting the young man. Upon further investigation, the young man's mother had sent him to check on his sick grandfather. *God forgive me. How can I follow you with so much sin clouding my vision?*

Jonah rubbed the back of his neck while he watched the EMTs load Montel into the ambulance. He took Katy by the arm. "Do you mind waiting in the car with Antonio while I talk to the investigating officer? I need to explain our involvement."

"Don't take too long. Antonio wants to follow the ambulance to the hospital."

After a quick explanation, Jonah told the officer he would catch him later. When he arrived at the car, Katy sat in the back with Antonio. She was bent over with her head resting on her knees. Both Antonio and his brother had been to the Bible study. He understood her concern. Knowing the boys personally elevated them to a whole different level.

"Jonah, we need to pray."

Katy turned to the young man and placed her arm around him. "Do you remember what Jonah told you about God loving Montel?"

Antonio shook so violently he struggled to answer, "Yes'm," he mumbled.

Jonah looked up, petitioning the Holy Spirit to pray through him—he was at a loss for words. "Heavenly Father, we come to you in the name of Jesus. You are the God of miracles and you see Montel fighting for his life. Free him from this addiction. Surround him with people who will love and care for him until he is completely free. We ask you, by the power of your Holy Spirit, to destroy the works of darkness in this neighborhood. We pray for truth, comfort, and peace to prevail. Put your arm of love and protection around Antonio and his family. In your Holy Name we pray. Amen."

Katy trembled as they waited for the ambulance to pull out. She placed her hand on her bouncing knee. This wasn't the first time she'd witnessed a drug overdose. She wanted to scream at the injustice of young lives destroyed by circumstances not always of their doing.

She'd watched at least one young man die before the emergency personnel arrived. Another barely survived. She hadn't bargained for this kind of drama when she chose to work in the neighborhood. Her dream had been to provide services for women and children in crisis, not watch young men wasted on drugs.

Now, she spent a good portion of her time rescuing addicts, persuading the court to send them to drug rehab, and educating the young people about the use of harmful substances. Those who did survive had a fighting chance at the drug rehabilitation centers, but she worried about their return to the same hostile environment. Many rejoined the community with their minds wasted from drug abuse. Others didn't have the strength or courage to refuse the next temptation. The suppliers were like filthy flies swarming around, offering a good time along with a free fix. But where were they when the child stood at death's door? Probably out searching for their next victim.

As if he understood, Jonah reached back and covered her hand. He squeezed gently before putting the car in gear and pulling out behind the ambulance. Jonah's confident reaction puzzled Katy. He'd either become immune to violence or he possessed something she didn't have.

Though the prayer had been her idea, the intensity shocked her. She expected a quiet petition, not a fiery declaration of war. Moments into the prayer, his tone changed to compassion and understanding. The man had two faces, and she wasn't sure she liked the bold, preachy one.

Katy's body stopped shaking as a calming presence filled the interior of the car. Antonio must have felt it as well. He released his tight grip on her hand and relaxed against the back of the seat. The peace stayed with her as she walked the boy through the doors of the emergency room.

When they checked in at the desk, the receptionist handed Antonio a clipboard with several forms. Katy shook her head when the boy stared at the blank lines. "We need to call your mother. Do you know her number?"

Antonio released a breath. "She works at the chicken packing plant, but she keeps her cell phone turned on."

He rattled off the number, lowered his head, and stared at his hands. Katy dialed the number and passed the phone to Antonio. "Mama, something's happened to Montel. We're at the hospital." From Katy's spot a few feet away, she overheard the mother's loud keening.

The grinding of the revolving doors drew Katy's attention. The impatient Jonah forced the slow-moving doors to a faster pace. She waited until he had freed himself. "Antonio is talking to his mother. I wish we had told her in person. She's so upset."

Jonah didn't hesitate. He walked over to Antonio and took the phone. "Mrs. Thomas, this is Jonah Abbott. I'm so sorry about Montel, but I believe he'll be all right. I'm on my way now to pick you up. I understand you work at the chicken plant."

Jonah checked his watch. "Can you meet me outside the plant entrance in fifteen minutes?"

Katy envied Jonah's calming influence. Without the least hesitation, he knew what to do and reacted with such peaceful assurance that even the mother had quieted by the time she hung up.

"Keep praying, guys. This battle won't be easy, but we have God on our side. I'll be back in a little while with your mother. Hang in there, buddy."

With that pep talk, he rushed to the doors and exited with the same effort. Katy and Antonio stared after him. From the moment Jonah arrived, everything changed. He had rocked Katy's world a few short weeks ago and had kept her reeling since.

Katy tried to do as Jonah suggested, but her prayers felt as if they evaporated before reaching the ceiling. She'd never been a television fan and inactivity didn't suit, but there was nothing else to do. She longed to change—or at least mute—the twenty-four-hour cable news channel for something more calming. Antonio paced the area near the receptionist. He looked up occasionally as if in prayer. Good boy. At least someone's prayers would be effective.

Katy's head hurt, and acid burned her empty stomach. She abandoned the television and plopped into a red plastic chair. The only news she wanted to hear was a report on Montel. She followed Antonio's movements as he continued to pace. He needed words of comfort, but she had none to give.

She looked up as the revolving doors growled. Jonah walked in with his arm around a tall woman. A hairnet covered the woman's short brown curls and her work clothes were streaked with bloodstains. Making her way across the room, Katy searched for something to say, but the grieving mother only shook her head and moaned.

"I told that boy to stay away from those guys. Older men hanging out with youngsters is never a good idea. Lord, what will I do if something happens to my boy?" She grabbed Antonio and held him in a tight hug. "My sweet boy, thank God you're okay."

After Mrs. Thomas consoled her younger son, she went to the desk to finish the paperwork and inquire about Montel. A nurse led her down the hall, leaving Katy more frustrated than ever. Jonah ignored her in favor of his cell phone. He paced back and forth near the elevator. Antonio sat quietly on the other side of the room. Oh, for a good tension-releasing scream!

When they'd waited what seemed like half the night, Antonio's mother returned and approached her son. Together, they walked over to Katy. "Our boy's going to make it. I'm so glad you found him when you did. The doctor says he's lucky, but I know the good Lord watched out for him."

Jonah joined them, then accompanied Mrs. Thomas and Antonio to see Montel. Alone, Katy cried tears of relief. Restless, her mind wandered to the plight of the other young people. She grieved for them and the obstacles they faced. Along with drugs came violence, poverty, and neglect. Her compassion for the kids freed her to pray. God, please show us what to do.

Not once since meeting Jonah had she considered facing the future alone. Regardless of their differences or her preferences, they were a team. Her thoughts were interrupted when a warm body took the seat next to her. Jonah put his arm around her and whispered in her ear. "Are you okay?"

Katy smiled through watery eyes. "I'm worried about these kids. What did the doctor say about Montel?"

"Fortunately, the drugs were only beginning to seep into his system when I gave him the Naloxone. He's going to be fine. They're giving him additional meds to neutralize the heroin and fluids to combat dehydration. He'll have to stay a few days for observation and psychological assessment."

Jonah brushed her hair back and kissed her cheek. Katy leaned against his shoulder. "I'm glad he's okay, but they can't release him to return home. I plan to stick around until I get permission to send him to rehab. We can't throw him back to the same wolves who are determined to destroy him."

When Jonah offered to wait with her, Katy looked at her watch. "It's already late. You need rest and nourishment before you report for duty in a few hours."

Jonah protested until Katy touched a finger to his lips. Jonah nodded in agreement, kissed her forehead, and left with the promise to call the next morning.

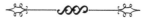

Jonah wanted to question Montel's mother and brother regarding the people he hung with, but Katy was right—he was exhausted. As he left the hospital, he thought of the strength she brought to the situation. Even though she was upset, she pulled herself together and began planning for Montel's release and recovery. A combination of God, the boy's brother, and the medical staff had saved Montel's life. But Katy would make a way for him to avoid a reoccurrence.

Jonah tossed and turned on his bed, sleep eluding him. He tried to distinguish the knowns from the unknowns in the complicated drug world. There had to be a connection between the attempt to frame Katy and the opposition to her social work. Situations such as Montel's would continue if they didn't dry up the drug source.

When his ideas kept hitting a dead end, he rolled out of bed and landed on his knees. Regardless of the odds, Jonah believed in prayer. He didn't know how effective his prayers were, but only a short time later, he crawled back into bed and drifted into a deep sleep. With the morning light came the reassurance that God would be with him.

CHAPTER TEN

Montel had been released from the hospital that morning. The overdose had frightened him enough he agreed to three months of rehab instead of taking his chances before a judge. After his lengthy interview with Jonah and his team, Katy drove Montel and his mother to the drug rehabilitation center and walked them through the admission process.

Katy realized her actions would be considered another interference by the drug dealers, but she didn't care. Montel was one of her boys, and she planned to use every resource available to give him a fighting chance.

When Montel realized they were leaving, he clung to his mother and cried. "You can do this, Son. I know you haven't thought much about God lately, but it's time to trust him. Your brother and I will be praying for you."

Even as the car backed out of the parking space, Katy saw Montel staring out the window. She reached across the console and squeezed his mother's hand. "I have a good feeling about this, Mrs. Thomas. Just like you told Montel, we need to trust God."

The sun was changing the sky into a radiance of colors when Katy stopped at a popular family restaurant. Over southern fried chicken, Mrs. Thomas shared some of her struggles. "I thought if I took my boys to church and worked hard to provide for them, they wouldn't get in trouble. Guess I was fooling myself. Antonio's a different kid and he'll be all right, but the temptation was too much for Montel. He said he was tired of being poor."

The fragile woman wiped a tear from the corner of her eye and shook her head. "I make enough to take care of their basic needs, but Montel isn't satisfied. I wish I knew how to get through to him."

Katy took the woman's dark hand and noticed her calloused skin. An ugly scar ran across the top of her hand and into her palm. Life wasn't easy for the single mother. Mrs. Thomas butchered chickens to provide for her boys—one of the most strenuous and dangerous jobs at the packing plant.

Before releasing the work-worn hand, Katy gave it a gentle squeeze. "Tell me about the boys' father. Is he in the picture?"

The woman shook her head. "No, he left us right after Antonio was born. He didn't like being tied down. Don't know how a man can walk out on his own flesh and blood."

Mrs. Thomas frowned at her hands and hid them in her lap. "Let's talk about something more encouraging. I can't tell you how much I appreciate what you and Mr. Jonah did for my boys. I never saw them so excited after the Bible study."

"We care about your boys."

"I know you do. They told me everything your man said in his talk. He sounded like a preacher who should be wearing a dark suit and tie. The night he came to pick me up outside the plant and got out of his old beat-up car, I almost ran back inside. He looked more like a drug dealer up to no good."

Katy chuckled at the truth behind the woman's assessment. "I wasn't going anywhere with him until he put his arm around me and began to pray. No drug dealer prayed like that. When I relaxed and cried in his arms, he assured me that he would do everything he could to help my boys. He's a good man. I hope y'all keep telling the children that Jesus loves them. They need to know that someone cares."

Katy wiped the moisture off her glass of sweet tea. "We have lessons planned for the next couple of weeks. I had never studied the Bible, but I'm learning right along with the kids."

Katy leaned toward the woman. "I would love to have a friend in the neighborhood. Would you mind calling me Katy?"

Mrs. Thomas smiled through her tears. "Only if you call me Cora. I've never had a friend so young or who didn't look like me, but I'm willing if you are."

Cora grinned and tilted her head to the side. "You probably go to church on the other side of town, but I'd be honored to have you go with me and the boys sometime."

"Why, thank you. I usually attend church with my parents, but I will definitely consider your invitation."

Two evenings later, as the clock on the mantel chimed eleven, Katy closed the mystery thriller and reached to turn off the gas fireplace. She kneaded her neck to relieve the pain working its way into the back of her head. Until recently, she'd never been afraid.

Walking through the house, she turned out lights, checked the lower-level windows and double locked the doors. Katy stopped in the kitchen and gulped down a large glass of water. Rarely did a week go by without someone from her neighborhood making the news. They'd either been arrested for an act of violence or been sent to the hospital or morgue as another unfortunate victim.

The drug pushers had warned her against "interfering in their business," but she had considered the threat little more than bullying. Now, she didn't know what to think.

Katy checked the last window downstairs and headed for the staircase. At the sound of a scraping noise on the back porch, she stopped. Afraid to breathe, she felt her heart pounding against her rib cage. Hearing nothing but the faint sound of crickets, Katy rebuked herself. She lifted her head and gripped the stair rail, refusing to give in to fear. More than likely, a stray cat or bird was the culprit.

With warm thoughts of her own cat distracting her, Katy continued toward the bedroom level. The harsh sound of breaking glass coming from the kitchen paralyzed her. Between long slow breaths, Katy prayed for protection. She grabbed the stairwell to keep from falling.

Belatedly, she wished for one of those guns Jonah had suggested. While longing for a weapon, Katy remembered the statue on the foyer table. The heavy piece might work if she could get to it before the intruder found her.

She eased down the stairs. At the bottom step she brushed against something solid, foul smelling and highly suspicious. "Well, Miss Katy. We meet again. Nice of you to find me so's I don't have to search the house for you."

"What do you want? Get out of my house before I call the police."

The man laughed and grabbed her by the arm. Katy's kick missed its mark. Her assailant slapped her across the face. She fell against the stair rail and struggled to remain upright.

With her attacker pressing the weight of his body against her, Katy feared for her life. "I'm going to kill you, but before I do, I'm going to show you what it's like to have a real man. That weasel who hangs around here is nothing compared to me. You been a lot of trouble, and I'm going to do us all a big favor by ridding this neighborhood of you and your do-gooder kind."

Katy struggled against powerful muscles. Any resistance only increased his wrath. She heard buttons bouncing down the stairs as the evil man ripped off her blouse. Shivering with the sudden chill, she resigned herself to the inevitable.

Amid the fear and hopelessness, the craziest thought popped into her head. Pray as loud as you can.

"Insane," she thought, but she'd try anything. When the man touched her breast, Katy shook with anger and shouted as loud and high pitched as possible. "Send your angels, O God, and defend me against this wicked man. Come save me, Lord Jesus."

The man stumbled back and cursed. At least she'd halted his sexual advances—if only temporarily. Her attacker's mood changed from drunken lust to angry wrath. He pummeled Katy's head with powerful fists. With each blow, evil vulgarities spewed from his mouth.

Katy grew weaker with each blow. His next punch sent her reeling against a table. When she realized they were in the foyer, she reached behind her and fumbled for the statue. At the next strike, he missed her head and staggered to the left. With her right hand, she swung the statue with all the strength she had left.

As the weapon hit the back of his head, her attacker stumbled backward to the tile. Katy bounded up the stairs, surprised at her sudden surge of energy.

She climbed the second flight of stairs into the attic before she stopped. Opening the door to the storage area, she felt her way to an old wardrobe left behind by the previous owners. She had used the piece of furniture to store winter coats donated during the spring and summer months. Pushing the few items aside, she huddled as far back in the corner as possible. Whether from the cold in the unheated attic or from paralyzing fear, Katy shivered so hard the wardrobe shook. She yanked one of the coats from its hanger to cover her exposed body. With her arms wrapped around her legs, she sobbed into the rough wool.

Still trembling, Katy located her phone in the pocket of her slacks. Katy thought of only one person, Jonah. Before she hit the call button, she heard someone on the stairs.

"Katy, Miss Katy, you are a bad, bad girl. When I find you, you're going to pay for what you did."

As the attacker called her name, the voice grew closer and closer. Katy heard closets opening, furniture splitting, and angry cursing. The door to her hiding place flew open with a loud bang. Katy curled into a tighter ball and prepared for the worst. God, please.

Praying silently, she held her breath as the intruder swiped aimlessly through the closet, missing Katy by inches. Had she somehow become invisible? The intruder gave up in disgust and swatted the door closed. Before she could release her breath, she heard heavy breathing and felt the cabinet move as if he'd leaned against the door. She heard another set of footsteps on the stairs. Her hopes dashed, she pulled herself into a tight ball.

"The woman's disappeared. I can't find her anywhere. Are you sure she's not on the second floor? The boss man's liable to kill us if she gets away. What do ya think we should do?"

The voices faded, yet Katy remained still until she heard heavy footsteps on the stairs. Taking a deep breath, she pressed the button to call Jonah.

Jonah and Joe brainstormed in a back booth of an all-night pizza joint. Finishing the last piece of the everything, jumbo pizza, they compared notes and discussed options. Nothing made sense. Their usual contacts acted suspicious and refused to cooperate.

They had gathered their notes and prepared to leave when Jonah's phone rang. Above the noise of the restaurant, he strained to hear the whispers of a woman in distress. Breathy words were scattered between sobs and sniffles. Fear gripped him when he checked the caller ID. He stood so fast he turned over his glass of iced tea.

"Katy. What's wrong."

Motioning to Joe, he continued, "I'm on my way."

"This guy broke into the house through the kitchen and he, he ... I'm hiding from him. He's with another guy and they're tearing my house apart. I prayed, Jonah."

Katy paused a minute before continuing with a gravelly voice. "You won't believe this, but I knew exactly where to hide. They were searching the whole house, even my hiding place, and didn't find me."

Jonah's heart rate accelerated. "Are they still there?"

"I'm not sure. They could have given up and left, but I'm afraid to leave my hiding spot. Please be careful when you get here. They might still be outside."

Katy sniffed. "They said they were going to kill me."

Jonah shook with anger at the thought of anyone wanting to harm Katy. He calmed himself with a few deep breaths. *God, please protect her and give me strength to control my anger. We need you.*

"Where are you now?"

"I can't tell you. What if they've hacked my phone? Call my name when you come in, so I'll know it's you."

Jonah sighed in frustration. "What if one of those guys comes back and calls your name? Don't do this to me. I need to know that you're okay."

Jonah recognized the exasperation in her voice. "Jonah, really? Believe me, I know your voice."

Her words warmed his insides like a cup of hot chocolate. "Joe and I are in the neighborhood. Be there soon."

When Joe slammed on the brakes at the curb, they both jumped out moving in different directions. Gun drawn, Jonah entered the house through the kitchen and followed the trail of broken glass and opened cabinet doors. He almost tripped over the pots and pans scattered about the floor. He'd moved into the dining room before he remembered her instructions. Instead of calling out, he checked to see if they were still connected.

"I'm downstairs, Katy. Are you still on the phone?" Jonah whispered.

Katy answered with clipped mutters. "Please be careful. They may no longer be inside, but they could be outside waiting."

"Are you going to tell me where you are, or must we play hide and seek?"

"When you get close, I'll find you."

Jonah shook his head as he mumbled under his breath, "You're killing me, woman!"

"I heard that. You love me and you know it."

Katy had calmed down enough to tease him, but he was in no mood for teasing. Jonah tightened his hold on the stair rail. His whole life had changed following the death of Monica, and he hadn't loved her the way he loved Katy. His heart pounded against his rib cage when he considered a different outcome—he might very well be searching for a dead body instead of a living, breathing Katy.

After searching the last bedroom on the upper level, Jonah started up another flight of stairs. When he looked up, Katy stood at the top wrapped in a man's coat about two sizes too big. Mischief twinkled in her eyes. Did she not understand the danger? He wanted to shake some sense into her and at the same time kiss her senseless.

"It's about time, officer." She glided down the stairs and flew into his arms. He chose to kiss her senseless.

In the middle of about the fourth kiss, he remembered his partner. His kisses moved near her ear where he whispered through his heavy breathing. "I hate to end this, but I need to check on Joe. I haven't touched base with him since we left the car."

Arm in arm, they walked down the stairs. When he took her face in his hands for one last kiss, his breath caught. Her left eye and cheek were swollen and already showed signs of bruising. Streaks of dried blood marred the corner of her mouth. Jonah pulled her tight against his chest. He wanted to kill the person who did this to her. "Why didn't you tell me you were hurt?"

"I'm okay. You'd better go."

Jonah grumbled under his breath. "You're not okay, but I do need to go. Stay in your bedroom until I get back. While you're waiting, call your parents. You can't stay here alone another night."

Katy crossed her arms and gave him her rendition of a determined pout. He tried not to smile while he waited for her to lock herself in the bedroom. At the sound of the click, Jonah took the stairs two at a time, rushed through the house and out the front door.

Sprinting in the direction he'd last seen Joe, Jonah tripped and fell headfirst over something blocking the path. He stood, turned on his flashlight, and spotted his partner lying in a pool of blood. Oh, God. Please let him be alive.

Jonah released a breath when he detected a faint pulse and saw Joe's back expanding with shallow breaths. He called 911 and requested an ambulance along with backup.

"Joe. Are you with me buddy?"

When he received no response, Jonah examined his friend closer. Except for the blood pouring from a cut on his forehead and swelling around his right eye, he found no other serious injuries. To staunch the heavy bleeding,

Jonah pulled off his T-shirt and applied pressure to the head wound.

Jonah kicked at the ground, angry with himself. While his lips were locked in passionate kisses, his buddy had been left for dead. Jonah wasn't fit to be anybody's partner, much less a police officer.

Joe moaned and opened his eyes. "What happened?"

Jonah readjusted his hold on the blood-soaked T-shirt. "From the looks of it, I'd say you ran into a couple of brick walls."

"That's right. While you were inside looking for your rich little princess, I was out here fighting for my life. Is Katy okay?"

The banter coming from Joe sounded better than a rap song. "She's a little bruised in the face, but feisty as ever."

Jonah had taken a lot of heat from the guys about his association with the mayor's daughter, but he didn't let their teasing bother him. They were just jealous.

The sound of sirens interrupted his thoughts of Katy. "Let's get you to the hospital. Backup is on the way, but I suspect the intruders are long gone."

Katy rushed out of the house and knelt next to them. "Let me help."

"I thought I told you to stay in your room until I came for you. Those guys are probably still out here. Get back in the house now."

With a raised chin, Katy huffed. "You can't tell me what to do. You and Joe are in as much danger as I am, and I want to help. So, get over yourself, Abbott."

She pushed his hands aside and applied pressure to Joe's head wound. His injured friend grinned at Katy. "This girl's good for you, man. She doesn't let you get the upper hand nor does she back down from a fight. You'd better hang on to her."

Jonah huffed. "She's going to get us both killed if she isn't more cautious."

"Don't talk as if I'm not here. I heard those guys' threats, and I understand the danger, but I refuse to live in constant fear. If I did, I wouldn't be able to help anyone."

Despite the worry and aggravation, Jonah admired Katy's courage—one of the many things he loved about her. Besides, life would never be boring with Katy.

Joe had resisted going to the ER, but his head wound had bled through the T-shirt plus a roll of paper towels. The emergency personnel ignored his objections and transported him by ambulance to the hospital. Jonah and Katy followed in the car. She had accepted an ice pack from the EMTs but refused further treatment.

"You should have your face x-rayed. What if you have broken bones in your cheek or those heavy blows gave you a concussion?"

Katy rolled her eyes at him and stared into the mirror on the visor. She winced at herself. "I'll be all right. After we check on Joe, you can take me home. I won't be able to sleep, and I want to clean up the mess."

Jonah gritted his teeth and rubbed the back of his neck. "Why didn't you call your parents?"

"My father would go ballistic if he saw me like this. He'd fire you and close down my program. Please don't tell him until my face heals."

"I won't tell him, but I can't promise what my chief might do."

Katy and Jonah sat with Joe until a room was available. "I can't believe I let those guys get a jump on me. They came out of nowhere."

"I'm sorry I left you so long, buddy."

Joe again brushed him off and grinned at Katy. "At least I know who has priority with you. Are you sure you can't sneak me out of here? We should already be searching for those guys."

"I know. I have Chip and Tony searching the house and grounds for clues. We'll rendezvous when I drop Katy off."

Joe raised an eyebrow when he realized Katy intended to return to her house, then glared at Jonah as if he had a say in what she did. Jonah shrugged, beat his cap against his leg, and ushered Katy out of the hospital. She seemed determined to send him to an early grave.

Katy recounted the details of the intruders' conversation to Jonah. Someone with considerable influence wanted her dead. But even after days of investigating the break-in, none of their leads panned out.

Although they'd managed to shelter Katy from the press and the wrath of her father, the chief dreaded his next meeting with the mayor. Jonah bounced from one bit of information to another, so stressed he chewed a cuticle until he drew blood. Those in charge of the illegal drug business were either exceptionally good at hiding their identities or they had a tight foothold in the community.

CHAPTER ELEVEN

Jonah prayed for guidance as he prepared for the Wednesday evening Bible study. He felt at peace with the topic and looked forward to seeing everyone, especially Katy. Though her battered face looked somewhat better, she had to wear heavy makeup to hide the lingering yellow and green bruising.

As promised, Katy had the fire pit going and two huge subs spread out on the picnic tables. Extra benches and chairs were scattered around the fire. Keeping her promise of healthier food, she paid extra for the oven baked chips. Instead of soda, she served fresh-squeezed lemonade.

Jonah pulled back the edge of a cloth napkin and grinned. "So, are these brownies on your healthy choice list?"

She hit him with her empty paper plate and whispered. "Got to have something to keep my man happy."

Jonah didn't care who watched them. He pulled her into his arms and whispered in her ear. "Do you realize how much I love you, Ms. Wilson?"

Katy pushed him away and began filling plastic cups with ice and lemonade.

While the students ate, Jonah played his guitar, starting with a lively song featuring difficult runs. Depending on his mood, music either stirred his emotions or calmed him down. Why had he abandoned his music at a time when he needed it most? The song lifted his spirits and made him want to dance. He tapped his foot and bobbed his head to the rhythm. Some of the kids clapped to the beat while others boogied around the patio, air-playing their "instruments."

Realizing the need to rein in his audience, he remembered a worship song he'd heard on the radio. The young people settled down as he sang the powerful words declaring the greatness of God. A few of the young people sang along, filling the backyard with a heavenly chorus.

The song finished, everyone grew quiet and Jonah opened with prayer. Antonio had shared about his brother during the meal. Their concern led to prayers for their friend.

As Jonah focused on each young face, he clutched his Bible to his chest. An uneasiness enveloped him—an urgency beyond description. Though they were good kids who wanted to do the right thing, they were born with several strikes against them. Almost daily, he heard of shootings affecting their age group. Often the violence involved drugs—overdoses, as in the case of Montel, were too common.

A few students were missing from the week before, but most returned for the second night, some bringing friends. That said something about their commitment and their hunger for more of God. Surely, they weren't just interested in the food as Katy had suggested.

Katy and Jonah exchanged concerned looks when a small group from the adjoining neighborhood came through the gate. With increased gang activity in the area, Jonah worried about their intentions. Katy jumped up and motioned them toward the food table. She pulled out another giant sub from a cooler. Jonah smiled at her tendency to over plan. The latecomers filled their plates and moved to the folding chairs he had opened near the fire.

Since kids from different cultures rarely attended the same events, Jonah watched to see how the others might react. They shifted uncomfortably until Willy stood and picked up a dish from the food table. The young man approached the new arrivals with a peace offering—Katy's brownies served with a wide smile.

Jonah relaxed and returned to his guitar. He played the worship song again with another reason to be thankful. The potential for conflict had drifted away with the calming music and a generous offer of friendship.

Not wanting to disturb the peaceful setting, Jonah kept the group outside for the study. What he had to say would be a hard word, especially for the virile young men. But he trusted God to give them grace to receive.

"I see most of you have Bibles, thanks to Ms. Katy. It might be hard to see, but don't you love it out here? If there are no objections, I would like our beautiful hostess to pass out the miniature flashlights I found at Walmart."

At the mention of 'beautiful hostess' Katy received a round of applause and a few wolf whistles. She accepted the compliment with a shy smile and quick bow.

"Sorry guys, but she's taken."

Katy responded with a defiant frown. Would he ever learn how to handle this independent woman?

With Jaylen's teasing grin, his teeth sparkled in the firelight. "Mr. A, you're in big trouble now."

Everyone laughed, except Katy. Surely, she knew how he felt about her. Jonah looked at her with an apologetic smile. He mouthed the word, later. In the meantime, he had to control a bunch of rowdy teenagers.

He regained their attention with a loud whistle. "Any volunteers to read?" he asked. As hands were raised, Katy passed out the slips of paper. Several attended the neighborhood church and easily found their way through the Bible—probably better than Katy.

When the shuffling of pages ceased, Jonah motioned to the person who had Genesis 2. The last verse described Adam and Eve as naked without feeling shame. Lewd remarks flew from every direction. Before he lost complete control, Jonah brought them back with a question.

"Why are you surprised to find verses like this in the Bible? Did you think Adam and Eve were created fully clothed? Let's not get sidetracked. Before the first couple sinned, their thoughts were pure. They walked with God through the garden and admired the beauty of his creation, including the bodies God had given them.

"Adam and Eve were married by God in the beautiful setting. He instructed them to be fruitful and multiply. They worked together caring for the animals, plants and the children their union would bring about."

To keep the kids focused, Jonah refrained from asking more questions. "The next verse comes from Proverbs, which I have memorized. 'The man who finds a wife finds a treasure, and he receives favor from the Lord.' From this verse we see God's approval of marriage between a husband and wife."

"Why do you have that verse memorized, Mr. Jonah. You in need of a woman?"

Jonah ignored the laughter at his expense and Kelvin's question and asked the person with Matthew 5:32 to read. "Thank you, Sierra. In this one verse, Jesus talks about the importance of commitment in marriage. No hopping from one person to the next, and no divorce without good reason. The Bible calls our actions adultery when we have sex with someone other than our spouse."

Jonah watched the kids lean forward with genuine interest. "At weddings, we often hear the words, 'What therefore God has joined together, let no man separate.' In other words, marriage is a sacred institution ordained by God and meant to last for a lifetime.

"The next verses are even more clear. Katy, do you have the verses from Hebrews?"

Not wanting to embarrass her, he had given them to her when he first arrived. She cleared her throat. "Give honor to marriage, and remain faithful to one another in marriage. God will surely judge people who are immoral and those who commit adultery."

Jonah closed his eyes and took a few deep breaths. He prayed for wisdom to explain the Scriptures in a way that the young people would understand. "We see from the verses Ms. Katy read that when we choose a mate, God expects us to stay true to that partner for the rest of our lives. Unfaithfulness in marriage brings dishonor to the injured party, whether the husband or wife. God ordained marriage as a sacred institution, and he called it good. He expects married couples to take their covenant seriously. In other words, no sleeping around."

"Since we aren't married, why are you telling us this?"

The kids whispered to their neighbors. With one question from Jaylen, Jonah had lost their attention.

To make eye contact with everyone, Jonah took a few steps closer to the fire. "Don't brush these verses off as not applying to you. Most of you will marry one day and in the meantime the apostle Paul has something important to say to you."

After one of the kids read from 1 Corinthians 6:18–20, Jonah challenged them. "Whether we like it or not, casual sex violates the person."

The kids stared at him with blank expressions until he listed some of the consequences—such as disease, unplanned pregnancy, and abortion. Unable to cover each topic in detail, he continued. "The apostle Paul described our bodies as a place for God's Spirit to live. Can you imagine the Holy Spirit participating in casual sex? The next time you are tempted, ask yourself what pleases God. Go a step further and see your body created to be holy, pure, and dedicated to the worship of God."

Jonah stiffened when Jaylen raised his hand. "That's a little scary, Mr. A. I don't want God anywhere around when I'm doing my thing. You know what I mean?"

Amid laughter and high fives, Jonah whistled to regain their attention. "I understand more than you might think, but I know that obeying God brings a freedom that far outweighs a few hours of sexual lust. So much evil and sin are committed in the dark, but God wants us to step out of the darkness into the light of his truth. John says that when we walk in the light, we have fellowship with one another, and the blood of Jesus, his Son, purifies us from all sin."

Jonah looked at the young people with new eyes. They had needs far beyond what he saw on the surface. "Take a look at the people around you. Are we not enjoying one another? We're not doing drugs or planning to steal enough money for our next fix. We aren't engaged in sexual sins or plotting how to get revenge on someone who's mistreated us. Instead, we're learning how to serve God and others. Your presence alone lets me know you want to know more about God and his word.

"In the last Scripture of tonight's study, Paul challenges the people of Thessalonica. 'God's will is for you to be holy, so stay away from all sexual sin. Then each of you will control his own body and live in holiness and honor—not in lustful passion like the pagans who do not know God and his ways.'"

Closing his Bible, Jonah sat on the high stool from Katy's kitchen. "I know this is new for many of you. The world tells us if something feels good, do it and sex is something we have a right to explore. Women are often deceived by the lie that claims sex outside of marriage is okay if you love the person and are committed to them. Do you realize, girls, that while you are letting a guy have his way with you, he's probably planning how to escape the relationship and move on to that good-looking babe he saw on the street corner."

Jonah watched as a few boys lowered their heads. "When I was fourteen and noticing girls, my dad sat me down and gave me these same Scriptures we read tonight. He encouraged me to save my body for the one girl who would agree to be my bride. Tonight, we discussed some of the consequences of premarital sex—painful consequences that often last a lifetime.

"My father said he wanted something far better for me. He pointed me to a day when I would stand before a beautiful young lady and say, 'I saved myself for you because I don't want to think of anyone else when we are together.' For over ten years, I've kept that promise to my father and to my future bride. I would like for you to consider making the same pledge to yourself and to God."

Jonah noticed some of his audience shifting uncomfortably. At least one of the girls wiped her eyes. "You might say, 'But I am already sexually active. I can't go back and change what I've done.' Regardless of your past, the same Bible that tells us sex outside of marriage is sin, also tells us that Jesus forgives. He made a way for our purity when he became the sacrificial lamb and died for our salvation.

"I know it's a radical way to live, but it's God's way. My heart longs for all of you to live for Jesus. Come to him and let him make you pure and clean. He will wash you whiter than snow."

Jonah had stunned them into silence. The only sound came from the crickets in the shrubs. He'd told the kids the truth. Now, only God could help them believe for themselves. Jonah played softly on the guitar and began to sing, "All Who Are Thirsty," by Kutless.

When the song finished, Jonah prayed for them to have courage to stand up for truth—keeping themselves pure and holy for the person God wanted them to marry.

Katy stood and waited until she had their attention. "Next week, as a follow-up to Jonah's teaching, I'll be sharing my own story. Jonah may have that bad boy look, but we learned tonight that his sex life is squeaky clean. Join us next week to hear more about the woman at the well."

When Katy sat down and most of the young people had left, Jonah whispered in her ear, "You don't have to do this, you know. You're not the person you used to be, and I love you just the way you are."

Katy looked at him with watery eyes. "I know you do, but the kids need to hear the flip side of the story—that God gives second chances and forgives. Several are sexually active—I know because I've provided condoms for them. Some will expect me to continue, and I don't know what to do. Some of my supporters would be appalled at your teaching. Please pray for me—I need divine guidance. I don't know what I will do tomorrow, but I know what I'm supposed to do next Wednesday evening."

"Only God knows," Jonah said as he pulled her to him. Before he could kiss her, he noticed Willy waiting at the edge of the patio.

Katy gathered the empty bowls and headed toward the kitchen. Jonah walked over to the teen and put an arm around his shoulder. "What can I do for you, my man?"

Willy looked around as if afraid to speak. "I need to tell you something, but you can't tell anyone."

"I'm afraid that depends on what you tell me. Sometimes we need others to help us with problems that are too big for us to handle. How can I help?"

"Well, you can't tell anyone I'm the one who told you. They would kill me."

The fear he saw in the young man's eyes spilled over on Jonah. Adrenaline had his heart pumping and his feet shuffling impatiently. If he was reading the situation correctly, he was about to get the answers he and Joe had agonized over for weeks.

"I'll protect you any way I can. You're too special to be wasted."

"I know who wants Miss Katy dead."

Jonah had expected something big, but this was over the top. He tried not to look greedy as he gave the boy's shoulder a reassuring squeeze. "Go ahead. I'm listening."

"I overheard my mama's boyfriend talking to a couple of thugs when I came home from school today. They kept mentioning this guy Damien who wanted the woman in that white house dead, except they didn't say woman. They called her a bad name. Miss Katy is one of the kindest women I've ever known. She cares about us like you do, Mr. A."

Jonah gave the boy a hug, "Thank you. That took a lot of courage. Don't worry. I promise to be careful how I use the information you shared. I'll do all I can to protect both you and Miss Katy, but please don't discuss this with anyone else. We wouldn't want your information to end up in the wrong hands."

Jonah watched Willy make his way back down the street, then went to find Katy. "I'm sorry I can't help you with the cleanup. Something's come up, and I've gotta find Joe ASAP. I'm worried about you, though. After what happened Saturday night, and now this information from Willy, I'm even more concerned. Would you please ask someone to stay with you or go spend the night with your parents?"

"What did Willy say?"

"He says he knows who wants to kill you. It took a lot of courage for him to come forward. I'm concerned for Willy's safety along with yours. Please go stay with your parents."

Jonah watched the color leak from Katy's worried face. Her smile transformed into a look of horror before she regained control. "God took care of me last week, and I know he will again. But I don't want you to worry while you're out on the street searching for answers. I'll spend a few days with my parents. They'll be happy to see me, but I'm not sure how to explain my late-night arrival."

Releasing an anxious breath, Jonah realized how much Katy meant to him. He took her face in his hands and looked into her eyes. "I don't know what I would do if something happened to you. Please be safe."

Jonah gave her a gentle kiss on the lips and rushed out of the house, speed dialing his partner on the way. He prayed they would soon find and arrest the suspects before they made another attempt on Katy's life.

CHAPTER TWELVE

Katy parked her car in the driveway of her parents' home and let herself in the front door. Since she hadn't called, she used her key and slipped into the foyer. She started for the stairs, rehearsing the placement of the squeaky steps. Before she reached the first landing, a commanding voice stopped her. "Is that you, Katy?"

Katy jumped and almost tripped. Leaving her overnight bag on the landing, Katy met her father at the bottom of the stairs.

With concern in his eyes, he hugged her and searched her face with a raised eyebrow. "What are you doing sneaking in here so late? Is something wrong?"

"No, Daddy. Everything is fine. I just wanted a few days away from all the people coming and going and to spend a few days with you and Mother. Is that okay?"

"You know you're always welcome here, but tiptoeing into the house this late at night seems a bit strange. You could have at least called first."

"I know, but I wanted to surprise you at breakfast. Wouldn't that have been fun?"

"Sorry to spoil your surprise, but my indigestion makes me restless. I didn't want to disturb your mother, but I needed my antacid tablets from the study. Your mother had a tiring day getting ready for the church bazaar."

"Well, I'm glad I'm here to help. I'd better get to bed if I plan to volunteer as her gofer."

Katy gave him a quick kiss on the cheek and started back up the stairs. Just when she thought she had avoided further questioning, her father stopped her. "How's that policeman coming along with the investigation? You'd think I had asked him for the moon instead of the simple truth as to who wants you out of the neighborhood."

Katy didn't dare look at her father for fear he'd notice her worry for Jonah. The man might be a lot of things, but she couldn't deny his perception. Learning to read people and understand their problems probably contributed to his successful reelection every four years.

"Could we talk about this in the morning? I'm tired, and you need to get some sleep too. I'll get up and have breakfast with you."

The look he gave her said she hadn't fooled him in the least. He might let her off for now, but she dreaded breakfast where she would be forced to juggle the truth around her father's scrutiny.

Regardless of the truths uncovered, she had to hide her interest in Jonah. Or better still, shock him with the truth—that she'd fallen in love with that bum of an imbecile and planned to spend the rest of her life with him. That would be enough to take his mind off her dangerous neighborhood. Katy shook her head. Better not. That shocker might give her father more than indigestion.

When she arrived in the kitchen the next morning, her parents were already at the table, anxious for an explanation. She took her plate from the warming oven and found her usual seat. Her mother narrowed her eyes. Katy anticipated the questions reeling in her mother's mind.

"This is a surprise. Is everything all right?"

"I'm fine, Mother, but I do look forward to spending time with you and Dad. What's on the agenda for today?"

Katy heard the paper rustle. "Wait just a minute, Princess." Her father peered over his morning newspaper. "You promised to talk over breakfast, and you are not skipping out on me. I can tell something has you upset, and if I had to guess, I'd say it has to do with that hoodlum cop who arrested you. You haven't tangled yourself up with him, I hope."

Her father stared at her. She had tried to hide the remains of her bruises under a thick layer of makeup, but apparently not well enough. Katy sighed.

The newspaper smacked against the table. "Tell me that incompetent fool didn't hit you. I'll wring his neck.'

"Daddy, Jonah is not a hoodlum or a fool. He's one of your best undercover police officers, who's working hard to discover those responsible for bringing drugs into your precious town. If you must know, he is the one who suggested I come home for a few days."

Katy debated how much to tell him. She released a slow breath. "Jonah received word of some people who want to hurt me. I didn't want him worrying about my safety while searching for answers. Please give him a break."

Father wrinkled his brow. "How are you so familiar with this guy? I hope you aren't shacking up with him."

"Now, Conor, that was uncalled for. Katy is an adult, and we need to treat her like one. After all, we raised her right. She wouldn't even consider hooking up with someone like that policeman. She only goes out with nice boys from fine homes. How could you even suggest such a thing? She knows he's not good enough for her."

Katy shifted in her seat. She refused to sit still while her parents criticized Jonah. "You're wrong about him, Mother. He's the best thing that ever happened to me, and I'm in love with him."

Her mother's mouth jarred open while her father nearly choked on his coffee. "Get a hold of yourself, girl. Do you realize what you just said?"

"I said I love Jonah Abbott and everything about him. You don't know him, Daddy, but I do, and I've never met a finer man. So, do not tell me he's not good enough, because I know differently. When you get to know him, you will love him, too."

The paper hit the table again. "You can't be serious. He's just charmed you with that sexy smile, but he's not going to get away with it. I'm going to have him fired as soon as I get to the office. If he thinks he can manipulate my little girl, he has another think coming."

What have I done? Breaking the news of her relationship with Jonah had the opposite effect of what she intended. Now, she wished to recall her revelation—talking about what happened the last few days would be much easier than fielding questions about her love life.

Her father acted like a bear when he got in a tiff, and on this occasion, Jonah would reap the consequences. "Don't you dare fire him. If it weren't for Jonah, I would have had to leave that neighborhood before now. He's right at the point of making arrests, and you'll destroy everything he's worked to accomplish. Daddy, please give him a chance."

Mrs. Wilson cleared her throat and reached across the table. Ever the peacemaker, she patted her husband's hand. "Conor. Listen to yourself. Seems to me you're the manipulative one. Have we ever doubted Katy's judgment? She has always made us proud. She cares about other people, and if she cares about this young man, we'd better get to know him for ourselves."

Her father shook off his wife's hand. "Well, maybe I won't fire him today, but I do plan to call him in and have a little chat. I want to know what's going on with his so-called investigation, but mostly with his relationship with my daughter."

When provoked, her father became unreasonable—the discussion was over. He checked the wall clock, threw his napkin in the center of his empty plate, and pushed back his chair. He headed for the stairs gearing for a fight. Katy didn't have to guess who the victim would be.

Her mother's placating was redirected toward Katy. "Don't worry about your father. He'll come around. Now, tell me about your young man. Who are his parents, dear?"

Here it comes. Her mother had been born into a family of southern elites who only married southern gentlemen or belles. Nothing and no one else passed muster. Katy didn't know the first thing about the genealogy of Jonah or his parents.

"All I know, Mother, is he credits his parents for teaching him to be a man of good character and integrity. His father is the pastor of the Community Church on Shell Island where Jonah grew up. Apparently, they have lived there since his father's ordination. Jonah's a good man, and I can't imagine life without him."

Her mother fanned herself. "I hope you're still on your birth control pills. You don't want to find yourself pregnant before you're ready to be a mother."

Katy tried to hide the laughter produced by her mother's unnecessary concern. "Birth control won't be necessary. Jonah and I are waiting until we are married for sexual intimacy."

The woman cocked her head to one side. "Really? What's the matter with him? He's not gay, is he?"

"No, mother. He's very much in love with me, but he believes what the Bible says about casual sex, and he's committed to remain pure until he marries."

"And you're okay with that? That's quite a change from your free-spirited thinking. Are you sure about this man?"

"I'm very sure. In fact, we're teaching a Bible study together on Wednesday evenings with the young people in my neighborhood. For the first time in my life, I'm learning what God says about some of the issues I've defended with such passion. I can't believe how wrong I've been."

Katy cringed at her mother's worried expression. "Honey, I'm afraid you're turning into the kind of person you used to call intolerant."

"I'm okay. If anything, I have become more tolerant. God has given me an even greater heart for the poor, the lonely, and the despised. What I can't tolerate are the people trying to destroy them with drugs and crime."

Uncomfortable with the conversation, her mother rearranged her place setting. "I know we seem hard on you sometimes, Katy, but we want what's best for you. We only want you to be happy. You should invite Jonah over for dinner while you're here so we can meet him."

"I would love to. He's going to surprise you when you look past the surface and see the kind, considerate man that I've come to know and love." As warmth spread over Katy, she grabbed her plate and stood. "Okay, enough about my love life. How can I help with this bazaar?"

While Katy and her mother went over details for the church bazaar, Jonah waited outside the mayor's office, wondering what he'd face on the other side of the wooden door. Around nine o'clock that morning, Chief Morrison informed him Jonah had been ordered to report to Mayor Wilson's office by ten for a meeting with the man himself. One thing about Katy's father, he didn't waste time, especially regarding his daughter.

Joe whooped with joy when Jonah related Willy's news. After examining the tip from every angle, they put a tail on the four men, including his mother's boyfriend.

Jonah wanted to shake Willy's mother until she understood her responsibility to her son. Getting to know the young people had awakened Jonah from a self-imposed lethargy. Face-to-face encounters were far different from viewing the young people in the neighborhood as statistics on a computer screen or headlines in the daily news. Willy seemed like a young man who wanted to serve God, but he needed someone to come alongside him. With a little extra attention, Jonah saw the young man rising above his present circumstances, and he wanted to be the man to guide him.

Katy had already identified at least two of the names Willy mentioned. With her life in danger, Jonah was relieved that she had agreed to stay with her parents for a few days. He didn't need his worry over her distracting him from the investigation. The slightest thought of Katy sent his mind wandering in the opposite direction.

Jonah grinned at their unlikely relationship and wondered if Katy had mentioned him to her parents. His thoughts turned sour when he remembered her father's dislike of him—the man would burst a blood vessel if she confessed to spending time with "that imbecile!" Jonah paused at the idea of dealing with the man long term.

Harnessing his thoughts, Jonah remembered the look Katy had given him during the Bible study. They never did get around to that "us" talk. Obviously, she wasn't as far along in their relationship—certainly not ready to introduce him to her parents. Jonah shuddered at the craziness. Pacing before the closed door, Jonah prayed the mayor only wanted an update on the investigation.

Further thoughts were interrupted by the loud intercom, "Sally, send that young hoodlum in here, and he better be ready with some answers."

Sally smiled apologetically and opened the door to the inner office. Jonah braced for the worst. "Mayor Wilson. Good to see you. I hope you are well, sir."

"I don't need to give you my medical report, young man. I need to know what you're doing to my daughter. My wife tells me you apparently have brainwashed her with your God-talk. What do you have to say for yourself?"

"Katy is a fine young woman, and I'm in love with her, sir."

Jonah stopped and stared. He hadn't meant to share so much so soon, but he didn't know any other way to let her father know where he stood—or why he was so concerned for Katy.

"What is this? Did you two get together and decide to tell me the same thing? If you're shacking up with my daughter, I'll have your hide."

Jonah wiped perspiration from his brow with the sleeve of his hoody. "Sir, did you not hear me? I said I love her. That means I value and respect your daughter. Until the day you walk her down the aisle, I promise to stay out of her bed. She is beautiful inside and out, and I am blessed that she chose to love me."

Mayor Wilson's mouth dropped open. He stared through narrowed eyes. Jonah changed the subject to the real danger they were facing. "My concern, sir, is that there are people who want your daughter dead. Not just out of the neighborhood anymore, but dead. Some of the drug dealers see her as a threat to their success. They don't like the influence she has on the young people nor that she sends some addicts away for counseling and treatment. Every time another user kicks the habit, they lose business."

Jonah was on a roll. He leaned forward and continued. "The pushers prefer to keep their clients close. They don't care what happens to the young victims as long as they line their pockets from the lucrative drug sales. Katy defies their very existence, and they are furious with her.

"I know you don't like the way I look—I'm not too fond of my appearance either. But if it helps me get the information I need, so be it. Just in the last few weeks, your daughter has become my life. I'm afraid you'll have to put up with me for an exceedingly long time, sir."

Jonah thought he'd made a mistake with his blunt speech when he saw fear wash over the mayor's face. His eyes grew wide and his hand shook as he rubbed his chest. Was the man having a heart attack? "Are you okay, sir?"

"I'm fine. It's just this blasted indigestion. I need a couple of Tums."

Katy's father pulled a bottle from his desk drawer and chewed the tablets slowly as if searching for a response. Jonah squirmed under the man's intense look and braced himself for another round of criticism. He knew he wasn't cut from the same cloth as Katy and didn't deserve her love, but all he cared about for the moment was keeping her safe. At least that would put him on the same page with her father.

Jonah stared at the apologetic look coming from Mayor Wilson. The man sat back in his chair and formed a tent with his fingers. "Officer Abbott, I know I seem harsh at times, but I love my daughter. I don't understand what she sees in you, but I can see we both have her welfare at heart. Have you made any progress in finding the persons behind this latest threat to her life?"

"Please call me Jonah. It only seems right since we are to be related one day." Jonah grinned, but wondered if he wasn't pushing his luck a little far, too soon.

The mayor dismissed Jonah's attempt at levity with a swipe of his hand. He wrinkled his brow and waited for Jonah's response. "The answer to your question is yes. Just last night after the Bible study, one of the young people told me about a conversation he'd overheard that afternoon. As a result, we have been tailing four individuals since late last night. Katy had already named two of them as persons who objected to her work with the drug addicts."

"What Bible study? Katy didn't tell me anything about a Bible study. I didn't hire you to preach to that neighborhood. You're supposed to be arresting them."

"God uses all circumstances. Obviously, the Bible study has helped in this case. That young man would have never approached me on the street to share that kind of information. He doesn't even know that I'm a police officer, but he cares about Katy and knows how I feel about her. He needed to tell someone he trusted—someone he knew would keep her safe."

Major Wilson tightened his face. "I hate to admit it, but you seem to know what you're doing—though you certainly made a mess of things when you arrested my Katy."

"I have to disagree with you, sir. God wanted me to meet Katy, and if I had to look the fool, I'd do it again. I can never thank him enough for that morning when I made the biggest mistake of my career. That disastrous day turned out to be the best day of my life."

Mayor Wilson shook his head and laughed. "You're a strange one, Abbott, but for the sake of my daughter, you and I are going to have to get along. Welcome aboard, Son."

Jonah rubbed his chin. Had the mayor just given him permission to date his daughter or had he invited him to keep his job? What difference did it make? Confessing his thoughts to her father had freed him to really love her and not be afraid of who might object.

As for the job, Jonah wasn't sure how much longer he would last. Most of the people in the drug world were all about hiding their deeds. His own job description required a certain level of deceit to uncover the truth. Jonah preferred being up front with people—especially where love was involved.

As Jonah left the mayor's office, a wave of guilt came over him. He had just spilled his guts to Katy's father while the relationship with his own parents had been strained for years. He hadn't had a serious conversation with them since he decided to leave college and become a police officer. He'd distanced himself—emotionally and physically—to avoid dealing with their disappointment.

When he'd left the island, he swore he'd never return. He had purposely hidden the clean-cut young man who prayed and trusted God behind a wall of anger and bitterness. Rebelling against everything his parents had taught him, he went to war. Though he claimed his fight concerned drugs and the people responsible for Monica's death, his war was more with himself and God.

Since he didn't want to talk about Monica or let his parents see how far he'd drifted from the faith, Jonah rarely called. He only saw them a few times a year when they came into town and insisted he meet them for lunch. The pain and disappointment he saw in their eyes matched his own. Now, when he felt free to share about his recommitment to the Lord, he worried about exposing Katy to their strict scrutiny.

Katy had come a long way in a short time, but she still wouldn't measure up to his parents' expectations. Although they were loving and forgiving, they had high standards regarding the women their sons dated. Somehow, he doubted Katy would fit their mold.

CHAPTER THIRTEEN

Jonah arrived at the precinct as drained as the coffee cup he'd just tossed. Whether from the intensity of the last few hours or sleep deprivation, he needed a place to crash. He'd been up for more than twenty-four hours and would never survive if he kept going. Finding a cot in the back room, he fell into a deep sleep.

What seemed like moments later, a ringtone pulled him into consciousness. Jonah blinked to clear his vision and noticed the time. Why had he slept so long with so much at stake? Shaking his watch, he checked again—still after three o'clock.

"Hey, Joe. What's up?"

The excitement in Joe's voice shook him from his lethargy. "Big news! Meet me in fifteen at that coffee shop near Katy's house, and I'll fill you in. Don't be late."

They had barely sat down before Joe spouted information so fast Jonah struggled to keep up. "You won't believe what happened while you were sleeping. Our guys followed the woman's boyfriend and one of his cohorts to Willy's house around one-thirty. With audio surveillance, they overheard a heated argument. The suspects had somehow gotten wind of our tail and blamed the boy's mother.

"All hell broke loose about the time Willy showed up. When the kid jumped in to protect his mother, the thugs turned on him. Our men smashed the door at the same time the boyfriend pulled a gun. One of our guys took a bullet before he saw the weapon."

Jonah's breath caught at the thought of losing a fellow officer. "Is he okay?"

"When I last checked, the bullet passed clean through his shoulder. He'll be fine."

"What about the suspects?"

"Arrested without a hitch. When I arrived with backup, the cowards threw down their weapons and surrendered."

Jonah made a mental note to obtain warrants for the other two suspects. "I hope at least one of those arrested will turn states' evidence and put the big guys away."

"You and me both."

Relieved that Katy's enemies would soon be in custody, Jonah still worried about the young people subjected to such violence almost daily.

"What about Willy and his mother?

"They're still alive, but in critical condition."

After he got off the phone with Joe, Jonah scrolled through his phone to find the number for the hospital. His desire to protect Katy had put Willy in intensive care, fighting for his life. The charge nurse gave little hope for his mother. At a great cost to her and her son, the woman had chosen bad company. As Jonah prayed for Willy, he remembered the promise he'd made—to encourage the young man to rise above his circumstances. Now, the boy needed a miracle merely to survive.

Jonah's next thoughts were of Katy. He dialed her number, confident she'd know what to do. "Jonah, you didn't call me this morning, and I missed you."

"I know, honey, but something big has gone down. I need you to pray. Willy and his mother are both in the hospital almost beaten to a pulp. The mother isn't expected to live, and our boy's in critical condition. Can you meet me there in about an hour?"

Jonah heard the catch in Katy's voice. "Oh, Jonah. That's terrible. We've got to help them."

"Just meet me at the hospital. I'll tell you more when you get here. I love you."

"Love you too."

Jonah rushed home for a quick shower. Although he'd need to keep the undercover grunge look a while longer, he could at least wash away the stench of street grime. Remembering Katy's last words, Jonah doubted a little body odor would deter her—she loved him. With thoughts of her love pounding his heart, the shower never felt better.

Jonah scrolled through his news feed while he waited for Katy to arrive at the hospital. He looked up in time to see Katy walk through the door. A wide grin spread across his face as he detected every eye in the waiting room follow her fashion model walk—to him. Jonah pulled her into his arms and noticed the confused looks staring at the beauty embracing the bum. One day he would dress like the man she deserved.

"Hello, handsome. Have you been waiting long?"

"I would wait for you forever." His voice sounded husky and out of place considering the circumstances.

Katy directed him to a chair and sat beside him. "I telephoned a few of the young people and asked them to pray for Willy and his mother. I also called the pastor of the Methodist Episcopal Church in the area. I thought Pastor Peyton might like to know what happened. When I gave him the details, he seemed genuinely concerned. The minister called him William and said the boy had recently started attending his church. He'd never met the mother. Said he'd come as soon as he contacted his emergency prayer chain."

"You've been busy, princess."

Katy grabbed his arm and smiled. The first time he'd used the term of endearment, she accused him of being snarky. The term had always been her father's pet name for her. She must have moved him up a notch because her warmth spoke of nothing but pleasure.

"After my conversation with the minister, I thought I might try his church instead of driving across town with my parents. That's where the Thomas's attend. Cora invited me the day I drove Montel to rehab."

"You might very well be the only White person in the congregation."

"So what? Segregation was outlawed in the sixties, and it's time the churches were open to all. Besides, I like the name. Sounds ecumenical. My parents are Methodist, and my grandparents are Episcopal. I could be a little of both. What are you, Jonah?"

"I haven't given much thought to denominations. My father pastors a Community Church. Because it's the only church on the island, parishioners from many religious backgrounds attend. While in college I went to a large evangelical church near the campus. Since I started working for the police department, I haven't had time for church or anything else. I've worked every Sunday for the past three years."

Katy looked at him and frowned. "Jonah, you haven't been home in three years? Shame on you."

Jonah stood and pulled her up with him. "I don't want to talk about my family—we need to get upstairs. Both patients are in intensive care. If we can't see them, we'll go to the ICU waiting room. I'm not sure if Willy has other family members, but we'll be on hand in case someone shows up."

Jonah put his hand on the middle of Katy's back and guided her across the threshold of the elevator. "Umm, you smell good."

The smell of fresh flowers in the small space messed with Jonah's senses. Noticing they were alone, he pushed Katy's hair back and kissed along her jaw line. Katy shoved him away. "Behave yourself. The door will be opening any minute. Instead of making out in the elevator, we should be praying."

Jonah laughed at her response.

"What's so funny? We've got one of our kids fighting for his life up there." Katy tapped a finger against her cheek. "I can't figure you out. One minute you are trying to seduce me—the next, you're laughing. And that's only one point of confusion. You refuse to talk about your past, yet you quote Scripture like you have been to seminary. Your personality changes so fast I cannot keep up. Just who are you, Jonah Abbott?"

"I'm sorry. I wasn't laughing at you, but your reprimand reminded me of how suddenly our roles have reversed.

You've become the passion police while I can't seem to take my hands off you."

The ding of the elevator announced their arrival on the intensive care floor. Before the doors opened, Jonah gave her a quick peck on the lips and faced the door.

Jonah led Katy toward the reception desk. He showed his badge to the nurse sitting behind the counter and asked about Willy and his mother. "Your name wouldn't be Jonah, would it?" Jonah pointed to the name on his badge.

"Willy's been asking for you." The receptionist peered at her chart. "He's regained consciousness but remains in a lot of pain. Since he has no other relatives here, the doctor thought seeing you might relieve some of his anxiety. You may only stay for ten minutes though."

The woman glanced at Katy. "Your friend will have to wait in the room reserved for family. I can't break all the rules at once."

Jonah left Katy and followed the nurse to Willy's bedside. Gripping the railing with tight fists, he choked back anger at the damage those thugs had done to his quiet, young friend. Purple bruises covered Willy's cheeks, neck, and arms. His face looked as if someone had taken a meat cleaver to it. Though Jonah wanted to lash out at those responsible, his own guilt silenced him.

Jonah reviewed the details in his mind. Where did I go wrong? He shouldn't have indulged himself with an afternoon power nap. How could he sleep when so many lives were at stake? In his rush to protect Katy, he had brought vengeance upon the head of an innocent young man.

From the short time Jonah had known Willy, he had seen nothing but a gentle soul who went out of his way to befriend others. He'd been the first to welcome the new kids to Bible study. The boy didn't seem to have the first thought of malice toward anyone.

Willy's typical wide smile didn't hide the fear and concern he had for his mother. The first night of the Bible study, he left the group early to check on her. Jonah didn't even ask if his mother was sick. He had been so caught up in what he thought was God's will that he didn't see the greater need. After reading the report of the woman's history of drug abuse and choice of male friends, Jonah understood. Had Willy ever had a chance to be a child?

Jonah moved to the head of the bed and called his name. Despite the IVs and tubes, the boy turned toward the sound of his voice. "Willy, I'm so sorry."

"Mr. A., you came."

"Of course, I came, buddy. I feel responsible for what those thugs did to you and your mama. I would give anything to be the one battered and bruised instead of you. Do you remember what happened?"

"I don't know for sure. I didn't tell anyone, like you said. Where is Miss Katy? Is she all right?"

Jonah looked at the boy in disbelief. "She's perfectly fine. Don't worry about her. When my time is up, I will sneak her in to see you. She's right outside in the waiting room."

"My Mom. She's not dead, is she?"

"No, but she's pretty bad off. Do you have someone you want me to call?"

Tears leaked from the slits of Willy's swollen eyes. "Would you call my grandma. She needs to be here for Mama. Can you let her know?"

"Where does she live?"

"She's in Wilmington. I don't know her phone number or address by heart." Willy paused and swiped his hand across his face. "Could you get in my house and find Mama's address book. She keeps it near the phone."

"What's your grandma's name?"

"Matty Walters."

Jonah squeezed the boy's shoulder. "Don't worry. I'll find her."

"One more thing, Mr. A. Could you please call me William? Willy sounds like I'm still a little boy."

"I'll be happy to call you William. You've more than earned the grownup name. Can I pray for you before I leave?"

Jonah grabbed one of William's hands. He waited for his mind to clear and to feel God's presence in the room.

"Father, we don't understand why this happened, but you know. Please touch William and his mother with your healing presence. Surround them with your love and peace. Show us how to bring those responsible to justice. In Jesus's name. Amen." Jonah squeezed the boy's hand before releasing it. "Rest now, Son and we'll check with you later."

Whether from the pain meds or the prayer, Willy, or William, faded into a relaxed sleep. Katy would have to visit later after they made a quick trip to the coast.

With the limited information on William's grandmother, Katy began a search on her iPhone. She had the address and telephone number within minutes, and after stopping at the precinct to pick up a car, they headed east on Interstate 40. The GPS indicated they would arrive at Mrs. Walters's home in a little over two hours. After the stressful day, Jonah needed the quiet drive with Katy.

"Did my father call you today?"

Jonah laughed. "That's an understatement. This has been one of the longest days of my life. The chief called me at nine o'clock and told me to report to your father's office by ten. When I arrived, he looked like he was about to explode. He wanted to know what I'd done to his daughter."

Katy chewed on her lower lip as if afraid of what he might say. "What did you tell him?"

"I told him I was in love with you and planned to marry you someday."

Jonah watched for Katy's reaction. Her wide smile said everything as she reached over the console to cover the hand resting on his thigh.

Katy raised an eyebrow and chuckled. "I basically told him the same thing. I bet that went over well."

"Probably as well as for you." Jonah moved their joined hands to the console and grinned. Seeing Katy's response brought a peace he hadn't felt for several hours.

"Since I didn't want to get into another war of words with your father, I turned his anger toward those trying to kill you. After I told him about the information from Willy, his mood changed significantly. He loves you, you know."

"I know. Both my parents love me and want me to be happy, but my father controls everything with his hot-headed

Irish temper. Thank God, mother plays the peacemaker so well. Otherwise, he would still be blasting me for falling in love with you."

Jonah chuckled as he thought of his own parents. His father held the role of peacemaker in his family. His gentle, trusting spirit calmed the roughest storm. "Thanks for that useful bit of information. Now I know who to kiss up to."

Katy turned serious. She looked out the window so long, he thought he'd lost her. "I was wondering, Jonah. Did your parents grow up in the South?"

"No. They were both born in New York. My grandparents still live in Brooklyn, but my parents have been down south for so long, they've adopted North Carolina as their home."

"You're a Yankee?"

He glanced in her direction, then turned back to the road. "Since my birth certificate indicates I was born in Wilmington, I hardly qualify as a Yankee."

Katy pulled her hand from his and scrunched her face into a worried frown. "Please, don't tell me you root for the Yankees?"

Jonah scratched his head. "You mean, the baseball team?"

"Of course, the baseball team. What did you think I meant?"

Jonah reached behind him and grabbed the baseball cap he'd thrown on the back seat. "You mean this team?"

Katy groaned. "My parents will disown me."

"Let me get this straight. Your parents will be upset that I might be a Yankee fan in addition to the fact that my parents were born in the north? If I recall, Lee surrendered a long time ago."

"It's not that they're still fighting the war." Katy hesitated.

"Tell me then. Help me understand."

"Girls from the old south do not marry northerners. Southern girls marry southern gentlemen who come from parents with roots burrowed deep in sandy soil. Their families have lived for centuries surrounded by moss covered live oaks and southern charm. I'm afraid you don't qualify."

Jonah laughed in disbelief. "You aren't serious. Are you?"

"I'm afraid so. When you meet my mom for the first time, a little southern charm wouldn't hurt. Would you consider talking with a little twang and using your best manners? That flirty smile might also help."

"You're kidding me. Right?"

Katy moaned and shook her head. "I wish. But, just for the record, your pedigree doesn't change the way I feel about you. You mean everything to me, Jonah. No southern gentleman could ever compare to you."

She reached over and recaptured his hand. She didn't let go until he had parked in front of the home of Matty Walters.

CHAPTER FOURTEEN

Matty Walter's house had the appearance of a well-maintained cottage. A white picket fence surrounded a manicured garden. Despite the late fall temperatures, jasmine and wisteria vines spilled blossoms over each end of the porch. Pots of chrysanthemums lined the walkway and baskets of ivy framed the wide brick steps.

After the knock, Jonah and Katy didn't have to wait long for the door to open. An attractive older woman greeted them with a wide smile. Her almond skin showed only a trace of wrinkles around her twinkling eyes. Her short curly hair had streaked naturally with tints of gray.

"Well, hello. What can I do for you this fine day? Are you here about the reverse mortgage?"

Jonah shifted, hating to break the peaceful mood. "Mrs. Walters, I'm afraid we have some bad news. This afternoon, your daughter and grandson were severely beaten." When the woman only stared, Jonah continued. "William asked us to let you know. He said you would want to come. If that's true, we will drive you to Raleigh."

The woman's calm demeanor faded. She silently cried into her handkerchief before lifting her eyes toward the ceiling—her palms opened in a receptive posture. Unlike Jonah who was familiar with God's presence, Katy shifted uncomfortably. She moved to the woman's side and rested her hand on the wrinkled arm.

William's grandmother looked at Katy and patted her hand. "My boy's going to be all right, but my girl needs to go on to Jesus. Life has taken its toll on her. Come in and let me pour you some sweet tea while I get my things together."

Katy shifted nervously. "We'll be fine, Mrs. Walters. If you don't need us, Jonah and I will take a walk around your garden."

Before she left the porch, Katy turned back to the woman. "I hope you're wrong about your daughter."

Mrs. Walters shook her head. "She's already in the arms of Jesus, but my grandson needs me. You enjoy the fall flowers while I manage in here."

Jonah and Katy stared at each other briefly before making their way down the steps and into the garden. "What do you suppose Willy's grandmother meant?"

Jonah shook his head. "I don't know, but I have a strange feeling."

They had barely left the walkway before his cell phone rang. After a quick glance at the caller ID, Jonah sent a worried look toward Katy. "This is Jonah Abbott."

When the nurse relayed a message from the doctor, Jonah raised an eyebrow. "What time did Ms. Walters pass?"

Jonah's voice tightened when the answer registered. "Thank you for calling. I'll let her mother know."

"Jonah, what happened? Between you and Willy's sweet grandmother, you're scaring me."

"Everything's going to be okay. Just like the woman said, her daughter died a few minutes ago. How she knew, I'm not certain. But I do know this: Matty Walters is acquainted with someone who knows all things—a God who shares secrets with those he can trust. That woman is a true friend of God, and I feel blessed to be in her presence."

Jonah walked around the garden with Katy tucked into his side. Words were not necessary as they enjoyed the beauty of the sun fading below the horizon. The colorful display cast an eerie glow over the plants and flowers. By the time they had circled the house, Mrs. Walters stood waiting on the porch. She held a couple of grocery sacks while a small well-used suitcase sat at her feet.

"You young people about ready to go?"

Jonah took her things and put them into the trunk of the unmarked car. Deferring to the elderly woman, Katy invited her to ride up front with Jonah. "I'll be fine in the back. I need to spend some time with Jesus."

Mattie settled into the back seat with the handle of her black purse circling one arm. She'd insisted on keeping a plastic Walmart bag with her. It now sat on the seat beside her. Jonah wondered what that bag held.

He watched in the rearview mirror as Mrs. Walters abandoned her purse in favor of the mysterious bag. Gingerly, she reached in and pulled out a black leather-bound book. She placed the book over her heart and closed her eyes. As she did, tears seeped from the corners. Understanding replaced Jonah's curiosity. In her hands she held the key to a strong connection to God—the one who comforts those who mourn.

Katy turned in her seat to speak to Mrs. Walters. "Did you get a chance to have supper?"

"Thank you for asking, dear, but I'd just finished eating when you came for me. Seems like the older I get, the earlier I rise in the morning and the earlier I eat my supper. If you need to stop for yourselves, go right ahead. I'll just sit here in the car and do me some praying."

"No, that won't be necessary. If you're fine, we'll keep going. Are you okay with that, Jonah?"

Hunger pinched his stomach, yet Jonah hesitated to delay their return to the hospital—not even for a drive-through sandwich.

"I like your name, young man. Are you anything like that Jonah in the Bible? He was one angry prophet on the run from God." She smiled at his reflection in the mirror. "No. I can see you aren't like that at all."

Jonah laughed at her perception. "I confess to having my moments, but with God's help, I'm working on it."

Katy wrinkled her brow and stared at him. Jonah ignored her and returned his attention to the backseat. "How did you and that lovely accent end up on the coast of North Carolina?"

Mrs. Walters cleared her throat and slid back into the leather seat. "Since we're going to be friends, you must call me Matty."

Jonah watched a faraway look come to her eyes. "My mother grew up in the French quarter of New Orleans. Her ancestors had arrived in the Americas in the early 1700s and helped establish the French settlement. As an established port, New Orleans flourished, shipping valuable goods all over the world. By the mid-1800s, the Dupré family had gained both wealth and status as shipping magnates.

"She was born into a traditional Catholic family. My mother's outward beauty, combined with her family's influence, afforded her every opportunity. But she was never satisfied. Her wild streak gave her the courage to rebel against her strict upbringing. My grandparents were helpless against her strong will. Stories of her rebellion remind me of my own daughter."

Jonah heard a sniff and watched Matty wipe her eyes. "My grandparents went to Mass along with their neighbors, but they never learned to trust God with their daughter.

"One night, my mother sneaked out of the house to attend a party with some of her friends. Noticing her dressed in finery, one of Grandfather's dock workers followed her into a secluded area and assaulted her. All mother's strength failed against her strong assailant. The Black man raped her and left her for dead in an alley not far from their home."

Katy looked at Jonah with alarm. He reached for her hand while Matty continued her tragic story. "When a servant found her the next morning, he found she'd been severely beaten. She had a weak pulse and shallow breathing, but he rushed her home to her parents. After the doctor patched her up, my mother quickly recovered from her injuries. But only a few weeks later, she discovered her assailant had left his seed behind.

"My grandfather was appalled that anyone would do this to his daughter. He wasted no time in hiring a detective and bringing the man to justice. But the deed had been done and nothing would cover the embarrassment my mother's rebellion had brought on her family."

Matty stopped for a moment and looked at Jonah's face in the mirror. She gave him an apologetic smile before clearing her throat. "To avoid further humiliation, my grandparents sent Mother to live with an uncle who had settled in the Wilmington area. Even after my birth, Mother remained with me in North Carolina."

Matty chuckled under her breath. "My features resembled my mother, but the color of my skin didn't quite fit into my uncle's White neighborhood. Though Mother loved me and wanted me to be happy, she didn't object when I spent most of my time playing with the children of our Black help.

"Upon graduation from high school, I attended a predominately Black college where I studied to be a teacher. My college years were some of the happiest of my life. That's where I met my Howie, a handsome young African American who was majoring in school administration. After a few classes together, he asked me for a date. I couldn't believe my good fortune—to be so accepted and loved. Before long, he took me home to meet his family."

When he saw the twinkle in Matty's eyes, Jonah looked at Katy with a sparkle of his own.

"Culture shock didn't begin to describe my first impression. Though I'd played with the Black children and gone to school with the young adults, I wasn't prepared for the way his people worshipped. Jesus wasn't just a statue behind the altar, but someone they trusted with every area of their lives. The religious training I'd experienced seemed preschool compared to what I observed in his family."

At Matty's pause, Jonah glanced at her image in the rearview mirror. She took a deep breath and tightened her hold on her Bible. "Howie's father pastored a small congregation in Wilmington. I stared in awe the first time I heard him pray. He talked to Jesus as if they were together in the same room. Not only did he know God, but he understood what God expected of him. He loved all people, even those who scorned him. Forgiveness came easy when he realized how much God had forgiven him.

"Observing Howie's father made me want the same kind of relationship with God. I knew about God and had been taught simple prayers, but I didn't really know him. Nor did I realize how much he wanted a relationship with me."

Matty folded her arms. "Howie wouldn't marry me until he knew my faith was real. The stubborn man dragged me to one Bible study after another to make sure I understood what I believed.

"After we married, my faith continued to grow until our only child ran away at the age of sixteen. Maggie broke our hearts. At first, we exhausted our resources trying to find her, but we finally gave up and released her to God's care."

Jonah watched as Matty's head shook in sympathy. "All her life, Maggie complained of being caught between two different worlds—my wealthy, White grandparents and our middle-class Black family. When my grandfather died, his company had to be sold to pay the heavy debt of a business that failed when larger companies moved into his once strong monopoly.

"Since Maggie left us thirty something years ago, my only contact has been through William. He found my address a couple of years ago among some of my daughter's papers and wrote to me. William said he always wanted a family. He didn't even know which of the many men was his father. The longing in his letters nearly broke my heart."

Jonah looked back at Matty and ached along with her. But she wasn't through. "My grandson described a deplorable life of poverty, hunger, and a mother addicted to drugs. Each return letter I included a little money, hoping it wouldn't contribute to my daughter's drug habit. I wanted to rescue him from what I considered the 'pits of hell.' William insisted his mother needed him. I wanted to shake my daughter for putting that kind of responsibility on a young boy. Before I called a lawyer, something, or perhaps someone, stopped me. God has a plan for my William and only he knows what the future holds. As for Maggie, she's finally found her way home."

By the time Matty finished telling her story, sniffles could be heard throughout the car. Katy handed Jonah a tissue when she noticed him reaching for the hem of his T-shirt.

Without words to respond, he remembered something his own father had said. "Parents do all they can for their children, but some still walk away."

Two loving parents had not been enough for Maggie, and it hadn't been enough for him either. He couldn't imagine how much more difficult life in a single parent home must be—with only one parent to cope with all the problems life throws their way. Thank God, Jonah had come to his senses before he reached the point of no return.

Jonah and Katy were so captivated by Matty's intense story that neither were aware of the miles gobbled up by the black sedan. After Jonah parked, they took the elevator to the ICU floor and introduced William's grandmother to the nursing staff. Before the nurse took her to see her grandson, she took her hand. "I'm sorry about your daughter, Mrs. Walters. We didn't tell William about his mother. We thought it might be better for you to tell him."

Matty patted the nurse's hand and walked with her to William's cubicle. Katy and Jonah waited behind the drawn curtain, listening to every word.

"Looks like the devil has been beating on you, Son."

"Grandma. Is that you? I'm so glad you're here. I need you."

Jonah squeezed Katy's hand when they heard William's sobs of relief. The grandmother he'd never seen had come to his rescue. For the first time since they'd met Matty, she sounded close to losing her quiet self-control. Jonah had to stop himself from rushing into the room. Instead of his comfort—they needed the strength and comfort of family.

"I know, dear boy. Your mama went to be with Jesus, and I'm so sorry."

"It's okay, Grandma. God told me. He said he would make things easier for both of us from now on. I'm gonna miss Mama, but I can't help her anymore. Can I come stay with you now?"

"Of course you may. After we clean out your mama's apartment, we'll take her home with us. She'll rest real good next to her daddy. As for you, young man, God and I will take care of you from now on. There are some fine young people in my church who would love to meet you. They'll take you under their wings and introduce you to a different kind of life."

"I wish I didn't have to leave Mr. A. and Miss Katy. They've taught me so much. I want to be just like them when I get older."

Jonah's breath caught as he thought of the hundreds of young people like William. "Well, I bet we can count on them coming to see us, and we can even come back here to see them. In just a couple of years, you'll have your driver's license, and I'm going to buy us a car. I'll even sit in the back so you can pretend to be driving Miss Daisy."

Matty snickered. "Only difference is, you'll be driving a Black French woman instead of an old Jewish lady. I loved that movie. It just goes to show that no matter how different folks might be, they can still be friends."

Jonah's heart swelled with love for the dear woman who had given her grandson hope. "Jonah, I know you're out there waiting. Why don't you and Katy come on in so we can pray for William? He needs to get well so he can go home with me."

Before he and Katy were halfway across the room, Matty began to pray, "Lord Jesus. You are the God of miracles and my boy needs a big one. You have great plans for him, but he needs to be well so he can continue telling others of your love."

When Jonah thought the woman finished, she moved from praying for William's healing to praying for the others in the hospital. She then placed her hands over his and Katy's and prayed for their future together. Before she finished, her prayers had extended to the whole world.

"Lord, you came to show us a better way—a way of love instead of hate. Raise up people like William, Jonah, and Katy who will teach forgiveness and love. Let the fruit of the Holy Spirit shine through their lives so they reflect the glory of Jesus. You are the only one who has the answer to life's problems. Thank you for the army of believers who choose love instead of hate, peace instead of war, and prayer instead of complacency. Oh, mighty Father, protect us from the evil one who wants to use others to harm or destroy your children as they did my Maggie and William. They are far from truth, and they need to be set free to love and serve you. Thank you for hearing our prayers and for your holy presence we feel in this room. Remain here with us until William is completely healed. Amen."

Several minutes passed before anyone said a word. Jonah had never heard another person talk to God with such power and authority. He didn't know about Katy, but when Matty prayed, he had goosebumps running up and down his spine.

Katy broke the silence when she put her arm around Matty. "Why don't you come home with me? You must be exhausted. I have plenty of room at my house, and I would love to have you."

"That's sweet of you, dear, but my place is here with my grandson. We have years of catching up. You two skedaddle and get some rest. Jonah looks about ready to fall asleep on his feet."

Matty was right. Not counting the power nap, he'd had no sleep in the last forty-eight hours. Hopefully, a few hours undisturbed would restore his mind and body before continuing his assignment—to take a couple more criminals off the street.

William's grandmother might be a saint, but she was a stubborn one. No cajoling on their part convinced her to accept Katy's hospitality. Acquiescing to Matty's wishes, Jonah talked with the head nurse to encourage the hospital staff to take care of her. The nurse told him that William would soon be moved to a private room downstairs where his grandmother would be allowed to stay with him. The woman was an angel who accidentally came into their lives, and Jonah would do all in his power to welcome her.

CHAPTER FIFTEEN

William's grandmother not only nursed her grandson back to health in record time, but she also visited every patient—praying and encouraging as she made her rounds. The beautiful lady with the French accent broke several hospital rules, but always with a smile. Nobody complained about the visiting angel.

Katy had renewed her offer of hospitality, but Matty never agreed to go home with her. Ten days after the beating, William was released from the hospital. Katy drove him and his grandmother to Wilmington and stayed for Maggie's memorial service. Jonah came with Joe for the service but planned to ride home with Katy.

The graveside service spoke of Maggie as a little girl and the joy she brought to her parents. Though she had lost her way, the minister told of the Good Shepherd who laid his life down for his sheep. "He searches everywhere for those who are lost and returns them to the fold."

At the graveside, Jonah and Katy clung to each other. Matty stood next to Jonah with her arm around William. While the boy stared at the coffin, his grandmother turned her eyes toward heaven. Her face glowed despite the black hat shading her from the midday sun.

After the burial, most of the guests returned to the church for the reception. The tables groaned with southern delicacies furnished by members of the congregation.

"I know you need to get back to Trenton," Katy said, "but I want to see Matty and William settled before we leave. Do you mind?"

"Of course, we'll stay." Jonah's stomach growled as he eyed the heaping platters of fried chicken, ham, and barbeque. The donut he'd consumed at six a.m. had long disappeared.

The sun had painted the sky with an ever-changing picture of pink, red, and orange by the time Katy and Jonah headed west. "Do you mind driving? I don't know about you, but I'm beat—emotionally drained."

Jonah took Katy's hand and rubbed her knuckles. "What did you think of Matty's friends and relatives?"

"Relieved. None of them spoke of the painful years. They only remembered the bright, little girl of Maggie's childhood. We don't have to worry. William is in good hands."

"I'm happy for him. Did you see the look of contentment on his face when he sank into the porch swing and set it in motion?"

Jonah relaxed as he followed the signs to I-40. "How was your overnight with them?"

Katy touched her hand to her chest. "Oh, Jonah. His eyes glistened with tears when he first saw his grandmother's little cottage. I don't think the child has ever really had a home. I'm so happy for him. He walked all through the house and into the garden with me hovering like a mother hen. I was so afraid he'd fall on the uneven flagstones, but he did well.

"This morning I set him up for physical therapy. In no time at all, he'll be walking without assistance."

Jonah watched Katy wiggle in her seat as she jumped from one subject to the next with hardly a breath between. He wasn't surprised when she confessed she'd been ready to adopt William if they'd failed to find his grandmother. She would need to get in line behind him. The young man had impressed them both, and Jonah couldn't wait to see what God had planned for his future. Jonah needed more people like Matty and William in his life.

Several weeks passed before Jonah and his team found and arrested the two other suspects in Maggie Walter's murder. After further investigation, those arrested were also charged with the influx of drugs into the Raleigh area. Jonah breathed easier when he had them locked behind bars.

With the pressing workload, Jonah hadn't seen much of Katy. He regretted missing her talk on abortion and was anxious to hear her take on it. At his first break the following day, he stopped by her house.

Katy opened the door along with her arms for a hug. "I thought you were too busy to see me."

"I am, but I had to hear about last night. How did the kids react to your story?"

Katy lowered her head. Jonah reached for her, fearing the worse. "What happened?"

"The meeting went well, but today, I regret sharing such a painful experience that I haven't even told my parents."

"I understand. You and I suffer from a similar dysfunction. While trying to shield our parents from disappointment, we put up barriers instead. We'll pray for each other, but I'm still anxious to hear about the meeting."

"The kids were never so attentive. I saw a few guilty looks, but they were full of questions—some I didn't know how to answer. I missed you and your expert knowledge. The kids complained when they realized you wouldn't be there with your guitar."

Jonah guided her to the sofa and anchored her head against his chest. "I'm proud of you, honey. You'll know when the time is right to talk with your parents. As far as the Bible study, I'm afraid I will have to miss a couple more weeks. Can you carry on without me?"

Katy moved away and wrinkled her brow. "What would we study? I can't imagine coming up with something on my own."

"We still have several topics to address from the Gospel of John, but we should move slow and allow the kids to apply what they've already learned."

Katy's eyes brightened as she scooted to the edge of the sofa. "I agree. Several talked about how God had helped them overcome temptations. Some confessed to bullying other kids, to disrespecting their parents and using foul language.

"Antonio went into more detail about his brother. The room was so quiet I could hear the dripping faucet in the kitchen.

"After the silence, the boy looked at each person in the room and issued a challenge. 'Some of you are doing the same things Montel was doing. You need to turn your life around before you end up dead.'"

After a long sigh, Katy folded her hands in her lap. "I'm praying they will heed the warning before it's too late. I have never seen them more motivated to change not only themselves, but to support one another."

Jonah squeezed Katy's arm. "Wow, that's great. I won't be there, but I can pray. Since I know you're uncomfortable leading the group alone, what about asking the youth pastor at the neighborhood church to teach for the next couple of weeks?"

Katy thought a few minutes before answering. "That's a good idea. I had already planned to attend their church on Sunday. I'll make an appointment with the minister and ask his advice. Thank you."

Jonah pulled her back into his arms and let his fingers run through her long hair. He would never get enough of this beautiful woman. Just when he was enjoying the feel of her body molded to his, he looked at the time and winced. With a quick kiss, he darted for the door.

"Sorry, but I'm already late for a meeting with the chief."

The Wednesday night Bible studies continued into the cold winter evenings, forcing the crowd back into Katy's living room. Jonah had rejoined the team which now included Jeremy, the pastor's son who served as the youth pastor at the church, and his wife, Trish.

Every week, Jonah felt closer to Katy, while she drew closer to God. Her mission to the people in her neighborhood had turned into a ministry as she added prayer and Scripture to her classes. On Jonah's days off, he and Katy spent hours planning and studying together. They remained at odds on some issues, but the more they prayed together, the more the gap between their opposing views decreased.

On Jonah's first Sunday off, he attended church with Katy. The southern gospel music was a bit different from the familiar hymns he had sung on Shell Island. As they sang the spirited songs with gusto, he couldn't be still. He swayed with the music and clapped to the beat.

The sermon hit him with a boatload of conviction. "Are you following God's plan for your life, or are you making your own plans?" That question bothered him all afternoon, along with the secrets he'd kept from the people he loved. For years, his parents had been his go-to source when he needed guidance, yet he hadn't talked with them about Monica and how her death changed his life. Their few conversations since he'd left college had ended in uncomfortable silence.

Without realizing it, he had done the same with Katy—skirting the issue every time she mentioned his family. With their relationship moving forward, he had to tell her why he abandoned college for the police academy.

Since they both had afternoon meetings, Jonah had originally planned to leave her at the door. His nagging conscience kept him shuffling his feet and hanging on the doorframe. "Katy, I know you have a busy afternoon, but may I come in for a few minutes?"

"Of course." She pulled him inside and melted into his arms. After their brief kiss, Katy looked at him with concern. "What's wrong?"

"I need to talk to you. I haven't been completely honest."

Katy frowned and led him to the couch in the living room. "Please tell me you don't have a wife hidden away somewhere."

Jonah laughed. "No, nothing like that. It's just that I never told you why I left the university and became a police officer. As a survival mechanism, I pushed that painful time deep inside."

Katy stroked his arm while he talked about how Monica's death affected him—how he'd built a wall between him and his parents. By the time he finished, they were both in tears. When she hugged him, and he heard her pray aloud for the first time, he knew he'd done the right thing.

"Father, you know Jonah wants to serve and obey you in everything. Instead of running away from your best, give him the courage to face his fears and follow wherever you lead him. Restore the relationship between him and his parents. Help them understand and forgive him for shutting them out. Give him the grace to receive their support and encouragement. In Jesus's name. Amen."

As the flowers began to bloom and the trees turned from winter sticks to a lush green, his team learned they would be presented with a special service award at the Grand Gala in early June. The mayor hosted the annual ball to honor the men and women from the police and fire departments. The party was fine for people who liked that sort of thing, but Jonah had never attended and didn't plan to—no matter who might be honored. The idea of dressing up and parading his men before the town's elite grated on him. Their undercover operation wouldn't work in the limelight.

During the investigation and trials, his chief had kept the press at bay with regular press releases and news conferences. Just because they'd made a few arrests did not mean the town was drug free. Such publicity would work against them and compromise their operation. Only William, Antonio, and Montel from the Bible study knew of his position, and they had agreed to help him remain incognito.

Jonah fumed at anyone who would listen. "The man doesn't care what happens to us after he parades us before the whole town."

When his objections drifted to the higher echelons, the mayor shut him up with his message through the chief. "You tell that hoodlum I expect to see him at the gala. Not only will he show up, but he will be on time and look presentable on the arm of my daughter."

Along with the message were strict orders defining what he should wear and how he should look. According to the mandate, he had to lose the facial hair and ponytail. Jonah hated the thought of starting over. That disguise didn't happen overnight. He'd be forced to hide at the precinct office for weeks before he looked grungy enough to move about the streets. His chief, however, would be happy to finally have someone pay attention to administration.

Jonah packed most of his clothes and uniforms in his old Mustang and left the apartment to Joe. He'd be forced to live away from the neighborhood. He was taking a risk even going to Katy's house. She'd returned home following the last wave of arrests. Despite her father's insistence he appear "presentable," he agreed to do so for Katy. His objections to her father's unreasonable demands led to their first major argument.

"I know you love your father, but he's nothing but a showoff. He wants to turn our successes into a political circus."

"How can you say that? If you knew him, you wouldn't suggest such a thing. So far, you have thwarted every attempt my parents have made to get to know you. Every time they've invited you to dinner, you've canceled at the last minute, citing a hot lead."

Jonah paced back and forth, making his point. "I'm sorry, but everyone knows when you get a lead, you have to move quickly. Otherwise, another bit of information is wasted while I brownnose your father."

Disgusted with his excuses, Katy put her hands on her hips and got in his face. "You're a coward, Officer Abbott. Every day, you face hardened criminals, yet you're afraid of my father."

Jonah chuckled as he pulled Katy into his arms. He kissed her until he knew she had given up the fight. She would be even more furious if he told her what he really thought of her father. He considered the man a controlling tyrant who took every opportunity to make Jonah's life miserable. Who would want to sit through an entire evening with the man? But for this occasion, he'd run out of excuses and would be forced to cater to the mayor's unreasonable demands.

CHAPTER SIXTEEN

Jonah waited until the day of the big event to change his appearance. He made a big mistake when he chose the closest hair salon instead of a barber shop. Before he even gave his name, three women descended upon him like vultures. Determined to give him the ultimate makeover, they spent most of the day working their magic.

First, they stripped him of his long hair and shaved his beard. Then the attendants insisted on a manicure and pedicure. They relieved him of cuticles and buffed his nails. He stopped them short when they reached for his shoes. Jonah threw a wad of bills on the counter and dashed out the door, slowing when his apartment was in sight.

Jonah arrived at the precinct later than he'd planned. He threw his garment bag over the door of a restroom stall and pulled out his rarely used dress uniform. While he fumbled with the brass buttons, he did a double take when he noticed a wide-eyed well-groomed police officer in the mirror. He hadn't seen that clean-shaven face in over three years.

Although he objected to the event, he anticipated the look on Katy's face when she saw him. She'd be pleased, and despite his animosity toward her father, he wanted to make her happy. The time and expense would be worth every cent. As he remembered his more recent look, he grinned at the reflection. Not bad. Not bad at all.

His attitude improving, he sang "I'm a Happy Man" by The Jive Five. Jonah had rented a classy red Mustang so Katy wouldn't have to ride to the formal ball in his "dumpster." He ran his hand along the clean lines of the leather console. Nice ride. When he noticed the time on the display, he pressed the accelerator and felt the rush as the car surged forward.

Even with his hot ride, Jonah's transformation had made him over an hour late. He shrugged. Refusing to abandon his happy mood, he whistled as he walked the path to the front door. No longer dreading the occasion, he looked forward to a romantic evening with Katy. Before he could knock, the door flew open, and an ethereal vision glared at him. She had the look of a warrior—ready for battle.

Jonah ignored her angry scowl and forced himself to keep breathing. The light reflecting off the overhead fixture gave her gown a sparkling glow. The slim lines silhouetted her figure too well. He stared like an imbecile while his mind planned ways to skip the gala.

"You're late—whoa!" Speechless for a moment, Katy sized Jonah up and down. With a tap to his shoulder, she turned him around and he did a full three-sixty with a bow. "My, my. You do clean up well."

"You look amazing yourself. I will be the envy of every guy in the ballroom." He attempted one last out "Are you sure we have to go?"

"Of course, we are going. You and your team are the guests of honor, and you can't get out of escorting me. Pull yourself together."

Easier said than done. His blood boiled as he pulled the enticing woman into his arms. He wanted to devour her. Amid the third passionate kiss, Katy pushed him away.

She glanced at the hall mirror and moaned. "Now look what you've done. We're going to be later than ever. I will need to repair my makeup and look at you—you have lipstick all over your face. That should make a great impression on my parents."

While Katy glided back upstairs, Jonah went into the downstairs powder room and splashed cool water on his face. Traces of her lipstick clung to the corner of his mouth and reignited the fire the woman stirred inside him. As he reached for a tissue to remove the last bit of lipstick, he wondered how long before he could convince Katy to accept a marriage proposal. He needed that trip down the aisle sooner rather than later.

Katy wasted no time when she returned to the lower level. She rushed him out the door but stopped when she noticed his wheels. "Wow, what a great car. I know you rented this for me, but I would have been fine with a clean version of your Mustang."

"I know, but there wasn't time with all your father's demands on my appearance."

Jonah spotted Joe and his team as he and Katy entered the hotel ballroom. He snarled and whispered through clenched teeth, "Why did your father have to pick on me? Look at those guys. Their hair and beard only saw a glimpse of the razor while I've been scalped."

"Stop whining. You look great. This night is important to us and my parents. They want to be proud of the man their daughter plans to marry."

That shut him up, but the thought of marriage to such a beautiful woman made him want her more. As Jonah looked around the room, he noticed almost every eye focused on Katy. He wanted to scoop her into his arms and flee. The demon of jealousy taunted him until he remembered she belonged to him. The other fellows were just wishing they were in his shoes.

Speaking of shoes, after the comfort of Nike's and flip flops for months, his rarely worn dress shoes were pinching his toes like they were caught in a vise. Katy poked him and directed his attention to her parents. "Mother, I would like you to meet Jonah. Jonah, this is my mother, Saundra Wilson."

"How do you do, Mrs. Wilson? It's a lovely evening. I understand you are partially responsible for making the event so special for the service personnel. Thank you."

Jonah felt as if he were under a microscope as the woman looked him over. "Well, it's good to finally meet the elusive Officer Abbott. Katy tells me you're from Shell Island. That must have been interesting growing up in a resort area."

"I had a blessed childhood, Mrs. Wilson. It wasn't until I had a couple years of college under my belt that I realized how idyllic my life had been."

"Katy didn't tell us that you attended college. Did you major in criminal justice?"

Jonah pulled at his collar and squirmed at the mention of his painful past. When Katy recognized his discomfort, she placed her hand on her mother's arm. "Not now, Mother. Jonah had an interesting change of careers before graduation, but we'll have to discuss it later."

Her father had finished a conversation with a few of the Trenton business leaders and turned toward them. "Officer Abbott, I hardly recognized you without the hoodlum look. I'm impressed. Katy obviously saw something hidden under all that hair and dirt. For the life of me, I certainly didn't see it. You two make a handsome couple. Get out there on the dance floor so our friends can admire my Katy."

Jonah's feathers ruffled at her father's remark, but Katy smiled and pulled him toward the dance floor. As the orchestra played, "When I Fall in Love," Jonah pulled her closer than the waltz intended and whispered his own version in her ear, "I have fallen in love with you, Katy. It will be forever. I have fallen in love with you." Jonah nuzzled her neck and whispered, "My Katy, how will I survive another day without you?"

Love shining from Katy's eyes melted him as she moved even closer. When the song ended, she kissed him gently on the mouth and held him a moment longer. The romantic moment was lost when she whispered in his ear. "If you want to win my mother's approval, ask her to dance."

"I'd rather not leave you free for that long."

"Why? Are you jealous? You know I'm not interested in anyone but you. Besides, I plan to dance with my father."

"In that case, I'll release you for one dance, but that's all."

Jonah ushered her to her father and reached his hand toward Mrs. Wilson. "May I have this dance?"

The woman gushed with pleasure as he led her out on the floor. A familiar sweet smell drifted toward him—the same perfume her daughter wore. Breathing deeply, he sighed while wishing he held Katy instead.

Jonah's mind wandered as he moved across the dance floor with Katy's mother. He winced at the thought of the curious woman questioning him further about his past. "You dance well, young man."

Good—a safe topic. "Thank you, Mrs. Wilson. I will forward the compliment to my mother. She taught her boys the art before we were old enough to attend our first junior high dance."

The woman raised an eyebrow. "You have brothers?"

"Yes. I'm the youngest of three. My older brothers are twins."

"How interesting."

Mrs. Wilson grew silent for a few moments. "I always wanted a large family, but God only gave us Katy. She's special. Please don't hurt her."

Jonah looked at Katy as she and her father glided past. "I love your daughter, ma'am, and I would never harm her. She's precious to me."

Katy's mother squeezed his arm as they walked off the dance floor together.

Jonah danced the remainder of the evening with Katy—even the unfamiliar dances where he struggled to stay off her pretty toes. Joe teased about her clumsy dance partner. Toward the end of the evening, Katy's father interrupted the orchestra with a tap to the microphone.

"Before this pleasant evening comes to a close, we would like to honor a few of our service personnel."

Jonah gritted his teeth, dreading the next few minutes. The mayor recognized several firefighters, followed by a few policemen in other departments before mentioning his team. To Jonah's surprise, the mayor refrained from calling them forward.

"The last group I would like to recognize is a team of highly qualified officers who work undercover in our police department. Recently, they worked almost twenty-four/ seven to uncover a plot against my own daughter. They arrested several persons responsible for distributing drugs to our young people. Due to their need to remain anonymous, we will not call them forward nor mention them by name. This impressive trophy will sit in the hallway at police headquarters in acknowledgment of their dedication to our town and its citizens."

Jonah released a pent-up breath and wiped the sweat trailing down his face. He hoped the low-key ceremony would protect his men as they continued their undercover assignments. Surprised by the mayor's wisdom, Jonah took another look at the man. Had he misjudged Katy's father in other areas as well? Perhaps he should give her parents a chance.

When he finally had Katy alone in the car, he leaned over the console and breathed in the smell of her. "I need to apologize to your father for misjudging him. You were right. I shouldn't get paranoid over his attempt to protect his daughter. In the future, I promise to stop avoiding him and will try to get to know him along with your lovely mother."

"Would you mind saying that again, please?"

"You mean about getting to know your parents?"

"No. The one that said something about me being right."

Jonah laughed and tweaked her nose. "I hate to admit it, but yes, you were right, and I plan to make amends as soon as possible."

Katy's eyes twinkled. "Thank you. See, I told you the dreaded evening wouldn't be nearly as difficult as you feared. You had my parents eating out of your hand, especially my mother. She thinks you're very handsome."

Katy stretched across the console and snuggled into his neck. He ran his fingers through her hair and again breathed in her sweet smell. "The main thing I liked about the evening was you. Though I don't deserve you, the most beautiful girl chose to be with me. I felt like a million bucks with you on my arm. As for your parents, I like your mother's perfume. She smells just like you."

Katy tapped him with her evening purse. His chest swelled with love at the pleasure he saw shining in her eyes.

When they arrived at her house, she unbuckled the seat belt and waited for him to open her car door. He wanted to kiss her until neither of them could breathe, but, with his feelings so raw and vulnerable, he didn't trust himself to be alone with her. With her hand in the crook of his arm, they strolled up the sidewalk.

At the porch, Katy pulled him into a tight hug. "Thank you for dressing up for me. I felt like a princess, escorted by a very handsome prince. You made the evening more than special."

"I'm the lucky one. I know I don't deserve you, but thank you for loving me."

Jonah gave her a quick kiss on the lips and took her keys to open the door. When he knew she was safe inside, he turned toward the street. His steps were lighter as he whistled the tune that lingered in his mind, "When I Fall in Love."

About halfway to the car, his steps slowed. Something didn't feel right. He stopped and peered into the shadows. Despite the deserted street, Jonah's sense of danger remained. He shuddered as the hairs on the back of his neck prickled. He looked back toward the house. Katy waved from the window. He waved back before moving on down the walkway.

The next moment chaos erupted—running footsteps followed by rapid gun fire. A strong force exploded in his abdomen, his vision blurred, and his legs collapsed beneath him. He heard himself screaming Katy's name.

CHAPTER SEVENTEEN

Katy locked the door, rushed to the window, and pulled back the curtain. With his hands in his pockets, Jonah bounced down the sidewalk to the tune of a faint whistle. Tapping her hand over her heart, she sighed. Did Jonah have any idea how he affected her?

As if sensing danger, Jonah stopped and turned in every direction. When he saw her watching from the window, he waved and continued toward the gate. On heightened alert now, his carefree bounce became steady, cautious steps.

A popping sound pierced the darkness and sent chills up and down Katy's spine. She screamed as Jonah's body crumbled to the sidewalk. Without a thought to her own safety, she rushed out the door.

"Someone, please call the police!" Katy yelled toward the house next door.

"Oh, God. They've killed my Jonah. Please, help us."

Kneeling beside the motionless form, she put her hand over his chest and released a shaky breath when she felt movement under her hand. Blood had already dampened his uniform. Her heart skipped a beat when she looked down and saw blood oozing between her fingers. Katy pushed back his hair and whispered, "Jonah, please don't leave me. I need you."

A strong hand grabbed her arm and pulled her across his chest. "Get down."

She muffled her cries against Jonah's bloody jacket. Since they'd met, he had done everything to keep her safe. Now, at the brink of death, he only thought of her.

Katy's breath caught, and she choked back an anguished cry. If Jonah hadn't dressed to please her, he would not be fighting for his life. That formal uniform might as well have been a bull's eye. Why, oh why, had she made him attend the gala?

As guilt gripped her insides, Jonah's hold on her weakened, and his hand dropped to the walkway. If not for the gradual rise and fall of his chest and the faint heartbeat against her ear, Katy would have thought him dead.

She lifted her head in relief at the sound of sirens. The ambulance, fire, and police vehicles soon blocked the street. A police officer lifted her to her feet, his eyes focused on her blood-stained gown. "Were you also shot?"

Katy shook her head. "No, Jonah left me at the door and was on his way to the car when I heard the shots. I saw him fall."

Katy looked down and saw Jonah's blood staining the front of her gown. Sweet visions of their night together competed with guilt and anger. She cried, "Oh, Jonah. What have I done?"

The paramedics loaded Jonah into the ambulance and jumped into the rear with him. "Please let me be with him. He can't go alone."

The ambulance crew agreed to let her ride up front. As if in a trance, Katy watched the two paramedics hovering over Jonah, inserting IVs, and hooking him to machines. When she realized the driver had started the engine, she rushed toward the passenger seat.

Katy braced herself against the door as the ambulance flew through town, lights flashing, horns blaring. She wanted to cover her ears. The frantic conversation of the paramedics blurred with the beep, beep of the machines keeping Jonah alive and the shrill of the siren. She froze at the one-sided conversation. "Adult male in critical condition. Gunshot wounds to the abdomen and right femur. Speed it up, Mike. We'll lose him if we don't stop the bleeding."

Katy bit her lip to keep from drawing attention away from Jonah. Her emotions raged like a storm as she searched for a haven of peace. Where was her newfound faith? Surely God wouldn't take Jonah from her—not when he meant so much to her. Because of him, she had found meaning and purpose for her life.

When the ambulance pulled into the emergency entrance, the medics rushed Jonah in one direction while a volunteer directed Katy to the reception desk. The attendant handed her a clipboard. Her vision blurred when she saw the pages filled with blank lines. She handed the papers back with only Jonah's name filling the top space.

"You don't even know his address?"

Katy shook her head and shrugged. Without an explanation, she walked toward the waiting room. A heaviness pushed against her chest. She had barely taken a seat in the hard plastic chair when a nurse rushed through the open door. "Is there a Katy here for Officer Abbott?"

Katy stood on shaky legs and met the nurse in the doorway. "I'm Katy. Please don't tell me he's dead."

"No, but he's bad and making himself worse. He thinks you were killed. His blood pressure rises every time he screams your name. Maybe you can calm him while we prep him for surgery."

As they ran through the double doors, Katy heard him before she reached his cubicle. "Katy, stay down. Where are you?"

"Jonah, I'm here. I'm okay. Shhh. Let me pray for you."

Katy whispered in his ear as the anesthesiologist waited for the two nurses to place IV lines in his arm. Katy's soft touch and soothing words of love relaxed Jonah even before the drugs took effect.

The nurse released a long breath and motioned for her to leave. Near the door, Katy saw the remains of Jonah's tattered, bloody uniform piled on the floor. No longer pretending, she fell to her knees. Her keening wasn't loud, but it came from the depths of her soul. Katy pulled the bloody strips to her chest and cried. She gagged at the raw smell of Jonah's blood.

"I'm so sorry, Miss Katy. Let me help you."

They didn't even know her last name. The nurse took her by the arm and helped her to her feet. She didn't let go until she had seated Katy in the surgical waiting room. "Is there someone we can call for you?"

Katy shook her head. The only person she wanted had been rushed away on a gurney.

Within minutes, Chief Morrison stepped through the door. His clothes looked as if he'd slept in them. Worry lines wrinkled his brow as he searched the room until his eyes locked with hers. "Ms. Wilson. Are you all right?"

Katy swallowed and tried to clear her throat. "I wasn't shot if that's what you mean, but Jonah—he's hurt bad. Who would do this to him?"

The chief scratched his thinning hair. "I'm not certain what happened. I thought we'd arrested everyone involved in the plot against you. What happened after the two of you left the gala?"

Katy recalled the events of the bittersweet evening ending with the ambush. Chief Morrison took her hand and squeezed it gently. "I know this is hard, but I need your help to find the persons responsible. Did you see anything suspicious?"

Katy shook her head. The chief wouldn't be interested in the things she remembered with such clarity—the oneness she felt in Jonah's arms, his passionate kisses, or the love shining from his eyes. They were precious memories to her, but they wouldn't bring the chief any closer to bringing in the persons who'd shot Jonah.

His eyes softened while he waited for an answer. "I don't remember seeing anything unusual when he brought me home, but I'm certain Jonah did. As he was leaving, he paused and checked in all directions." Katy sobbed and shook her head. "Jonah had been in such a good mood all evening until ..."

Bent over, Katy wept into her shaking hands as she recalled Jonah crumbling on the sidewalk in a pool of blood. How had the evening changed so fast? One moment he was whistling a tune, and the next, he was fighting for his life.

Katy sniffed and took the tissue Chief Morrison handed her. He patted her hand and excused himself. He disappeared through the door with his cell phone to his ear. After a few minutes, the chief returned and took the seat across from her. He said little though he was in constant motion—making notes in a folder, shuffling through pages of material, and then returning to the hallway.

Shifting positions every few minutes, Katy vacillated between fear and trust. With her faith so new and fragile, she struggled to follow Jonah's example—relying on an unseen person for strength, comfort, and peace. Remembering the stories she had read in his Bible, Katy tried to picture Jesus healing Jonah. The fear of losing him overpowered her fragile faith. Inside her head, she screamed at God. How could you let this happen to such a good man?

Several minutes passed before the door swung open, and Katy's father rushed in. She choked on her tears when their eyes met. He rushed forward and lifted her from the vinyl couch. In his comforting embrace, she burst into tears and shook with pent-up grief.

Katy sniffed a last few times and wiped her nose on a wad of tissues. She looked into her father's compassionate eyes. "Daddy, Jonah was shot."

"I know, honey. But, thank God, you're okay."

Her father held her at arm's length and noticed her soiled gown. "Here, take my jacket. Your dress is ruined, and you'll be freezing before the night's over."

As he helped her into his dinner jacket, she once again burst into tears. Her father put his arm around her and squeezed. "You just hang in there. Jonah seems like a fine young man, and I like him. He has an unusual strength that I'm sure will get him through this. Keep praying to that God you and Jonah think so highly of."

Her father held her a few minutes longer, kissing her hair and rubbing her back. When she stopped shaking, he led her back to her seat, then joined Chief Morrison. Katy strained to hear their muffled conversation. She rung her hands. Nothing would erase the bloody scene on constant replay in her mind.

A short time later, Joe arrived. "Katy, I'm so sorry. With all the arrests, I had no idea there'd still be a mad man roaming the streets. But don't you worry—I'm going to get him if it's the last thing I do."

Joe looked as miserable as she felt—his eyes were red from lack of sleep. "Pray for me. Jonah's been after me for years to seek God. Now might be the time to do something about it. Jonah would want us to have faith."

Joe gave her another hug before he turned toward her father and the chief.

Katy felt the room closing in on her. To find relief, she walked out to the nurses' station. The nurse looked at her with pity when she asked about Jonah. She patted Katy's hand. "I'm sorry, but since you aren't related to Officer Abbott, we're prevented from releasing information on his condition."

Katy clung to the reception counter. "You don't understand. We're closer than family. He means the world to me."

The nurse only shook her head and turned back to the computer. Katy pondered the brush-off as she returned to the waiting room. Every person in that room waited to hear a positive report about someone they loved. But none were next of kin. They could only relate to one another as the anxious moments passed.

Katy shook her head and walked toward the window. She watched the sun rising over the buildings to the east. Despite her aching heart, the sun awakened the day with the sound of cars and buses crowding the roadways, and life going on as if nothing happened. Katy leaned her head against the window and sighed. Her breath clouded the glass, and she drew a small heart with her finger.

At the sound of a door opening, Katy turned around. A doctor in scrubs stuck his head in the door. He glanced at her, then moved toward the men. Obviously, a person did not have to be related if he had a "need to know." Regardless of their inconsistent rules, Katy knew she had a need to know. She walked across the room and eavesdropped on the huddle. She had already missed the first few words of the report.

"He is far from being off the critical list. The damage to his organs required extensive repair and will need time to heal. Also, we had to remove a portion of his colon. With stomach wounds, the possibility of infection increases. While we had him under, the orthopedic surgeon worked on his damaged right femur. He's now in recovery but will soon transfer to ICU."

The doctor spotted Katy. "We'll need you again when he wakes up. We could have used you in the operating room. He awakened briefly, screaming for you. I don't know who you are to him, but unless he's drugged into oblivion, he's disoriented."

Katy put her hand over her mouth to muffle her cry. The doctor gestured toward her. "Come with me, and I'll take you to him."

The doctor held the door for her to enter recovery. The moment she saw Jonah's pale face, Katy rushed to his side. Restless, he strained at the confining straps. Tubes protruded from his nose and the right side of his stomach. Katy moved to his left side and whispered his name. She kissed his cheeks, nose, and eyelids. "Jonah, please come back to me." He opened his eyes for a moment and stared. "Katy?"

"I'm here, Jonah. I won't leave you again. Close your eyes and rest."

Without thinking, she moved into prayer—praying for healing, restoration, and strength. As she ended with a quiet amen, she felt peace for the first time since she'd heard the gunshots. Jonah's grip on her arm relaxed and his breathing leveled. Katy smoothed the worry lines on his brow and slumped against the bed in relief.

A few hours later, Jonah was moved into the critical care unit. Katy rushed behind the gurney to the next floor. When she tried to enter the room, a nurse directed her to the family waiting area.

"Sorry, ICU policy."

More strict rules—visitors only allowed in the room for ten minutes each hour. That might work for some people, but not when Jonah needed her.

Katy leaned against the closed door and cried when she heard Jonah screaming her name. She wiped her tears and rushed back to the nurses' station. "Don't you hear him? Please let me go to him."

The nurse patted Katy's hand as if brushing off the desperate cries. "The sedative will take effect soon, and he'll be fine."

Why would they give him a drug when all he needed was her? She recognized the fear in Jonah's voice and broke into action. Forget the unbending hospital rules, she leaned over the high counter. "Call his surgeon. I need to be with Jonah. After what happened, he fears for my life. The doctor said he should remain calm. Please, call him."

The nurse frowned, glanced toward Jonah's room and back at Katy. She sighed in resignation and picked up the phone. "There's a woman here who insists on being with your patient, Jonah Abbott ... I see. Yes, I'll take care of it."

She hung up, rolled her eyes at Katy, and addressed the frazzled nurse coming out of his room. "It seems we've been overruled. Please allow Ms. Wilson to stay with the patient, doctor's orders."

Without waiting for anyone to change their mind, Katy rushed into his cubicle and squeezed into a spot between Jonah's bed and the window.

"I'm here."

Katy heard his quiet whisper. "Don't leave me. I need you."

Jonah slipped in and out of consciousness for the next several hours. He called her name each time he awakened. Staying close to his side, Katy calmed him with words of encouragement and love. One of the nurses found her a Bible, and she read comforting words from the Psalms. When he hadn't stirred for some time, Katy yawned and stretched her eyelids, fighting fatigue. Giving in to the exhaustion, she laid her head at his side. With her hand covering his, she drifted into a peaceful sleep.

CHAPTER EIGHTEEN

Jonah woke confused, intense pain ripping his abdomen. He tightened his fist at the reminder of the gunman and the danger to Katy. As he opened his mouth to yell her name, he felt the warmth of her resting against his side. He trailed his fingers through her silky hair and remembered her whispered prayers and comforting Psalms. Her words had consoled him as he drifted in and out of consciousness, but nothing calmed him more than knowing she rested within his reach.

When the nurse came in to check his vitals, she frowned at Katy. Jonah shook his head. "Please don't—I need her here."

"So, I've been told. You know you're breaking all the rules. If the surgeon hadn't insisted, she'd be sleeping in the ICU waiting room with the other visitors."

Jonah winced as a sharp pain sliced through his stomach. "I'm sorry, I didn't realize ..."

"I have something for your pain."

After the nurse left, he gritted his teeth and waited for the medication to take effect. The door opened again. Why wouldn't they leave him alone?

Before he could protest, two teary-eyed individuals stepped into the room. His parents rushed to his bedside and cast worried looks over his battered body. His mother started around the bed but stopped when she saw Katy. "Jonah? Who is this? Have you forgotten to tell us something?"

Jonah squirmed at his mother's strict scrutiny. "Please don't wake her."

His mother squinted at Katy, stating the obvious. "She's wearing an evening dress stained with blood. Was she also injured? Were you together when this happened?"

Jonah moaned and watched his father round the bed. He put his arm around his worried wife. "I know you're upset, Deborah, but Jonah doesn't need us badgering him."

His mother reached for a tissue and wiped her eyes. "I'm sorry, Jonah, but I haven't had a peaceful night's sleep since you took this dangerous job. I just need some assurance that you'll be okay."

Jonah reached for his mother's hand and whispered through the pain. "I'm alive, Mama, but I can't talk now."

His mother looked down at Katy. "Perhaps you should wake the girl and let her go home. Your father and I are here now."

Jonah grabbed the corner of the sheet and twisted it into a tight ball. "Katy can't leave. I have to keep her safe."

Jonah's words slurred as his body relaxed under the heavy dose of medication. He stared into his mother's eyes and watched her worried expression fade into oblivion.

Katy awakened to the beeping of machines and quiet whispers. Her arms felt numb as she rubbed the base of her neck. At the sound of unfamiliar voices, she froze.

"I know you're worried, but he's going to be all right," a man whispered.

Katy heard sniffing before a woman answered. "How could he have found someone special without telling us?"

Katy didn't have to listen long before she guessed who might be visiting. Jonah's parents had arrived at the worst possible time. Bedraggled and covered in blood wasn't how she imagined their first meeting.

Since disappearing wasn't an option, Katy took a deep breath and raised her head. The surprised eyes of two strangers stared back at her. She looked at Jonah for an introduction, but he was still out. Katy tried to smooth her dress, then finger-combed her hair. She cleared her throat but choked on the sympathetic words she intended to express.

The couple waited for her to stop coughing before Jonah's father reached across the bed. "I'm Mark Abbott, Jonah's father, and this is his mother, Deborah."

Katy took the outstretched hand and tried to smile around the awkward introduction. "Katy Wilson. I'm Jonah's friend."

Mr. Abbott raked his fingers through his thinning hair and gave her a crooked smile. "I know you've had a difficult night, but we're glad you're here with Jonah. The way he looked at you—I suspect you are more than a friend. I can't imagine why we haven't met before."

Katy looked down at her soiled dress. "Please forgive me. I know I look awful, but ... uh, I need to go."

Lowering her head, Katy rounded the bed and skirted past the bewildered couple. At the door she looked back and whispered, "I'm sorry. Tell Jonah I'll return soon."

Katy rushed toward the elevator, but before she could press the down button, a voice sounding a lot like Jonah's stopped her. "Katy, is it?"

At her acknowledgment, Mr. Abbott continued. "I'm sorry we seemed distant back there, but your presence caught us by surprise. Jonah hasn't mentioned anyone special since he broke up with his college girlfriend."

Sadness and sympathy for Jonah's parents washed over Katy as she realized he still hadn't told them about Monica's death. Her parents might be basket cases at times, but at least they knew the current happenings of her life. Katy winced when her conscience reminded her of her own secrets. Maybe she understood Jonah's hesitancy after all.

"When Jonah recovers, you need to talk to him. I know he's kept you at arm's length for a while, but he needs to be the one to share his burdens with you."

"I can see why my son loves you. You're a very perceptive young lady, and I'm looking forward to getting to know you. It might take a while for his mother to come around, but I predict you two will become friends."

Katy smiled at the man's insight. "Well, I can see that you and I will also be friends. You remind me of your son."

Shifting uncomfortably, Katy remembered her destination. "I know you are anxious to hear about your Jonah, and I could talk all day about what he means to me. But I suspect you and your wife would rather hear the story from him. Let me tell you this—you will be extremely proud of the man he has become. I'm going home to rest and give you time to talk."

"What if Jonah's upset that we let you leave?"

"He won't like it, but I'm sure you'll think of some way to reassure him. Tell him I'll be back later, and I hope to look a lot better when I return."

Katy winked at Jonah's father before she pressed the down button.

Yes, they were going to be exceptionally good friends. Nothing like having a good-looking man on your side and a minister to boot.

Mark Abbott watched the elevator doors close, then wandered down the hall following the signs to the chapel. The last several hours were a nightmare. His nerves had been on edge since he'd been awakened by the early morning call from Chief Morrison—a call he had feared since his son took the position with the Trenton Police Department.

Waves of anger, disappointment and choking sorrow washed over him as he opened the door to the sanctuary. He knew all the right answers for others, but when the situation concerned his baby boy, he felt lost and helpless. Sitting alone in the early morning darkness, his son's life passed before him as if someone had opened a photo album of family portraits.

Jonah, their third son, arrived a few years after his twin brothers. Mark saw Deborah's disappointment when the sonogram revealed yet another boy. She received a double blow when the doctor shook his head and told them Jonah would be their last child. Postpartum depression paralyzed her for weeks and forced him into the role of caregiver. During those difficult months, Mark developed a special bond with baby Jonah. They had been close until Jonah left college and joined the police force. The loss wasn't in his change of career but in his withdrawal from his family.

Mark returned to the moment and sat in the front pew. He gazed at the polished brass cross hanging from the ceiling. The backlighting gave the structure the appearance of something unreal—something holy. He broke into tears of gratitude for a God who would give up everything for him. Instead of pouring out his fears and concerns for his son, Mark spent the next half hour thanking God for the cross and for the direction his life had taken. His confidence was restored when he remembered Katy's kind words about his son. Though Jonah might have withdrawn from his earthly father, his heavenly Father had been working overtime.

Jonah opened his eyes and looked around the room. His mother sat in a corner chair with her eyes closed, holding her Bible and journal. He looked past her toward the door. "Where's Katy?"

"Jonah, you're awake. Did you rest well?"

"Where's Katy?"

"Don't be upset. She needed to go home and get some rest. She promised to be back soon."

Jonah's heart rate increased, and perspiration beaded on his forehead. "You don't understand. People want to kill her. I've got to call Joe."

His mother rubbed her forehead as she stood and moved closer. She captured his hand and pulled it to her chest. "I'm so sorry, Jonah. If we had understood the situation, your father and I would have tried to persuade her to stay."

Spotting the hospital phone, Jonah stretched to pull the adjustable table closer. He moaned at the pain slashing through his abdomen.

"Let me help you. You're going to tear the stitches loose." His mother moved the tray closer and handed him the receiver. He dialed the number from memory.

Joe answered after the first ring. "Man, you scared us half to death. What's going on?"

"It's Katy. She ... she went home. Please don't let anything happen to her."

"Don't worry. We'll take care of Katy. All you need to do is stop tormenting yourself. Now, get some rest and leave your woman to us."

Frustrated with his helplessness, Jonah slammed the receiver down and beat his fist against the air-filled mattress. When he saw his mother wringing her hands, he recalled snippets of his earlier irrational behavior. His actions were far from that of a man who trusted God. Nothing justified making a spectacle of himself. He might survive the bullets, but if he didn't get control of his emotions, he'd worry himself to death. His only option was to trust God and his fellow officers. Both resources were better than becoming an emotional wreck. God, help me rest in you.

Jonah looked back at his mother's tear-filled eyes. "Are you all right, Mom?"

Deborah dabbed her cheeks with a tissue. "Yes, but I'm worried. If you don't relax and rest, your wounds will never heal."

"I know. Forgive me."

His mother had a dreamy look to her eyes. "Remember how you used to rush home from school anxious to talk about your day? I miss that little boy." She sniffed and caught a tear with her finger. "What happened to my open, trusting son?"

Jonah lowered his eyes and mumbled. "I've been through hell, Mama, and I didn't want you and Daddy to worry or be disappointed."

His mother raised an eyebrow. "Don't you know the silence makes us worry more? We need a good long talk. Your father and I missed so much of your last three years. But for now, you should rest."

His mother kissed him on the forehead and returned to her chair in the corner. After she picked up her Bible,

Jonah's mind drifted back three years to that painful time after he left the university. He'd arrived on the island consumed with guilt. When he realized his parents had somehow missed the news bulletins, he let them jump to their own conclusion—that Monica had broken his heart. Rather than disappointing them with the truth, he chose to wallow alone in self-pity and regret.

By the time he left, the guilt had turned to rage against those responsible for Monica's death. He vowed to never return until he had won his self-proclaimed war on drugs. He had failed on all fronts.

Jonah watched his mother write in her journal. His absence hadn't protected her, but had only added to her pain. One prayer lingered as he drifted back to sleep. Please give my parents the grace to forgive their prodigal son.

When Mark returned from the chapel, Jonah rested peacefully. Deborah sat solemnly in a chair by the window with her Bible open on her lap. She sniffed into a tissue and turned her eyes toward the ceiling. Her motherly instincts enabled her to see beyond the obvious.

Once she'd emerged from her depression, Deborah had referred to Jonah as her little warrior. Even his older brothers teased him just to trigger a response. The boy fought like an angry rooster. While the brothers forced him to "take it like a man," Deborah tried to protect him from the battles of life.

Mark's goals for his sons were practical—go to college, choose a profession that pays decent wages, find a good wife, and settle down to serve God. With none of his sons married, they obviously didn't pay much attention to his instructions. Mark smiled when he thought of Katy. His youngest son just might beat his older brothers to the altar.

Katy brought back memories of the girl who'd broken Jonah's heart. He didn't understand why Monica's rejection caused him to react the way he did. Dropping out of college had been disappointing enough, but becoming a policeman didn't make sense. Instead of allowing a girl to make him relinquish his dreams, they had counseled him to let the girl go. She obviously wasn't the one God had planned for him.

The day he'd met Monica, Jonah had called them so excited he could hardly talk. He had met the "perfect girl." From then on, she dominated his telephone conversations. He even brought her to the island for their first spring break. Mark and Deborah had no reservations about the young woman and expected the two to marry after graduation. After the breakup, Jonah refused to even mention her name.

Deborah's touch to Mark's arm released him from the painful memories. "Where were you?"

Mark winced. "For the past couple of minutes, I've been standing here wool gathering. Before, I was in the chapel spending time alone with the Lord."

"Did you say anything to Katy before she left?"

"Yes, we had a brief conversation, and she encouraged me. Seems we may have been out of Jonah's life for a while, but God was not. And I believe Katy might be part of the story." Mark studied Deborah. "She's a bit different from Monica. But I believe she just might be the one God has chosen for our Jonah."

Deborah looked at him with a worried frown. "With such strong feelings toward the girl, I am surprised Jonah hasn't mentioned Katy. A son's jumping from no girlfriend to someone he is obviously in love with would be difficult for any mother to understand. But who am I to question God? I jumped that hurdle about three years ago."

Mark threw his head back and laughed. Deborah referred to the teaching she gave at a women's retreat on relinquishment. During her preparation for the event, Jonah had called with his disturbing announcement. At the depressing news, her teaching took a dramatic turn. She struggled to keep up with what God revealed through his Word. Giving up control of her boys wasn't easy, but she was challenged to look beyond the present and trust God with the future.

Pulling Deborah from her plastic chair, Mark wrapped

his arms around her and kissed her with a passion he had neglected for some time. "Do you realize how much I love the mother of my three sons?"

"Well, that was quite the kiss, Pastor Mark. Would you like to rendezvous a little later at the hotel?" Deborah turned her head to the side with a seductive smile. When she heard the outer door opening, she looked over his shoulder to see who had caught them in their intimate moment.

The nurse gave them a kind but knowing smile. "I hate to disturb you, but we need to take your son's vitals and give him his medications. If he keeps improving, we will move him to a private room tomorrow. Not that it would make much difference. The ICU rules don't seem to apply where he's concerned. I see he finally let Katy leave without getting too upset."

"I'm sorry my son has caused such a disruption. He probably wasn't happy when he awakened and found Katy gone."

Mark looked to Deborah for an answer. "He was concerned at first, but he called his partner and asked him to watch out for her. After that, he seemed to relax."

The nurse finished putting information into the computer before she answered. "We haven't heard much from him lately. The anesthesia has worn off. The pain meds will help him relax. You'll all be more comfortable when he moves to a private room."

"Yes, and we'll be happy to follow the rules. I never did like rebellion. I even preach against it occasionally. Are you a believer, Ms. Hunt?"

The woman looked about with uncertainty. "I guess I am. I go to church every Sunday and try to do what the preacher says. Someone said you pastor a church on Shell Island?"

"Deborah and I have been there for some time. Jonah and our two older sons grew up on the island."

Mark studied the woman a moment. "Church is a good place to find friends. We need the encouragement and support of others, especially when we struggle with the disappointments of life. Regardless, I hope you have a close relationship with the Lord. We need him more than anything."

The woman smiled. "I'm working on it. A few weeks ago, we had a patient whose grandmother stayed with him the whole time he was hospitalized—a beautiful Black woman with a French accent. That sweet old woman made me want to be a better person."

The nurse looked at Jonah. "Now that I recall, your son and Katy were somehow involved with her. She spread her kindness and encouragement all over the hospital."

Nurse Hunt shut down the computer and picked up her clipboard. "I've got to go for now, but maybe we'll have time to talk later."

"We'll be praying for you."

When the nurse left, Deborah turned to him with a smile and a questioning look. "Looks as if there's a lot we don't know about our son."

Jonah heard his mother's final comment as he awakened from a fretful sleep. Though waves of guilt washed over him, he didn't have the strength to dig up the past. He took short breaths attempting to relieve the intense pain. When that didn't work, Jonah pressed the call button. He needed another infusion of mind-numbing medication.

CHAPTER NINETEEN

Jonah drifted in and out of consciousness for the next several hours. The combination of pain meds, antibiotics, and IV fluids messed with his mind. Each time he slipped into a restless sleep, a recurring nightmare haunted him. In the dream, he dialed Monica's cell numerous times without receiving an answer. When someone finally answered, a police officer gave him the dreadful news—his girlfriend was dead.

His body shook with spasms, and his mind struggled against the fog. At the grasp on his hands, Jonah awakened and saw Katy bending over him. "I'm here. Just relax." Her gentle touch and calming words lulled him back into a deep sleep.

After two agonizing days, Jonah awakened with less pain and confusion. The smiling nurse explained. "You're improving. For the last few hours, you've been able to sleep without pain medication. That's a good sign."

With his free hand, Jonah rubbed the three-days growth on his chin. "The nightmares are finally gone. How long before I can get out of bed?"

Nurse Hunt smiled. "As a matter of fact, you are scheduled for physical therapy this afternoon. The PT team will get you up and moving."

"That's great news, Son!" Jonah hadn't noticed his parents standing to the side.

After the nurse left, Jonah looked around the room. "Did Katy leave?"

"She left for an appointment after we arrived early this morning. She's exhausted but insisted on staying until you were sleeping without nightmares."

His father straightened the covers on Jonah's bed. "Your Katy is about as stubborn as your mother."

Ignoring his father's humorous observation, Jonah remembered the nightmares and the guilt they inflicted. No more excuses—he had to come clean about Monica. Since he'd met Katy, he'd buried that tragedy along with his guilt. But his parents deserved an explanation. *God, please give me the words and help my parents understand.*

"Mom, Dad, I'm glad you're here. I've put this off for a long time. Please forgive me for closing you out since Monica died ..."

Jonah halted midsentence when he heard the gasp. His mother's Bible flew to the floor when she jumped from her chair. Both parents stared in disbelief, their faces furrowed in horror.

Ashamed of his dishonesty, Jonah looked down at his hands. He still didn't understand how his parents had never heard about the incident.

"What on earth, Son? We had no idea. What happened?"

Jonah struggled through the details surrounding Monica's death. "Please forgive me. When I came home before my training to become a police officer, I was deep in depression. I never imagined she'd attend the party without me. If I'd been there, she wouldn't have accepted the drugged alcohol. She wasn't like that."

Jonah's father leaned against the foot of the bed. "You don't have to justify Monica's actions. We knew her to be a wholesome young lady, but you can't blame yourself. I still don't understand why you didn't tell us."

"I assumed you knew. The story was all over the local papers. I was relieved when you jumped to the wrong conclusion. Instead of facing the truth, it was easier to let you believe a lie."

Jonah shook his head at such immature and flawed thinking. His mother rubbed his arm. "I'm sorry you weren't able to share with us. Since you talked about giving Monica an engagement ring for Christmas, we assumed she had rejected you—the only explanation that made sense."

Jonah looked out the window to control his emotions. "You had a right to know, but you were already disappointed with me—I didn't want to hurt you more."

His father wiped at the corner of his eyes with his handkerchief. "We were disappointed when you dropped out of college, but we would have understood if you'd given us a chance. I'm sorry you had to face this alone."

"I know. I always depended on you to keep me grounded, but I was ashamed to admit such a failure. Becoming a policeman seemed the best way to fight the persons responsible for killing Monica."

Jonah's mother took Katy's usual place at his bedside. "What about your faith? You used to be so dependent on God."

"I not only turned from you, but I also rejected God. I blamed myself and the drug pushers—and God—for what happened."

Jonah's eyes blurred and his voice became hoarse. He coughed before continuing. "After the investigation into the threats against Katy's life came to a screeching halt, I finally cried out to God. Even after the shooting, I've had to remind myself that only he can keep her safe."

His father rubbed his chin. "You and Katy seem close. How did you meet?"

Jonah didn't dare tell his parents what initially motivated his return to God—the fear of losing his virginity for a night of pleasure. "Katy is the best thing that's happened to me in a long time. It doesn't seem possible, but I'm certain I fell in love with her the first time we met. Can you believe I arrested her for prostitution and dealing drugs?"

Jonah snickered at his mother's gasp. "Wait. That didn't come out right. Blame it on the pain meds."

"Tell me it was a mistake," his mother said.

Jonah nodded. "I thought I'd made the biggest mistake of my career, but I don't regret it one bit. Contrary to my assumptions, she lives in the neighborhood and assists the low-income families. Katy is an independent social worker who has rescued several of the young people from drug overdoses."

His father smiled and stepped closer while Jonah continued. "Apparently, the drug dealers weren't happy with Katy's interference and thought to thwart her plans by falsely naming her as the drug source. The operation escalated into a dangerous business before we finally arrested a few key players."

With his unencumbered hand, Jonah scratched his leg. "This latest attack makes me wonder if Katy isn't still in danger. Hopefully, the investigation will prove the shooter to be someone with a vendetta against me, personally, or against policemen, in general. The night of the gala was the first time I had worn a uniform since I went undercover. That's why I didn't want her to leave the hospital. With a guard outside the door, this room is the safest place for both of us."

Jonah's father nodded and crossed his arms. "I assume that your Katy is a Christian."

Jonah paused as he considered how much to tell his parents. "Katy and I have been teaching a youth Bible study together on Wednesday evenings. We're growing in our relationship with God ... and each other."

Content with Jonah's answer, his father leaned over the bed and hugged his neck. "You don't know what a relief it is to hear you talking freely about God. We need to pray for Katy's neighborhood and her work there."

His father took his mother's hand and started to pray. Jonah heard the door open and through narrowed eyes watched Katy walked gingerly toward them. Without missing a beat, his father reached for her hand and pulled her into their circle. Jonah watched for her reaction, but she dismissed his concerns with her warm smile.

Before the prayer ended, tears streamed down Jonah's face. How had he survived the last three years without his parents? They prayed with sincere anointing and urgency. They petitioned God for his healing and took turns praying for Katy's community and for the young people who came to the Wednesday night Bible study. William's grandmother was the only other person whose prayers stirred him as much.

After he'd spent three days in a private room, the doctors discussed Jonah's release. Katy had a meeting that morning and couldn't be there for the instructions from the social worker. Jonah's release was conditioned on his receiving consistent care. The wound to his abdomen required special care in addition to several weeks of physical therapy to restore his shattered femur. After discussing and weighing several options, his parents offered their home.

Jonah was reluctant to leave Katy with someone still wanting her dead or at least out of the neighborhood, but he was in no position to participate in the investigation. Every move he made hurt and reminded him of the long recovery ahead. Shifting to find a more comfortable position, Jonah tried to turn on his side. As he pushed with his good leg, pain ripped through his lower abdomen. The raw truth hurt—he would never pass the physical to return to the streets, and in his condition, he would be helpless to keep anyone safe.

Following another painful physical therapy session, Jonah's thoughts turned to his childhood on Shell Island. His senses heightened with the memories—the sound of the ocean crashing against the shore, the fishy smell of salty air, waves bouncing against the bottom of his father's boat, and the faint giggles of three young boys chasing seagulls.

Shell Island represented peace, security, and balance—a place to mend his broken body, his broken and shattered emotions, and to rethink his career. He was desperate for answers. The island would be the perfect place to find them.

Refreshed, Jonah awakened with renewed hope until he thought of leaving Katy. He hadn't planned to make life-changing decisions without her, but the details of his release had been worked out rather quickly. His parents were already on their way home with a lengthy to-do list—equip his old room with a hospital bed and turn their small home into a handicap-friendly space.

The Abbots had arranged for Jonah to return home the following morning with their family friend, Alex Caine, who was in Raleigh for a meeting. Since Alex had gone through cancer treatments a few years before, he would be sensitive to Jonah's needs. The long trip would require the maximum dose of pain medication, but hopefully sleep would claim him for most of the three-hour drive.

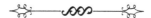

Katy arrived in Jonah's room in late afternoon and remarked on the empty chairs. "Did your parents go out for an early dinner?"

"No, they left after lunch to return to the island."

Katy pressed her lips together. "I can't believe they left without saying goodbye. I had no idea they would leave so soon."

She gave him a quick kiss and stepped back to check him over. "So, why did your parents leave so soon?"

Jonah shot her a quick glance before lowering his head. "Dad has to prepare for the Sunday service." He fidgeted with the sheet. "Uh ... there's something I need to talk about with you."

She noticed his uneasy shift away from her. What did he have to say? Had he decided she wasn't good enough? Was he breaking up with her? "Jonah, you're scaring me. What's wrong? Did the doctor say something?"

Jonah straightened the sheet in a tight fold. "No, no. It's nothing like that—I'm being released tomorrow."

When she gasped, Katy realized she'd been holding her breath. "Thank God. I thought something bad had happened or was about to happen. I'll come early in the morning and pick you up. You can stay with me until you're well enough to take care of yourself."

Jonah turned from her and gazed out the window. Katy reprimanded herself for such a ridiculous offer. In a million years, he would never agree to come home with her. She nearly choked when she realized the alternative.

"You're going home with your parents, aren't you? I may never see you again."

"How can you say that? You know how I feel about you."

"But what will I do without you? Who's going to help me with the Bible study?"

Katy paced at the end of the bed. "I hate how I've become so dependent upon you, and now you're leaving."

"Come here." Jonah pulled her to him and held her close to his heart. He ran his fingers through her hair, sending shivers down her spine. How would she survive without his gentle caresses? Even his touch spoke of love.

"A lot happened this morning in a brief period. I wish you had been here. The social worker first suggested I go to a rehab center, but I would go crazy for that long in a hospital type setting. My parents volunteered to provide the full-time care I will need and have gone home to adapt the house for me. Besides, I'd rather be in familiar surroundings with people who love me."

Katy moved away from Jonah to give herself room to think. She scrambled for a way to hold on a little longer. "Your parents have already left. Do you want me to drive you?"

"That won't be necessary. Dad's friend, Alex, is in town. He returns home tomorrow, and I'll ride with him. I've thought a lot about this. The island will be the best place for me to recover and help me get back on track."

Turning away, Katy grumbled. "I know what will happen. You'll return to your old life and forget I exist."

Katy twisted a strand of hair that had escaped from her tight ponytail. She wanted to bite her tongue for putting such pressure on Jonah, but she couldn't see beyond the wall rising between them. He had become everything to her in just a short time. He might not need her right now, but she couldn't survive without him.

Jonah grabbed her hand. "Look at me. I will never forget you. You changed my life and brought me back to God. I've come a long way in a few weeks, but God and I still have some unfinished business. I'm hoping he and I can get things settled while I'm recovering at home."

Jonah caressed her arm. "Do you remember Matty asking if I was running from God like the Jonah in the Bible? I've thought about that ever since. Pray for me—I don't want to miss God's plan for the future."

Katy's tears fell freely as she thought of how close they'd become, and how now, they were going their separate ways. Losing him to God didn't make sense, but that's exactly how she felt. How would she compete with such a formidable foe?

With his thumb, Jonah wiped a tear from her cheek. "Don't cry. I told you I won't forget you. I promise I'll be back. I can't say how right now, but I want you in my future. God brought us together, and I believe he means for a lifetime."

Doubts made her want to shy away. Her recent study of the Bible and prayer taught her that God did not always give a person what they wanted. Would God punish her for her past sins by taking away the one person she longed to be with?

As Jonah took her face in his hands, the love shining from his eyes gave her reason to hope. Pulling her close and caressing her mouth with his moist lips, he whispered, "I love you. Please wait for me. We can email and talk often, but if you really need me, I'll come. Can you let me go for a while?"

When Jonah finished kissing her with a passion that left her breathless, Katy could deny him nothing. Despite his confusing talk of the future, she knew he loved her. In his arms, she had no trouble believing him, but what would she have left once he returned to his island?

Katy stayed as late as possible. If not for her early morning meeting, she would have stayed with him through the night. Unlike Jonah, she wasn't a morning person. Her eight o'clock appointment interrupted her natural rhythm.

Tears formed in her eyes as she rushed from Jonah's room. Katy clutched her stomach against the empty feeling gnawing her inside. She didn't understand her strong reaction. Jonah had stormed into her life with his own agenda, consuming her thoughts and disrupting her plans. He had changed almost every goal she'd set for herself. Her dependence on him had nearly destroyed her self-confidence. Though she loved the man, she did not like what he'd done to her.

After the fiasco with her last live-in boyfriend, she had

vowed to never let another man get that close. The male species brought nothing but heartache and could not be trusted. Yet, she left the hospital sobbing like a blubbering fool at the thought of Jonah Abbott leaving her.

CHAPTER TWENTY

Jonah shifted uneasily in the wheelchair while waiting for Alex Caine to arrive. He had only met the man once during his last visit to Shell Island. At the time, Jonah had been in the grips of depression and had no interest in anyone but himself. Though he was closer to Jonah's age, Alex and his father had become the best of friends.

After a quick greeting, Alex left to bring his car around. A volunteer in a pink uniform pushed Jonah's wheelchair toward the hospital entrance. He felt like a criminal with the police guard walking ahead of them. To avoid stares, he pulled his ball cap down over his eyes.

By the time Jonah maneuvered his body into the front seat of Alex's car, spasms of pain were shooting through his abdomen and down his leg. He wiped the perspiration from his forehead and willed the last-minute dose of medication to take effect.

Jonah squirmed on the leather seat, searching for a more comfortable position. Why hadn't he asked Katy to drive him? They had barely left the hospital, and he already missed her. But he had to find the answers to his future, and he couldn't think straight with her around.

After Katy left the hospital the night before, Jonah wrote her a long email. Even as he promised to return, his conscience reminded him that he shouldn't make promises he couldn't keep. Jonah focused on encouraging Katy and her work in the neighborhood. He reminded her the residents still needed her, and she had much to give. He closed with a prayer that someday God might allow them to again work as a team.

He ticked through his career alternatives again. The police department was no longer an option. He wouldn't be able to pass the physical, and he'd go crazy sitting behind a desk at the precinct. Besides, his renewed faith and dependence on God were no longer consistent with his former information gathering techniques. While he respected his undercover teammates, he was no longer motivated to continue that line of work.

Every day he put his life on the line and often jeopardized the life of others to gain information. He thought of William, who almost died. Or Alfonso who played both sides of the fence. How many others had he endangered?

From now on, Jonah's war on drugs would be fought from his knees. He trusted God to provide the insight and direction for the young people. Arresting a few criminals didn't compare to what he envisioned. His original hatred toward the drug pushers, along with his need for retaliation, had been replaced with the realization they too needed God's love and forgiveness.

As the car merged onto Interstate 40, Alex interrupted Jonah's introspection. "Penny for your thoughts. Or are they worth more than that?"

Jonah's laugh sent a sharp pain through his abdomen. He held his breath to stifle a cry. Alex turned back to the road. "I'm sorry to be such a poor traveling companion, but I do want to talk." Jonah pulled the seat belt away from his stomach. "Since my father considers you one of his best friends, I'm sure he's shared his concerns over the last few years. Next to my other disappearing brother, I've probably been the subject of many conversations."

Alex glanced at Jonah. "Yes, I can't deny that your name comes up frequently, especially after your dad got me on track. I don't know where I would be today without his encouragement and friendship. How are you holding up, by the way?"

"The pain meds I took just before leaving the hospital haven't kicked in yet. They usually send me into oblivion. While I'm still conscious, I'd like to ask you something."

"I don't know if I can help, but I'll be happy to listen." Alex tapped the steering wheel.

"How did you know Sarah was the right person for you?"

Alex chuckled. "You might not believe this, but I was far from God when I first met Sarah. Oh, I felt a spark of physical attraction at our first meeting, but I didn't get to know her until I had to deliver her second set of twins. Talk about uncomfortable! I'd never been so stressed out."

"You're kidding, right?"

"I kid you not. Sarah was a rock, me a bungling idiot and a bundle of nerves. When I didn't know what else to do, I cried out to God. Before the day was over, I knew God had arranged for me to meet Sarah and her family. She and her children played a major role in my return to the faith of my childhood.

"The answer to your question is I knew right away Sarah would one day be my bride, but it took her much longer. God used her rejections to change me into a man worthy of her love."

Jonah cleared his throat a couple of times. "I heard some of your story when you and Sarah appeared on a morning show. I can see why you were drawn to her. She's not only a beauty, but her witty personality held the audience. That appearance must have hit an all-time high for likes, tweets, and shares."

Alex laughed at Jonah's accurate assumption. "They tell me the video trended for several days."

Jonah grew quiet a moment before resuming the conversation. "I'm sorry you didn't get to meet my Katy. She's also an attractive woman, and I felt the physical attraction from the get-go. It's her compassion and drive for justice that really attracts me to her. Regardless of my spiritual condition at the time, God made sure I knew what he saw in Katy."

Jonah's brow wrinkled as he stared out the window. "I hated to leave her knowing she's still in danger, but I've come to realize only God can protect those we love. I need to trust him with her life and our future."

Alex narrowed his eyes and glanced at Jonah. "I don't

know if your dad told you, but he became my lifeline when I needed a friend. I hope you will confide in your parents. It's true they were disappointed when you dropped out of college, but they were more concerned when you withdrew from their confidence. You have two incredibly wise parents who would have gladly shared your burden."

"I know. I was trying to shield them from the pain and ended up hurting them even more. That's one of my reasons for coming back to the island. I have some major repair work to do. Thanks for being there for Dad when I couldn't. He told me in the hospital how you prayed with him and helped him understand the mind of a frightened, immature son."

"After guiding me through months of confusion, I'd say your dad is more than prepared to handle you."

As his body relaxed, Jonah heard Alex laugh, but he couldn't rouse himself enough to respond. Whether from the influence of the drugs or the sun shining through the windshield, he drifted into a restful sleep.

In what seemed only moments later, the car hit the grid on the drawbridge, rousing Jonah from his slumber. He didn't have to look out the window to fix the location. The squawk of seagulls, a foghorn blast, and the squeak of the drawbridge told Jonah they'd arrived at the island. His heart quickened when he lowered his window and breathed in the salty, moist air. Home. Why had he waited so long to return?

Jonah craned his neck for the first glimpse of his childhood home. The small ranch style house sat back from the road, nestled in the shadow of the three-story house next door. Palms swayed in the breeze on each side of the driveway. The crabapple tree in full bloom filled the air with a sweet aroma along with pleasant childhood memories.

Unlike the sweet smell of the flower, the bitter fruit became a nuisance when they littered the lawn. His mother used to recruit him and his brothers to gather the small apples into garbage bags and set them out for the trash truck. Not willing to miss an opportunity for fun, the ripening fruit turned into ammunition, baseballs, or hockey pucks—whatever their current interest. Amid the fun and laughter, the battle with his older brothers left a bigger mess than the fallen fruit.

As Jonah waited for Alex to retrieve the wheelchair, he noticed a ramp to the left of the steps. His father had been busy, or perhaps he had recruited one of his talented parishioners.

Jonah's thoughts turned toward the man who had made the greatest impact on his life. Even those who didn't attend his father's church loved him. He never refused an individual or family in need of assistance.

Whether from thoughts of his father's faithfulness or the pain in his abdomen and leg, Jonah teared up as he slid from the car to the wheelchair.

Attentive to his passenger's condition, Alex said, "Let's get you inside before you pass out."

By the time Alex pushed the chair up the ramp, the front door opened to smiles of welcome from his parents—the two people he would be dependent on for the next few months. Jonah despised himself for the heavy burden he'd be to them. The small house closed in on him—more like a prison than his beloved home.

"Welcome home." Jonah winced at his mother's hug, then looked away to avoid her scrutiny. "Oh, Jonah. You're hurting. When did you take your last medication?"

Jonah released a slow breath. "Just before we left the hospital, but it's still too soon. If you will help me into bed, I'll be fine."

His father pushed the wheelchair into the bedroom while his mother turned back the fresh linens and fluffed his pillow. "Would you like a sandwich?"

Jonah shook his head. Despite the early afternoon hour, food had no appeal.

His mother straightened the covers and patted his hand as if reluctant to leave. "Perhaps later? We'll let you rest for now."

Jonah hated the worry lines he saw on their faces as they tiptoed from his room. Sleep might not come, but he needed time to himself. He tightened his fist against the pain and focused on the sounds coming through the open window—the cawing of seagulls, wind chimes on the front porch, and the steady beat of a halyard hitting the mast of a sailboat next door. The slight breeze blew the sheer curtains into a peaceful dance.

Jonah thought of Katy. He longed for her to be by his side, but he'd made the right decision. He couldn't move forward until he backpedaled to three years before—when his life had spiraled into regret and depression. Reliving those painful moments would not be pretty, nor would remembering them change the outcome. He determined to approach the memories from a more mature position. Instead of closing himself off, he would welcome his parents and God on the journey with him.

When Jonah awakened, the spasms that had racked his body for most of the trip home had disappeared. He hesitated to move lest he disrupt the new pain-free, peaceful state. Words of praise and thanksgiving overflowed him, and a familiar verse from Jeremiah popped into his head. "For I know the plans I have for you," says the Lord. "They are plans for good and not for disaster, to give you a future and a hope."

The pain returned as Jonah sat up and reached for the Bible that had been on his nightstand for as long as he remembered. He read the Jeremiah passage thoughtfully, pausing a couple verses later. "If you look for me wholeheartedly, you will find me." His future weighed heavy, yet he knew how he would spend the next few weeks of forced rest—he would seek God with all his heart.

"Jonah, you're awake."

He'd been so focused on what might be next for him, he hadn't heard his mother's soft knock or seen her tiptoe into the room.

"I've been awake a few minutes. It's nice to be back in my old room. I didn't realize how much I missed the sounds coming through the window."

His mother's face brightened with an approving smile. "Are you ready for something to eat?"

"I don't feel very hungry, but I suppose I should eat something. Would you help me to the deck? I'd love to sit outside a while."

Deborah pulled back the covers and helped Jonah slide into the wheelchair. They went through the kitchen to the rear deck where his father occupied his usual spot on the upper landing.

"I'll leave you two for a few minutes while I heat your soup."

His father put down his paper and welcomed Jonah with a smile. "You look better, Son. The rest must have helped."

Jonah wheeled his chair closer to the round, glass table. He had missed sitting there with his dad. "Thank you. Yes. I hadn't realized how difficult the ride would be."

As he gazed down the walkway toward the water, Jonah admired the flowers cascading from planters along the steps. "I'd forgotten how calm and peaceful it is here. I see Mother has been busy."

His father chuckled. "Since you boys left home, I'm her only helper. She keeps us both busy."

Jonah looked back toward his father. "When Mother returns, do you have a few minutes to talk?"

"I've been hoping you'd say that."

Jonah and his father carried on a casual conversation—fishing, the family boat, and island life. When Jonah asked about church, Mark went into a lengthy discourse on their new preschool.

"The church has gained several new families since we started the program. I have to brag on your mother. She's doing a great job as director."

Love shone from his father's eyes when the subject of their conversation walked through the door.

"Thank you. As you can see, your father is my biggest fan. But I can't take all the credit. We have amazing teachers, volunteers, and an extremely generous donor. With his contributions, we are able to hire well-qualified people for our team."

Jonah shook his head at her humility. "I'm sure the program wouldn't be nearly as successful without your leadership. I'm proud of you, Mom."

"Enough about me—here's your soup and sandwich. This should be mild enough for your fragile stomach. I hope eating this late doesn't spoil your dinner. I'm making striped bass from your father's latest fishing excursion."

Jonah grinned and rubbed his hands together. "I'll make sure I save room. I can't wait to get back out on the water and catch my own meal. I don't suppose fried foods were on that extensive diet the nutritionist gave you?"

"I'm afraid not. You'll have to settle for sautéed or baked for the next few weeks."

"Bummer!" Jonah groaned as visions of crispy fried fish, hush puppies, french fries and coleslaw ran through his mind. None of his favorites were allowed.

Jonah tightened his hold on the wheelchair. "Do you have time to sit down with us, Mom? I've neglected you guys for the past few years, and I never explained what happened after Monica overdosed on drugs."

Jonah took a bite of his sandwich and thought back on the most devastating year of his life. "I was so depressed—I didn't want to get out of bed to even go to class. It seemed wrong to prepare for a successful future when Monica's life had been wasted.

"When self-reproach didn't bring relief, I turned my anger and bitterness on those who'd supplied the drugs. They were responsible for murdering Monica and needed to pay. I wanted to retaliate. The police academy seemed like the best way. That's how I ended up in Trenton."

Mark and Deborah glanced at each other before his dad touched his arm. "We had no idea, Son. We knew you were going through a bad time, but you shut us out as if we were responsible for your misery."

Seeing his actions from his parents' perspective encouraged him to recall the most painful time of his life. "I was angry with God and myself, mostly. Since you represented God, I avoided you as well. And I knew you'd be disappointed with my decision. I was so angry I couldn't think straight."

Jonah wiped the perspiration from his forehead. "I claimed to be this strong man of faith, but when the difficult test came, I failed miserably. I'm sorry I didn't confide in you. You were the two people who would have spoken wisdom at a time when even a whisper might have made a difference."

His mother rose from her seat and leaned over the wheelchair. She hugged him from behind. "You don't know how often we wanted to come to your rescue. But when we were tempted to find you and drag you home, something always stopped us. All we could do was pray and trust God."

"Thank you for your prayers. In hindsight, I realize God used that time to reset my course, and he's still in the business of turning my life upside down. I've decided to leave the police force. My injuries will keep me from returning to the streets, and I would go crazy cooped up in an office. Although I know where I don't belong, I haven't the first clue about my future. I woke from my nap with Jeremiah 29 running through my mind. I don't know what the future holds, but I know God has a plan."

"We're proud of you, Jonah. Wherever God leads you, your father and I will be there for you."

CHAPTER TWENTY-ONE

Jonah's parents took turns driving him to physical therapy. The leg spasms continued but he gained strength with each session. Not only did he improve physically, but he also felt closer to God than ever. Unable to do anything else, he spent hours on the deck studying his Bible, making notes, and writing in his journal. As he mulled over what he had read, a plan took shape in his mind.

After scrolling the university website, he rolled out to the deck to find his parents. "You know I've been concerned about my future. I still don't have all the answers, but my heart keeps telling me to finish my education."

His mother leaned in with a quizzical look.

"I emailed the dean of students at the university and asked if he would consider reinstating me in the school of business. Those unfinished goals have tormented me for months. Please pray I receive a favorable answer."

His father stopped pushing the swing with his foot and peered at Jonah. "You said you didn't want to sit in an office at the precinct. How different would that be from working as an accountant or financial advisor?"

"I'm not sure, but I'd just like to finish what I left dangling three years ago. I've heard you say that if you get off-track with God, do the next thing he asks of you."

His father cocked his head. "You believe this is what God wants?"

"Right now, I'm uncertain about everything, but when I pray, finishing my degree is the only thing that comes to mind. I'm not sure where he's leading me, but I do feel as if I'm finally running with God instead of sprinting in the opposite direction."

Jonah looked out on the water and slapped the arms of his wheelchair. "I've got to get out of this confounded chair. I haven't seen Katy in weeks. I know you have your doubts about her, but we didn't meet by chance, and I can't let her go."

"I understand. Even though we haven't had much time together, I recognized something special in her that first day we met."

"I know. Her concern for the people in her neighborhood puts me to shame. She doesn't care what the person looks like or even how they act—she only sees their needs. I have spent the last three years fighting the war on drugs, but for every pusher I arrest, several others move in to take their place. Katy's way of working with people comes closer to God's heart than my method. I would love to work with her."

Jonah watched his parents for a reaction. His father nodded in approval while his mother seemed hesitant. She looked down at her hands and rocked aimlessly in her chair. Not willing to entertain anything negative about Katy, he returned to the original topic.

"I can finish most of the requirements online. I'm hoping the university will reinstate my scholarship for the tuition. If I work hard the next few months, I'll graduate by the end of the year."

His mother cleared her throat and sat forward in her chair. "But how will a degree in financial management help people trapped by poverty? That seems the epitome of an oxymoron. If the people are as impoverished as you claim, they have no need of someone to handle their finances."

"I don't know, Mama. All I know is that I want to spend the rest of my life with Katy."

His parents jerked their heads toward him. His mother cleared her throat. "You plan to marry Katy? From the little you've told us about her, you don't seem to have a lot in common. Are you sure you aren't putting your own desires before God's?"

"I can't imagine life without Katy, and I'm hoping God will agree."

Jonah stopped when he heard himself. Who was he to ask God to agree with his plans? His mother was right. He and Katy came from two different worlds. Ignoring his negative thoughts, he forged ahead—not knowing who needed convincing more.

"I admit it won't be easy. The biggest obstacle will be getting her parents' approval. Her father and I started off bumping heads, and our relationship went downhill from there. Katy's an only child and her parents have high expectations of the man they want her to marry. I'm quite sure I'm not that man. The mayor never liked me as a police officer. I can't imagine what he'd think of me as his son-in-law."

Jonah squirmed at his parents' concerned faces. "For months, I have asked God to show me how I might serve him—to give me his heart—a heart like Katy has for the people in her neighborhood. When we first met, her motivation stemmed from compassion and sympathy, but a few weeks later, I saw a shift in her priorities. She started including God in her programs. I'm proud of her."

Again, Jonah stopped himself. He knew God had placed Katy in his path. Had he presumed more than God intended? Had it only been to bring them both closer to God? He had dreamed of a future with Katy for so long that he couldn't imagine anything different. But until he knew for sure ...

"Regardless of my plans, I can't share them with Katy until I'm certain of God's will. I'm not sure she can handle a husband with minimum income. She is used to expensive clothes, jewelry, and plenty of money to spend. Neither of us knows what it means to be short of funds."

Jonah shook his head at the impossibilities. He chuckled when he remembered one of Katy's concerns about him. "Her mother thinks we're Yankees because you guys are from New York. Her father has referred to me as "that hoodlum" for so long, he probably doesn't know my real name."

The surprised look on his parents' faces would be comical if not for the truth behind his statement. "Forgive my exaggerations, but I'm sure you get the point—nothing about my relationship with Katy has ever been easy."

Instead of studying, Jonah mulled over the earlier conversation with his parents. He had never considered the challenges a marriage to Katy might entail. Jonah had told her about the online courses, but nothing else. Had he led her to believe him destined for one of the big accounting firms in downtown Raleigh? He had shut Katy out like he had his parents.

Frustrated over his future with Katy, Jonah gave a long sigh and stared at the spread sheet on the computer screen. No reason to worry over something that might never happen. Until he knew for sure God's thoughts on the subject, he refused to make promises he couldn't keep. Pushing back the laptop, he lowered his head to his crossed arms on the table. God, please don't take Katy from me.

A few afternoons later, his mother came out on the deck with a letter in her hand. She smiled as she handed him the pink envelope splattered with tiny white dots. He recognized the writing before he saw the address. Katy. Why the need for snail mail when they talked almost daily? He ripped open the envelope, dreading what Katy thought so important that she had to seal it in a letter.

Jonah,

I am sick with worry. It has been weeks since I've seen you. A short email or a strained telephone call isn't enough for me. I can't go on like this. I thought you loved me, but you brush me off every time I mention anything about our future. I worry that you no longer care.

Are you ever coming home so we can talk face to face? The Wednesday night Bible study continues to thrive, but it's not the same without you. The kids need you, and I need you.

Forgive me for expressing my doubts about us, but please don't shut me out.

Forever yours,

Katy

Jonah sobbed into the open pages. Relieved that Katy still loved him, he grieved over the pain he read between the lines. In the past, he had prided himself on his ability to fix things, but he had no remedy for a broken heart. All his plans included her, yet he didn't feel free to share them without asking her to marry him. And everything he'd ever heard about a godly marriage started with finding the right woman—one approved by God.

Even if he received the green light, he would first have to talk with her father—make that grovel. Stretching his useless legs, he groaned so loudly he disturbed the pelican resting on the dock. He had never felt so helpless.

Jonah swiped down his wet face before he buried his nose in the crisp sheet of paper. The faint scent of flowers sent warmth spreading through him. He pressed the letter to his heart and looked out at the water. A boat moved slowly up the intracoastal waterway producing little wake. Unlike the watermen on the island, his "boat" was in dry dock awaiting repair.

He returned to Katy's letter, wondering how to respond. What he wanted was to hold her in his arms and reassure her of his love, but the few hundred miles between them seemed like millions. Since holding her wasn't an option, he reached for the phone.

When she answered in her sweet southern voice, Jonah despised himself for not asking someone to drive him to Trenton. "Katy, I just read your letter. I love you and miss you, too. This isn't easy for either of us. Please forgive me."

"Oh, Jonah. I cannot go on like this. Let me come to you."

Jonah hit his head with the palm of his hand. How stupid of him. "Of course, you may come. I don't know why I didn't invite you before now. What was I thinking? When can you get away?"

"Would Thursday be too soon? I will have to cancel a few classes, but that won't be a problem. This week's Bible study will be over, and I'll have a long weekend before we prepare for next week.

"I haven't told you, but Pastor Peyton's son is planning a series of teachings on 'Total Commitment.' What do you think?"

"That's a great topic. I'm glad Jeremy and his father are supporting you. I like that the ministry has a strong connection with the neighborhood church. Perhaps that will motivate more of the young people to attend the Sunday worship services."

"I thought so too. I can't wait to see you. Will I be able to stay with your parents or should I make reservations at a hotel?"

Excitement built in Jonah's chest. "Don't worry about where to stay. I will take care of everything. You just show up here on Thursday afternoon and expect to be kissed senseless."

Katy got quiet until he heard a sniffle. "What's wrong?"

"I've missed you. When we are apart, I question your love. You're everything to me, and I can't bear these lonely weeks without you."

"Please don't worry. Next to God, you are the most important person in my life."

"That's what I'm afraid of. What if he doesn't want us to be together?"

Jonah froze. Katy had just spoken aloud his biggest fear. Every time he thought of mentioning his plans and marriage, something had stopped him. Surely God would want him to be with the person responsible for restoring his faith.

"I can't think of a reason for him to keep us apart. Come this weekend and we'll talk about the future."

"Are you sure you're up to this?"

Jonah did a happy dance with his fingers. "I'm doing fine and bursting with joy at the thought of seeing you. We need this time together."

Checking his watch, Jonah began stacking his books and closed the laptop. "My therapy appointment is within the hour, and I haven't even showered. Getting dressed is a challenge, almost as much as the PT. But the thought of seeing you in a couple of days will be all the motivation I need."

Jonah interrupted his conversation with Katy to call his mother. Without her assistance, he would never make it on time. The constant pain had eased, but he still struggled to accomplish simple tasks. He'd fallen so often trying to use a walker, he hesitated to leave the safety of his wheelchair. Each tumble strained the stitches in his abdomen and caused intense pain. He had hoped to be in better shape before he saw Katy, but after talking with her, he realized their relationship would not survive another week of separation.

With her suitcase in her left hand, Katy fumbled to open the trunk. Instead of being excited to see Jonah, she dreaded the thought of a superficial meeting. She longed for the connection they had shared before the shooting. They had danced through every day as one unit, sharing their thoughts and completing each other's sentences. But his leaving had ripped them apart—a divorce wouldn't be more painful. Was he just stringing her along to see if she fit into his future?

Worry and self-abasement made the road trip longer than the three hours Jonah insisted it would take. Katy tightened her grip on the steering wheel. She berated herself for caring so much.

"Take a left at the next light." The GPS interrupted her confusing thoughts. Ahead, she glimpsed the Atlantic Ocean glimmering in the sunlight. Jonah's description of peace washed over her. She exchanged her anxiety for a breath of calming ocean air.

By the time the car pulled into the driveway of Jonah's childhood home, her concerns had been replaced with giddy excitement. Then she saw Jonah waiting in the shade of the carport. Despite being confined to a wheelchair, he looked tanned, healthy, and relaxed. That familiar look of love calmed her fears as she drank in the sight of him.

Tempted to linger, Katy's desire for Jonah's touch propelled her from the car and into his waiting arms. Jonah pulled her onto his lap and held her for so long she worried that she might hurt him. When she pushed back and stood, she noticed tears streaming down his face.

"Oh, my goodness. Did I hurt you?"

"I'd like to blame it on the meds, but having you in my arms turned me to mush."

He reached for her hand and placed a kiss on her open palm. "Help me up the ramp. I want to show you my favorite spot."

Tired from driving, Katy struggled to push the heavy chair. "Why don't you have an electric scooter? If your arms weren't doing most of the work, I'd be flying backward down the ramp. Doesn't the exertion put a strain on your injured stomach?"

Katy grunted aloud and gave the chair one last push. They were both gasping for breath by the time they reached the level front porch.

"The manual chair gives me a good workout, but I can't do the ramp alone. I shouldn't have expected you to fill in for Dad. Sorry. I wasn't thinking."

"It's okay."

Following Jonah inside, Katy looked around, amazed that Jonah's parents had raised three sons in such a small house. The tiny living space looked homey and comfortable, tastefully decorated with pictures of the boys from infants to graduation.

She picked up one of the framed photos for a closer look. The three brothers were quite young—Jonah, only a toddler, stood between his twin brothers, holding a hand of each. Seeing him as a child, she dreamed of having children with curly blond hair and shiny blue eyes. She released a slow breath filled with longing.

"Katy, are you coming?"

"I'm admiring your mother's portrait gallery. You and your brothers were adorable little boys."

"But I'm the cutest. Right?"

"Of course you are." Katy grinned as she turned to follow the wheelchair through the kitchen, breakfast room, and out to the deck.

When she stepped through the door, Katy gasped at the scene. "Wow. No wonder you chose to come home."

The covered deck held a variety of hanging baskets. Green ferns complimented the colorful annuals cascading from planters. The wide steps ended with a flagstone patio also surrounded by a profusion of color. If that wasn't enough, the patio narrowed into a meandering walkway leading to a wide seating area near the water. More flowering plants bordered the walk and colored the area above the boat dock.

"The whole scene is breathtaking. Which of your parents has the green thumb?"

"They share the work equally now that their day laborers have moved out. As children, one of our summer chores included watering and deadheading the flowers. I'm sure they miss us, but the lack of help doesn't keep them from adding more plants each year. Dad says the backyard greets him like an oasis when he comes home."

Jonah looked out toward the intracoastal waterway. "I enjoy the flowers, but it's the water that inspires me. I sit for hours out here reading and studying. I can't wait 'til I'm well enough to go out on the boat again."

"What are you studying?"

Jonah shifted in his chair and looked past her, focusing on something in the distance. "This is my online classroom, but I've also been spending time studying the Bible. This is where I feel closest to God. Our future has been at the top of my prayer list."

Katy's insecurities forced her eyes off the view to see the expression on Jonah's face. His sweet smile raised her hopes. "Tell me."

Jonah opened his mouth to share when the familiar verse from Jeremiah stopped him. "I know the plans I have for you ..." *Are my plans the same as God's plans?* Though he had promised her before she came that they would talk, an invisible hand clamped over his mouth.

When he looked up, Katy bounced from one foot to the other like a little girl anxious for a surprise. He gazed back toward the water knowing she would not like what he had to say.

"I know I promised to talk about our future while you're here, but I'm not ready. For the longest time, I have been consumed with making plans. But the problem is, I had left God out of the equation."

He reached for Katy's hand. "Three years ago, I decided to change careers without the first thought of God. Bitterness, fear, and confusion motivated me until I met you. After that first disastrous meeting, I realized how much I needed to rely on God. Now, I find myself wavering at yet another crossroads."

Jonah watched Katy's lips pinch together in a tight line. He heard a sniff as she turned away and looked out at the water. He hated moments like this, but this time he had to put God first.

"I know this isn't what you wanted to hear, but I can't make the same mistakes I made before. Pray that I will continue to seek God until I know for sure what he wants and be willing to do whatever he asks. I hope you won't feel as if I'm excluding you, but I must do this without any distractions. To be honest, my insecurities about our future may have been the reason I didn't invite you here before. I hope you understand."

All the previous signs of happiness and excitement faded as Katy's eyes flooded and tears spilled down her cheeks. Jonah ached when she removed her hands from his and swiped hard across her face.

"I knew this would happen. Even God doesn't consider me good enough for you. You're no different from the men I've fallen for in the past. You make me fall in love, and then you dump me for someone else. Who knew God would be the 'someone else'?"

Jonah reached for her. "There is nothing wrong with you. I love you and so does God. I am the only problem. Give me time to work this out."

"I can't do this anymore," Katy mumbled as she rushed past him. He heard doors opening and closing as she ran through the house. He tried to catch her, but by the time he had wheeled himself to the front porch, her car was disappearing in a cloud of dust.

Let her go. The quiet words sent his body into spasms. God, I have hurt her again and this time, I don't know how to repair the damage. Again, he heard the whisper coming from the depths of his being. *Let her go, Jonah. Look to me and be healed.*

CHAPTER TWENTY-TWO

Tears threatened to obstruct Katy's vision as she followed the GPS commands back to the interstate. She gripped the steering wheel, her knuckles turning white, lest she turn the car around and race back to Jonah. All she'd needed was the assurance of his love.

In the middle of rehearsing their painful discussion, Katy realized how pathetic she sounded. Why had she allowed a man to dictate her future and render her powerless? As the truth hit, anger replaced any lingering hurt. What had happened to that strong independent woman she claimed to be? Not certain where to direct her wrath, she pounded the steering wheel until her palms burned. More than anyone, she blamed herself for allowing a man to sidetrack her. Without the benefit of an audience, she yelled at the person in her rearview mirror. "No more. You hear me? No freaking more."

Unconcerned with the staring drivers, Katy continued her tirade. Down with tempting men and their promises of love and a future. She'd been happy before Jonah arrested her and changed everything. She would be perfectly fine without him or his big plans. Since when did she need a man for her to feel contented and fulfilled?

Katy stopped the useless argument with herself when she thought of the changes that had occurred under Jonah's influence. Her social work had become a ministry. Many of her previous ideas had been set aside in favor of Jonah's way—letting God dictate her actions. God. The one she had blamed for destroying her relationship with Jonah.

Remembering that last look of anguish on Jonah's face when he realized how much he had hurt her, she pulled into a rest area and cut the engine. Why had his words been so painful to hear? *Please help me, God. I don't know what you want from me. Jonah led me to you, but I'm confused. If you're asking me to give him up, I don't know if I can. My whole life and even my work have become entangled with his. Please show me what to do.*

A quiet peace came over Katy. The only sounds were from cars zooming by on the expressway. She restarted the engine with the intention of turning around at the next exit. Noticing the signs ahead, she slowed her speed and turned on her right turn signal. Before she moved into the exit lane, a soft voice whispered inside her head. *Let Jonah go.*

Katy broke into tears. *Why God? I don't think I can.* As she struggled with doubt, one of Jonah's choruses popped into her head, "He's All I Need." *Are you all I need, God? Will you be enough?*

Katy didn't want to give up Jonah, but God wasn't giving her a choice. After only a few months of walking with him, she knew God as the one she couldn't live without. From now on, she would depend solely on him.

The following day, Katy moved about the house in a fog. Her mother called to ask if she was enjoying her time on the island. She hadn't meant to tell her parents, but as soon as she heard her mother's welcoming voice, Katy broke into tears.

She sobbed out the raw truth. "Jonah and I broke up. We both need time to consider our relationship, and since we can't be together, we are better off without the distraction."

"I'm sorry, Katy. Are you still on the island?"

"No, I left soon after I arrived. Please, let's talk about something else."

Katy didn't need her mother telling her how wrong Jonah was for her. Nor her recommendations of a more suitable replacement. Although she would never stop loving Jonah Abbott, she would grit her teeth and move ahead without him.

Before she put down the phone, she remembered her plans with one of the young mothers. She called Desiree to invite her and her young children to dinner. Katy had a pot roast simmering in the slow cooker.

Knowing that the single mother worked full-time to provide healthy meals for her babies, Katy had purchased a Crockpot for her. The gift would come with a few recipes that would fit within Desiree's meager budget. In the refrigerator, Katy had the fixings for her friend's first slow-cooked meal.

While she waited for her guests to arrive, Katy's mind returned to Jonah and the ache that continued to grow inside her. She rubbed her chest and reached for her Bible—Jonah's Bible.

Katy looked around the room and sighed. Almost every spot in her house reminded her of Jonah. The mantle where he leaned with his teasing grin. The entryway where they shared their first kiss. The dining room where they had scrolled his computer. The couch where they'd studied the Bible together. Swiping at the trickle of tears evoked by the memories, she opened the book of John and studied the Scriptures she and Jeremy had chosen for the next study.

As she turned the pages to find the Gospel of John, Katy's eye caught one of Jonah's notes at the end of Luke's gospel. Open Katy's mind to understand your word. Her breath caught as she realized how much that prayer had been answered. She'd felt lost the first time she opened the Bible. Now the words meant something, as if God turned on a light.

As she flipped through the pages, Katy pictured herself sitting at the feet of Jesus—a branch connected to Jesus, the vine. All her life she had longed for a sense of belonging. In college, her boyfriend had rejected her when she told him she was pregnant. Before he slammed the door in her face, he called her a slut and suggested she find the nearest abortion clinic.

Her parents had never understood her career choice. While they applauded her for earning a degree, they were appalled at her desire to live in a rundown neighborhood. A big office in downtown Raleigh better described their vision for her. Now, they were concerned that she had become a "Jesus freak."

A knock on the back door interrupted her painful memories. "Desiree, come in. Here, let me hold the baby."

Katy took Keisha from her mother and snuggled the baby against her chest. The sweet smell of baby lotion brought a wave of sadness. Would she ever hold a baby of her own? While catching a tear with the corner of the pink receiving blanket, she led Desiree and Shan into the living room. The little boy gravitated to the basket of toys she kept in the corner.

The young woman touched her arm. "Are you okay?"

"Yes. I'm just weepy today. I must have PMS. I can't seem to control my emotions. How are you?"

Desiree grinned. "I couldn't be better. I've only worked six weeks at the job you found for me, and today, they gave me a raise. My boss said I was a hard worker, and he wanted to keep me from leaving. He also said he would pay for me to take a computer class online. If you hadn't helped me, I'd still be sniffing coke and neglecting my babies."

"Wow, girl! I am more than impressed. You earned that raise. I just gave you a little push in the right direction."

Katy hugged her and offered a seat on the couch.

"When I invited you over, I had no idea we would have wonderful news to celebrate. If you need a computer, you can come here and use mine. I'll even watch the children if your mother isn't available."

"Thank you, but my boss offered me a laptop to take home when the time comes." Desiree grabbed a tissue and blew her nose. "I don't know what I'd have done if you hadn't rescued me. I felt alone and unloved, like no one cared. Thank you for caring enough to show me how much God loves me."

Desiree worried the tissue into a wad and reached for a fresh one. Shan came and leaned against her leg. "Mommy sad."

The young mother laughed. "No, baby, these are happy tears."

Satisfied with her answer, the little boy skipped back to his block wall. "You might not believe this, Katy, but even before you called, you had been on my mind. Do you realize what a bright light you are in this neighborhood?"

After her friend left for home, Katy mulled Desiree's words. She remembered reading in Matthew where Jesus called his followers the light of the world. That's what she wanted to be more than anything—if she could only free herself of this impossible longing for Jonah.

Wanting to remember Desiree's encouraging words, Katy rummaged through her desk drawer for a pencil. She cringed at the idea of making a permanent note in a Bible that didn't belong to her. But every time she thought about getting her own, she couldn't bring herself to part with Jonah's note-filled pages. Katy tilted her head and wondered why she felt so spiritually connected to a person who had rejected her.

Returning to the Bible, she heard a loud knock on the back door. The door hit her on the shoulder before she could step out of the way.

"Montel, what's wrong?"

Katy hadn't seen Montel since she brought him home from rehab the week before. The young man struggled to get out the words. "They arrested my mama, and social services took my brother. I sneaked out the back door before they saw me."

Katy rubbed her chin. "No way. Your mother is not a criminal. Why did they arrest her?"

Montel shifted on his feet. "They said she'd been selling drugs at the chicken plant."

"We both know that's not true. Your mother would never do such a thing. She fights against drugs."

Katy thought back to the time Jonah had arrested her. She hadn't been worried because she knew her father would take care of her, but who would defend Cora?

"Let me get my purse. We'll go see what we can do for your mama."

"What about Antonio?"

"First things first. If I have my way, you will both be home with your mother before the sun sets."

Katy turned the teenager around so she could look him in the eye. "Can you think of anyone who would want to hurt your mother?"

Montel scratched his head and looked sheepish. Katy tightened her hold on his upper arms. "What are you not telling me?"

The boy gave a long sigh. "Remember when I was a user? The man who furnished the drugs showed up a little late one afternoon. Mama came home and caught him in the house. She looked frightened at first, but the man flirted with her and insisted he came to see her. He claimed somebody down at the 7-Eleven told him how pretty she was, and he had to come see for himself.

"I wanted to slap his ugly face. But he made Mama blush. She liked the attention. Daddy never treated her right, but this man comes along with his pretty words, and she's a goner. They went out a few times, until he tried to force himself on her. She kicked his sorry ass out the door. I don't think he liked the way she did it."

Montel stopped and chuckled before explaining. "She'd taken a class in self-defense and kicked him in the ... you know what. Could he be trying to get back at her?"

Katy tapped her chin. "That's a possibility, but there's got to be more to the story. Someone may want to cast blame on your mother to keep the real pusher from suspicion."

"If something happens to Mama, it's all my fault."

"Don't waste time blaming yourself. We need to find the real culprit. Let's go."

Katy arrived at headquarters around four o'clock and asked to see Chief Morrison. "Wait here," she said to Montel when the receptionist motioned for her to follow her. The chief stood when she entered the room.

"How are you, Katy? What do you hear from Jonah?"

Katy swallowed hard before she could answer. "We aren't together anymore. The last time I saw him, he was still in a wheelchair."

Chief Morrison looked uncomfortable as he took her hand. "I'm sorry to hear that. I know you were close, but I'm sure Jonah isn't the reason for your visit."

"No. My concern is for Cora Thomas. She was arrested for selling drugs at the chicken plant where she works. I know her, sir, and I can attest to her innocence. Who was the arresting officer?"

Chief Morrison frowned and took refuge behind his desk before answering. "I'm not sure what difference this makes, but Joe Riley arrested her. That's his territory and he's been working hard to carry on without Jonah."

Katy bit the inside of her lip and sat on the edge of the chair. "Do you know what prompted him to suspect Cora?"

The chief stared over the top of his glasses. "I'm responsible. I received a call from the manager of the chicken plant. He had recently promoted a worker from the night shift to the position of supervisor on the day shift. Two days after his promotion, the man came to his office complaining about drug trafficking. He named Cora as the main suspect and threatened to quit if Mr. Buford didn't report her to the police."

"That doesn't sound right to me."

The chief wrinkled his brow. "The manager did say that Cora had been a stellar employee. But he claimed he couldn't overlook the evidence her supervisor had stacked against her."

The chief shrugged. "I had no reason to doubt the information either."

Katy frowned as she remembered Cora ranting about a scum bag getting promoted over her. "In other words, you let someone else do your investigating. What is this new supervisor's name?"

"I'm not sure you have a need to know, but I suppose it's public knowledge."

The man shuffled through some papers before coming up with a name. "A man by the name of Dewayne Gates."

Katy lifted a finger while standing. "Could you wait a minute? I need to check something."

Though concerned about revealing another of Cora's minor-aged sons, she had to trust her instincts. "Montel, did your mother mention a new supervisor?"

The boy looked at her with surprise. "Yea. She came home like a wild woman when she found out who would be her new boss. She said she'd quit if we didn't need the money."

"Is he the same man who furnished you the drugs and tried to force himself on her?"

Montel dropped his jaw. "Do you think he'd try to frame her?"

"I'm afraid so. Come with me."

Katy rushed back into the chief's office without even knocking. She pushed Montel forward. "Chief Morrison, this is Cora Thomas's sixteen-year-old son."

She put her arm around the young man and gave him an encouraging squeeze. "Tell the chief what you told me about your mother's new supervisor."

Montel looked as if he might faint. His pupils enlarged as he leaned against the desk and stammered. "He, he, he ..."

Katy understood the teen's reluctance to return to a time that had almost ended his life. She rubbed his back until his breathing felt normal under her hand. He leaned against the desk and told the chief what he knew of Dewayne Gates.

The chief's pupils enlarged, and his mouth dropped open as he gave Montel his full attention. Before the teen finished his story, Chief Morrison stopped him with one hand while reaching for the intercom with the other. "Sally, get me Joe on the phone."

"He's in the conference room interrogating a suspect."

"Get him. I want him in my office now."

Joe rushed in looking sheepish. The chief stared at him with such intensity, Katy and Montel cowered into the corner. "Are you interrogating Cora Thomas?"

"Yes, sir. But I don't think she's guilty."

"And what makes you say that?"

Joe looked around the room until his eyes landed on Katy and Montel. "May I ..." he stammered, "speak with you in private?"

"Katy, would you wait outside a moment?"

She put her hands on her hips and tightened her jaw. "No, I want to hear Joe's reason for arresting an innocent single mother."

The chief let out a long breath and signaled for Joe to continue. "I suspect Mrs. Thomas is keeping something from me, but my instincts tell me that she is more the victim than the offender."

The chief beckoned Montel forward. "Tell Officer Riley what you just told me."

Katy's young charge approached the desk with less trepidation and again related how Dewayne had threatened his mother. When he had finished, the chief looked as if he might bore a hole through the boy. "For goodness sakes, Son, why didn't you tell us about this when you nearly killed yourself with drugs?"

"Never mind." With a wave of his hand, the chief stopped Montel from answering and turned his attention to Joe. "Take this brave young man to his mother and come back as soon as possible. We have some backtracking to do. In the meantime, I'll call the plant manager. I want to know how a 'possum got himself promoted to supervise the chicken house."

Katy thought of Jonah as she left the precinct with Cora and Montel. She longed to tell him what happened and hear his response. Another tear slipped from her eye as she quietly grieved the loss.

CHAPTER TWENTY-THREE

A few weeks later, Cora knocked on Katy's door early one Saturday morning. "You still in bed, girl? Get dressed—we're going shopping."

Katy blinked a few times and rubbed her eyes. "Shopping? Did you win the lottery or something?"

Cora laughed and shoved Katy toward the stairs. "You have to play the lottery to win. I got this idea this morning from the boys. They were talking about how you dress like a rich woman."

Katy shifted uneasily and wondered what her friend had in mind. "What's this about, Cora? You have never skirted an issue before. Just spit it out."

"Listening to the boys, I thought about how you have tried to help us. Don't get me wrong, I appreciate how you've befriended me and all, but you will never understand some of our struggles."

"How so?"

Cora counted the ways with her fingers. "For starters, you were born into an upper-class White family who never went hungry a day in your life unless you were trying to lose a few pounds. Secondly, you will never be afraid of being bypassed for a promotion because of the color of your skin." A third finger went up. "You won't have to worry that your boys might be mistreated at the hands of a police officer. Nor will you be concerned about being falsely accused."

Cora stopped a moment and grinned. "We won't count that time Jonah took you off in handcuffs."

Katy did not consider anything about Jonah funny, but she motioned for her friend to continue. "You have no idea what goes on outside the doors of your upscale home. How can you teach the women to shop for clothes when you buy the finest from Nordstrom or Macy's? The cost of one of your silk blouses would feed me and my boys for a month."

Katy listened to Cora's reprimand, but still didn't get the message. "I know all that. But what exactly do you hope to accomplish by dragging me out of bed at the crack of dawn? The malls don't even open for another two hours."

"First, we're going to hit a few yard sales on the better side of town. Then we will visit some thrift shops for furniture and clothes. On our way home, we'll check the clearance rack at Walmart. You with me?"

"I am, but I still don't know why we have to leave so early," Katy whined.

The first stop more than enlightened Katy. Cars lined the streets of the upper middle-class neighborhood Cora had chosen. The two friends elbowed past others to grab designer clothes, accessories, and furniture. When the back of her SUV could hold no more, Katy pushed and shoved to force the rear lift to close.

"You've made your point, but what am I to do with all this stuff?"

"I'm going to wear the smart outfit I bought." Cora clung to an outfit she had insisted on paying for herself. Her mysterious smile made Katy curious.

"You have a date, don't you? When were you going to tell me?"

Cora gave her a snarky grin. "Maybe I do and maybe I don't. One way or the other, I'm prepared."

"Come on, girl. You haven't dated in years."

Cora's smug look had Katy curious. "Come on. Out with it."

The woman shuffled her feet. "I might be interested in Jonah's friend Joe."

"You mean the same Joe that arrested you?"

Katy had never seen her friend so animated. "He might have arrested me, but I have never met a kinder man. He sent my lonesome heart in orbit."

"I should have known. When Joe came back from interrogating you, that guilty look on his face didn't come from interviewing a criminal."

Cora shook her head. "I'm surprised he didn't arrest me for abusing an officer after I gave him what-for. I only wish Montel hadn't told him about me dating that scum bag."

Katy scoffed at Cora's concerns. "I'm fairly sure you'd have to do more than that. I'm happy for you. Jonah considers Joe his best friend."

Cora looked at her with sympathy. "Too bad things didn't work out for you and Jonah. You were so good together. Are you sure it's over between you two?"

"It's been over since that disastrous trip to the island. Now, we need to get back to this pile of stuff we picked up for almost nothing. I repeat—besides the outfit you bought to wear on your date with your policeman, what will we do with the rest?"

"We can use them as examples of how to shop on a low-income budget. The young working mothers need professional outfits before they go on interviews. Look how you helped Desiree when she found her job. You gave her clothes from your own closet to wear on her interview. There are other Desiree's who might not be your size."

A class on dressing for success took shape in Katy's mind. "How do I rate such a smart friend?"

The women laughed as they climbed the stairs to Katy's attic. After recording the prices, they organized their purchases on a long table. Katy surveyed the crowded room. "We need to order a couple of clothes racks online. We can invite the women up here to select their own outfits."

Cora shook her head as she shuffled shoes around to find a spot for handbags. "Good idea. This table can't hold another thing."

Katy's mind swam with ideas for the new class. With a finger on her chin, she looked at Cora. She would have to talk her into it, but this class, "Dressing for Success for Less," would have the perfect instructor. Her friend related to the women far better than Katy ever could.

Cora had been wrong about one thing though. Katy might not ever struggle for lack of funds, but the two of them shared a common goal—to care for the people in their neighborhood. And, together, they had come up with a fantastic plan.

Despite Katy's determination to control her temper and be a more loving daughter, her mother became a constant source of frustration. Her parents didn't hide their relief when she told them about breaking up with Jonah. Their remedy for a broken heart involved moving on—finding someone "more suitable than that hoodlum," were her father's exact words.

Her mother offered a comforting shoulder only long enough to resume her matchmaking skills. Without asking, she arranged a blind date with the son of a friend. Katy freaked out when her mother called with the details. "I can't believe you did this. The last thing I need is another man. Please call and cancel these ridiculous plans."

Her mother sniffed into the phone before taking advantage of Katy's soft side. "Please don't embarrass me with my friends. They were so excited when I told them you and Franklin were getting together."

Trapped, Katy showed up at the designated restaurant gritting her teeth and complaining under her breath. Her date didn't stand a chance against the angry thoughts toward her mother. Her guilty conscience stopped her at the entrance. Where had she left that "light" Cora talked about?

"You can do this, Katy." The little pep talk demanded she leave the anger outside the door before she followed the hostess to meet her mother's current choice. A handsome man stood when she arrived at his table.

Katy's anger threatened to return when she noticed his seductive eyes perusing her body. Had her mother thrown her to a wolf? Brushing off her concerns, she wondered if she hadn't misread his signals. He did have an outgoing personality and he certainly was a hunk. Katy gave him an encouraging smile and reached for his outstretched hand.

"Wow, Kathryn. Your mother was right on with her description of you. I'm Franklin Westerly, and I'm more than pleased to meet you."

Giving the doctor a little slack, Katy determined to make the most of the evening. "Thank you. Mother said you are a resident at the hospital?"

The man proved her original assessment correct when his long index finger made a sensual circle in her palm. Katy frowned and jerked her hand from his grasp.

Franklin chuckled in amusement while pulling out her chair. Determined to be honest from the get-go, Katy cleared her throat. "I'm sorry if Mother gave you the wrong impression. She means well, but I'm not interested in anything beyond friendship. If you aren't comfortable with that, perhaps we should skip the meal."

The young doctor sat back in his chair. He gave her a smug look as if unacquainted with a woman's rejection. Clearing his throat, "I understand, but since we're here, we should at least give our relationship a chance. We wouldn't want to disappoint our mothers. Would we?"

Franklin raised and lowered his eyebrows playfully. Though she didn't appreciate his flirtatious actions, his mention of her mother kept her glued to her seat. "As long as you understand the part about friends."

"I'm not sure I have time for friends, but if that's what you want? We'll see." He seemed pleased with himself as he scanned the lengthy menu.

Though the young doctor met her mother's requirements, it only took Katy a few minutes to know he didn't suit her. After his initial body scan, he showed little interest in her as a person. Not once did he ask about her social work or her views on injustice or politics. Instead, he bragged about his medical knowledge and complained bitterly about the long hours and heavy workload at the hospital.

Katy refused dessert, thanked him for the meal and stood to leave. Franklin jumped to his feet. "Would you like to go somewhere more private? The evening's still young, and we've only scratched the surface of getting to know one another."

Katy leaned away from him and frowned. The arrogant doctor had missed his chance. "I'm sorry, sir, but this won't work. What my mother failed to tell you is that I have recently become a Christian. I no longer sleep around, nor am I interested in casual relationships. Since we have little in common and friendship doesn't work for you, there's no need for additional plans. Thanks again for the delicious meal."

Katy fumed all the way to her car. The jerk only wanted a one-night stand. What was her mother thinking? Katy rummaged through her purse until she found her phone.

Without waiting for her mother to say hello, Katy released her fury on her mother. "Don't you ever do that to me again. The man does not want me—he only wants to get laid. Please stay out of my personal life."

Katy didn't give her mother a chance to respond. She hit the red button and threw the phone across the front seat. Her breath caught when she heard the convicting words in her head. *Forgive her. She only wants you to be happy.* What? She doesn't deserve my forgiveness. The voice wouldn't let up. *Neither do you.*

Katy wanted to protest, but she had read just that morning in her Bible that if she did not forgive others, her heavenly Father couldn't forgive her. She lowered her head against the steering wheel and cried.

After a bit of self-pity, Katy blew her nose and hit redial on the phone. "I'm sorry, Mother. Please forgive me. I didn't mean to take my anger out on you. I know you meant well, but please refrain from these attempts to plan my life."

"I'm sorry too. You are certainly capable of finding your own dates. I'm not sure why I keep interfering. Doris assured me that her son would be perfect for you. But what do mothers know? We're just a bunch of busybodies wanting our children to find happiness."

Katy recognized the remorse in her mother's hoarse reply. She had to laugh at her mother's assessment of her busybody friends. "I know you only want what's best for me. Are we okay? You are my best friend, and I wouldn't want anything to come between us."

Regardless of her agreement to refrain, her mother continued to introduce her to every available bachelor. Katy welcomed each introduction with a smile, but graciously declined their invitations. Jonah had withdrawn from her to wait on God—she would do the same.

As Katy went about her busy schedule, she considered how much her life had changed. She was no longer that rejected woman who'd abandoned Jonah on Shell Island. Instead of mooning over what might have been, she had replaced him with someone who would not disappoint— Jesus. She'd never been a morning person, but by nine o'clock each day, she had claimed her favorite chair in the sunroom. With a cup of joe, Jonah's Bible, and her journal, she waited in silence for her faithful friend.

Never having to wait long, peace soon filled the sunny room. With the guidance of God's Spirit, she studied the Bible lesson she and Jeremy had planned for that week. As she made notes in her journal, tears dripped off her chin and onto the pages. Regardless of their estrangement, Jonah remained close to her heart. She would never forget the impact he'd made on her life.

CHAPTER TWENTY-FOUR

Looking out at the fall foliage, Jonah identified with the wilted flowers that had struggled to survive the early frost. The jumble of words on his laptop overlapped with the haunting last glimpse of Katy's face. Her look of love when she first arrived had vanished. Doubt, rejection, and anger took its place when he hesitated to include her in his future. He didn't blame her for being upset. Her disappearing car still haunted his memories.

When he received no response after weeks of phone calls and emails, Jonah gave up. The stubborn woman had ignored every desperate voice mail. His laptop shook when he pounded the table. Why did he bother? He wouldn't know what to say if she did pick up the phone. Is this what the biblical Jonah felt like in the belly of the whale?

Instead of wallowing in what might have been, he returned his attention to the computer. Since he had doubted their suitability from the beginning, he didn't understand why he allowed her to keep messing with his head. Katy showed up in every prayer, especially those involving his future.

Jonah was determined to finish his degree and get back into shape. Miraculously, his dean had reinstated him into the school of business. He even went to bat for him with his professors. Jonah wasn't sure of their reasoning, but he suspected they reacted out of their own guilt over a student's tragic death.

By working hard over the summer, he had fulfilled the requirements for all but one of the classes he had abandoned weeks before finals. Amid painful therapy sessions, he took the required final exams and completed the projects. One hard-nosed professor refused to let him off so easily. The man insisted he retake the class his final semester. An additional class added to the already heavy workload left little time to mourn Katy. If they were ever to be together, he would have to deal with her in December—after he'd met all the requirements for his degree.

Wrestling with how to use the diploma, he kept returning to the struggling families in Katy's neighborhood. The young people lacked opportunities in education and training. The parents needed financial advice to stretch their inadequate salaries. Katy only scratched the surface when she trained them to make low-budget healthy meals; they needed more. Jonah rubbed his hand down his face and moaned at his dilemma. What made him think he had the answer to their problems?

Even if by some miracle his measly expertise helped, working pro bono wouldn't pay the bills—especially if he ever planned to have a family. Katy. She never moved far from the center of his future. He ached for want of a life with the beautiful woman.

He closed the computer, reached for his Bible, and picked up where he'd left off earlier that morning. Cawing seagulls on the dock below—squabbling over a dead fish—drew his attention. The war going on in his mind seemed as real as those birds fighting over a morsel of food.

Are you like that Jonah in the Bible? Matty's question had haunted him for months and now when he needed to focus on economics, her words again stared him in the face. That other Jonah struggled to forgive the people of Nineveh. He ran away instead of giving them God's message of repentance. According to the prophet, they didn't deserve God's forgiveness.

He sympathized with his namesake, then thumped the side of his head. Was that his problem? He had gone to war against the drug suppliers not once extending forgiveness and mercy. Holding them responsible for Monica's death, he had refused to accept anything short of justice. *God give me the grace to forgive, even my enemies.*

When he lifted his head, he felt as if heavy chains had been broken. The fog over his future had lifted. This new direction didn't in any way devalue the job of his fellow police officers who worked long hours to keep their communities safe. But working undercover wasn't for him. Before, he had fought the war with carnal weapons. Now, he would fight God's way—the way of mercy, forgiveness, and love.

Rebooting the computer, he researched the list of Christian colleges with online classes. He would work toward a master's in theological studies. Jonah dismissed most sites when he noticed their requirements included more on-campus hours than he was willing to spend. He refused to waste another two or three years. As his finger scrolled through the websites, he fidgeted nervously. Just the thought of moving forward spiked his adrenaline.

He pinpointed two universities that required minimal on-campus study. He applied to both and even applied for scholarships. Peace and contentment settled over him as he closed the computer. He would jump at the first positive response.

Returning to the book of Acts, he followed the apostle Paul throughout Asia Minor. In the book of Ephesians, Jonah made an amazing discovery. St. Paul went to work as a tentmaker because he didn't want to be a burden to the people. A tentmaker, huh?

Jonah massaged his jaw while considering the possibilities. *Do you suppose I could be a financial consultant? If I had a handful of profitable clients, I could devote most of my time to ministry.* He made a note in the margin. "God's answer!" followed by the date.

With a vision of his future taking shape, Jonah's thoughts returned to Katy. He took a sheet of paper and drew a line down the middle. On one side he wrote a plus sign, on the other a minus symbol. After a few selfish entries on the plus side such as beautiful, smart, smells good, romance. He cringed at the one glaring note on the minus side—*her father considers me an imbecile.* Moaning, he tore the page in half and wadded it into a tight ball.

Jonah picked up his Bible and reread the Scripture that had inspired him for years. "For I know the plans I have for you," says the LORD. "They are plans for good and not for disaster, to give you a future and a hope."

I'm tired of making my own plans, God. Show me how to step into your story. Jonah felt peace when he looked out on the water. He lifted his eyes past the horizon toward the clouds. Praise welled deep inside his chest. *Thank you, God, for Katy and for allowing our lives to intersect. Give her wisdom as she ministers to the people in her neighborhood. If you want me working with her, please bring us back together.*

The ringing of Jonah's cell phone interrupted his prayer. Before dismissing the call, he checked the screen. The face of his former chief urged him to answer. "Chief Morrison. How are you?"

"I called to ask you the very question. How's the recovery going?"

"I'm doing remarkably well. PT dismissed me a couple of weeks ago. I still use a cane for balance, but I'm hoping I can soon walk on my own. Thank you for asking."

"I don't suppose I might talk you into returning to the force?"

Jonah laughed at his chief's persistence. "I'm afraid not. I graduate next week with my bachelor of science in business administration. It's time to move on."

"I hate to bring this up, Jonah, but the mayor is furious with you. He came in a few months ago blasting you for hurting Katy. Yesterday, he called again."

Jonah frowned and let out a slow breath. Did everyone have to stick their nose into his business? "I know I've made a mess of things with Katy, but I'm working on it. I suppose Mayor Wilson had a specific reason for taking my name in vain?"

"As a matter of fact, he did. He wants to see you."

"Should I prepare for a dressing down?"

"It might be a good idea to wear your protective vest." The chief laughed while Jonah bit his lip in dread.

"Unfortunately for me, I will be arriving in town early next week to take finals and prepare for graduation. Guess this is a sign for me to make an appointment. He's one man

I'm not looking forward to seeing."

"I just wanted to give you a heads-up, so you'll be prepared."

"Thanks, Chief."

After a grueling week on campus, Jonah called the mayor's office for an appointment. He had put off the dreaded meeting too long. Now that God had given him peace about Katy, he knew what he should do. Getting her father's permission would be his first step.

Jonah walked into the city offices at nine o'clock the next morning. Lest he forget something, he carried a yellow legal pad under one arm.

The mayor's secretary smiled when he walked through the door. "Mr. Abbott. We haven't seen you for a while. Looks like you have healed from your injuries."

"Thank you, Mrs. Garret. I'm doing well." Jonah pointed his thumb toward the closed door with a sour expression on his face.

The woman laughed as she opened the door for him. "He's waiting for you."

"I bet," Jonah whispered under his breath.

"Mayor Wilson, it's good to see you, sir," Jonah lied.

"I ought to box your ears, Abbott, for hurting my daughter. Nobody hurts my daughter and gets away with it." The mayor motioned for Jonah to take the seat on the other side of his desk. A desk between him and the angry man didn't bring much comfort.

"Before you make mincemeat out of me, sir, I would like a few words with you." The mayor raised his eyebrows when he saw Jonah looking at his notes. While searching the page, Jonah prayed for the right words.

"First of all, sir, I love your daughter."

"You've got a lot of nerve. I ought to throw this book at you. Making Katy fall in love with you and then dropping her like a hot potato is no way to show love. You young people know nothing but hopping from one affair to the next. Have you ever heard of the word commitment?"

"Yes, sir, and that's why I'm here. I want your permission to marry your daughter."

The man gave a snarky chuckle. "Marry her? She can't stand the sight of you! You wouldn't get past her front porch."

Jonah lowered his eyes and studied his hands. Katy had shared more with her parents than he realized. "I know our relationship has been strained the past few months, but I hope to change that if you'll hear me out."

"Chief Morrison tells me you resigned from the police force. How do you expect to marry my daughter without a job or means of support? If you are marrying her for her trust fund, the answer is no."

"Sir, you don't know me very well if you think I would live off my wife's money."

The mayor looked like he might stare a hole through Jonah as he motioned for him to continue. "I wanted to share my plans with Katy when she visited last summer, but at that time, I didn't have a clue about where I was headed. I only knew I wanted my future to include her. Since I have committed my life to God, any plans I make must coincide with his story. I didn't want to presume anything. Not long after I returned to Shell Island, I started taking online courses through the university system to complete my degree. Next week, I will graduate with a degree in finance."

Jonah didn't miss the pleased smile the mayor tried to hide behind his hand. Knowing how the man felt about his daughter, Jonah knew the conversation was far from being over. "Have you found a job in that field?"

"Not a traditional job, sir. I want to work with Katy in her neighborhood. Among a host of other problems, the people struggle with little income. Together, God has given Katy and me the skills to help them. Over the next six months, I plan to recruit clients willing to trust me with their finances. Managing a few significant portfolios will provide the resources necessary to support my family. I'm hoping you might have a few suggestions."

Katy's father shook his head. "You're never going to be successful. Are you?"

"It depends on how you measure success, sir. What Katy and I desire has nothing to do with monetary or earthly rewards. Success and fulfillment come from God as we reach out to those he puts in our paths."

Unconvinced, the mayor smirked at him. "How do you know what Katy wants? She's washed her hands of you and moved on to someone who will commit to her and give her the things she needs."

The mayor knew how to rip Jonah's heart. Though he felt the ache deep, he shook his head. "I don't believe you."

"Suit yourself. If she doesn't throw you out on your ear, come back and bring my daughter with you. You don't have a chance in the world, but if you do succeed, we'll discuss your need of a few endorsements."

"That's all I can ask, sir." Jonah stood and reached his hand across the desk.

CHAPTER TWENTY-FIVE

In early December, Katy heard the doorbell and went to answer. The blood drained from her face as her past came back to haunt her. Standing on the porch was a person she'd never wanted to see again. But there he stood with a quirky smile and pushed his way into her living room.

"What are you doing here?"

"Katy Wilson, aren't you a vision of perfection?" He grabbed her by the forearms and forced her into an embrace.

Katy stiffened and turned her face to avoid his lips. She almost gagged on his overpowering cologne "Get away from me?"

"Now, Katy, don't be like that. We were so good together."

"What we did was murder a baby together. Get out of my house."

Max leaned against the mantel and grinned. "I'm only in town for the rest of the day. I thought we might pick up where we left off." His eyebrows rose and fell with a suggestive smirk.

"If you're looking to get laid, you've come to the wrong house. I am no longer that kind of person, and I'm certainly not interested in you. I suppose you've forgotten the last time we were together. You called me a slut and insisted I get an abortion. Leave now before I call the police and have you thrown out."

A hint of guilt crossed his countenance before his arrogance returned. Max stomped across the room and grabbed her. Katy struggled against his strong hold while he forced a harsh kiss against her mouth. With one last hurtful remark, he left, slamming the door behind him.

Katy repeated his hurtful words and broke into tears. "You'll never change, Katy Wilson. Once a slut, always a slut." She swiped her hand across her mouth, hoping to remove all traces of the ruthless kiss. His hurtful words wouldn't go away so easily. Only God could protect her heart from such abuse. She fell to her knees and wailed. *God, please help me.*

Spent, Katy dried her tears with the edge of her sweatshirt. As she relaxed against the couch, an unexplainable peace filled her. A Scripture from a recent study prompted her to reach for Jonah's Bible. "Do not be afraid, for I have ransomed you. I have called you by name; you are mine." In the margin she discovered another of Jonah's notes. "Katy is loved by you."

Her tears of remorse were transformed into tears of joy. God loved her. Nothing or no one from her past would make her doubt his love and forgiveness.

She read the words again and thought of Jonah. After weeks of deleting his voice messages and ignoring his persistent calls, the phone had stopped ringing. Now, she longed to see his handsome face lighting up her cell phone. Regardless of how he felt about her, she would never stop loving him. He had introduced her to a God of love, mercy, and forgiveness. Like God, Jonah had loved her, forgave her, and accepted her without criticism or prejudice. *God, please let him love me again.*

Katy rose from her knees and reached for the ringing telephone. "Mom. Is everything all right?"

"I'm fine, but I wondered if you had a visitor this afternoon."

Katy paused before answering. She decided to play coy. "What do you mean?"

"A young man called looking for you. He said you were in college together. His name was Max something. Do you remember him? Said he was in town on business and wanted to see you. The young man sounded so delightful—I knew you'd want to rekindle your friendship."

"Mother, how could you? That man brought me nothing but heartache and tragedy. Please don't give my address to anyone, regardless of how 'delightful' they sound."

Katy heard a long catch of breath, followed by dead silence. She wanted to be angry with her mother, but it wouldn't be fair. Her mother finally cleared her throat. "Katy, I had no idea. What happened?"

"I'm sorry I didn't tell you before, but that was a painful time for me. I really don't want to talk about it on the phone. We'll get together soon."

"If you're sure? I'm sorry I gave him your address."

"Please don't take this wrong, but I meant it when I asked you to stay out of my personal life. The only man I'd like to see is Jonah, and we both know that's a lost cause."

"I hate to see you like this Katy. Jonah has never been right for you. You have to move on."

"You're probably right, but I can't seem to get him out of my mind."

Katy checked her watch. "My after-school class starts soon, and I'm not prepared. I'll have to talk to you later. Give Dad my love."

Jonah stood at the gate and let his eyes roam over the peaceful setting. Katy's house brought back endearing memories. Some had been painful, he admitted, yet her home represented a place that changed his life.

On his last visit he'd been taken away in an ambulance. He approached the porch and paused at the spot where he'd fallen. That night, along with the last painful six months, had kept him separated from the woman he loved. He stepped onto the grass to avoid the stained flagstones. At the bottom step, he stopped and stalled for time. *Please help her understand.*

After breathing a silent prayer, he had the strength to walk across the porch and ring the doorbell. Jonah drummed his fingers against the frame with nervous energy. When he received God's approval to share his life with Katy, he had never felt stronger. Now that he had to face her, he was afraid of her reaction. What if her father had been right? Those painful words played over in his mind. "You think Katy's been waiting around for a loser like you? She's moved on, and I'm glad she finally came to her senses."

Jonah shook his head. He knew Katy, and he refused to believe her father's hateful words. God wouldn't have kept her in his heart if he hadn't meant for them to be together. Despite his warm leather jacket, a cold chill raced over his back. Where is she?

Katy put away the books from her last class. She frowned when the doorbell rang. The nerve. How dare he think I'd let him in again. Katy yanked the door open and screamed, "If you don't leave me alone, I'm calling ..." She stopped midsentence and burst into tears.

"I guess I deserve your anger, Katy, but please hear me out."

"Thank God," Katy whispered as she collapsed into Jonah's arms.

Katy couldn't speak for the man holding her, but her body was as limp as a wet noodle, filling every crevice of his arms. For months, she had longed for his embrace—a place of love and warmth—like coming home.

"That's a lot better," Jonah chuckled as he sprinkled kisses across her face.

She stepped back to see his face. Through the blur of tears, she smiled into his worried eyes. "What's wrong? Were you expecting someone else?"

"Never mind me. You're here now, and that's all that matters."

Katy placed her hand over his heart. All the questions, doubts, and fears of the past disappeared with the look of love shining through his eyes. After his long fingers traced the lines of her lips, he trailed kisses across her face. When his mouth claimed hers, fire ignited inside her.

With a frustrated groan, Jonah pushed her back and held her at arms' length. "I could kiss you into the night, but we need to talk. Are you free?"

"What? You want to talk at a time like this?" Katy doubted her ability to change gears that fast, but seeing Jonah's serious expression, she agreed. She took him by the hand and led him to their favorite spot before the fire.

Jonah took both her hands and gazed into her eyes. "Forgive me, but I had to do things God's way this time. I have wanted you in my life from the beginning, but I couldn't ignore the One who brought us together."

Jonah rubbed her knuckles with his thumbs. "The Scripture from Jeremiah 29 kept reminding me that God has a plan for my life. But before I aligned myself with him, I had to surrender my own plans. Finally, I am free to move forward with God and me on the same page."

A wave of fear started in her stomach and lodged in her throat. Katy withdrew her hands from his and massaged her neck. She choked on her words. "Please don't do this to me. I cannot take another rejection. If you think for one minute we aren't meant for each other, you've been getting faulty advice."

The hint of a mischievous smile tugged the corner of his mouth as Jonah recaptured her hands. "You think?"

"I know, Mr. Abbott." Katy gave his hands a sharp shake as if closing a deal.

"In that case, I'd better get to the point. I want you to be my wife, Katy Wilson. But before I make you a formal offer, I want you to understand what this might entail. When you hear what I have to say, you might not want to close the deal."

"Nothing you say would lead me to reject you."

"I'm glad to hear that, but I still want your agreement. My plans might not coincide with your vision for our future."

"You're as long-winded as some preachers. Just get to the point."

Jonah stared at her as if in a daze. What had she said that shocked him so?

"You, my dear, are a prophet and don't know it. I told you I was taking online classes to finish my degree at the university."

Eager for Jonah to get to his point, Katy signaled for him to move on. He grinned and hooked his thumbs in his jacket lapels. "You are looking at an honors graduate. I will receive my bachelor of science degree this Thursday."

"Congratulations! I'm proud of you."

"Wait. I'm not finished. What you don't know is I have applied to study online for a master's in theology. It will take a couple of years, but there may be a time when I need such a degree. It makes perfect sense when I consider the future."

Katy raised her eyebrows wondering what Jonah would reveal next. "Remember William's grandmother asked me if I was a runaway preacher like the Jonah in the Old Testament? The more I think about my choices, I wonder if I rebelled against God by not following in the footsteps of the other men in my family."

Katy squirmed away, her mind bursting with questions. Jonah caught her hand. "I know I've shocked you, but please tell me what's mulling around in that pretty head of yours."

"I'm not shocked at all. The financial degree sent me for a loop, but this theology degree doesn't surprise me in the least. You pray like a preacher and you sound like one—you might as well become one."

Jonah held up his hand. "Don't jump to conclusions."

He sat back on the couch and rubbed a hand across his face. "I've always loved your heart for the people in this neighborhood. I don't want to pastor a church, but I want to work beside you in ministry. We'll continue the Bible studies and counseling, but I have an idea how we might also use my degree in finance and accounting."

Katy moved to the edge of her seat in anticipation. Jonah tightened his grip on her hand. "What would you think about helping the people find jobs and teaching them how to get the most out of their small incomes? As for the young people, we need to establish a foundation to provide them with scholarships to colleges or trade schools."

Katy pulled one hand free and covered her chest. God had given them similar goals. Unable to control her excitement, she bounced with a giddiness she hadn't felt for months. "I love this. I have already been working on a jobs program for women. Can't you just ..."

Jonah interrupted with a raised hand. "Hold on, Katy. There's a kicker that I'm not sure you'll like. I will never be the successful financial advisor I had previously planned. How do you feel about a husband with little income?"

"Money isn't a problem. My trust fund provides more money than we'll ever need."

Jonah almost choked when he remembered her father's accusation. "I will not be a financial burden to my wife. You will just have to live within my income."

"I can see where this is going. You're letting pride and the opinion of others keep you from enjoying God's provision. For now, we'll have to disagree on the source of our income."

Lest he get the wrong impression, Katy smiled and closed the gap between their lips.

Jonah laughed. "You certainly know how to make a point. I don't like your idea, but I'll let it go for now. In the meantime, I'll pray about this pride issue you brought up.

"Whether you agree or not, I plan to have a few clients who will pay for my services. We won't be wealthy, but we'll have more than enough. Your father promised to suggest a few possible clients if I made it past your front door."

Katy narrowed her eyes. "When did you see my father?"

"This afternoon, before I came here." Jonah chuckled. "I couldn't ask his daughter to marry me without permission, could I?"

"Pretty sure of yourself for someone whose been in hiding for months."

"Not of myself, but I'm very sure of God. One last thing. May I come live with you in your beautiful home? After we're married of course."

Katy frowned as she thought of the logistics. "We won't have to wait until you earn this degree in theology, will we?"

"I certainly hope not. What about a June wedding?"

Her smile returned as Katy pressed the palm of her hand against his cheek. "If you're talking about the one coming." She exaggerated the clearing of her throat. "Wasn't there something you wanted to ask me?"

"Oh, yeah." Jonah slipped to the floor on both knees and pulled a black velvet box out of his pocket. "Kathryn Elizabeth Wilson, would you do me the honor of becoming my wife?"

Katy stood and pulled him up with her. She bubbled with joy as she clasped his hands. A long sigh escaped her mouth. Over a year of longing for this man would soon come to an end. "Nothing would bring me greater pleasure, Mr. Abbott."

Jonah looked into her eyes and pulled her to him. His kiss seemed different now that they were engaged. A kiss that spoke of forever—much greater than anything imaginable. Katy longed for the day he would make her completely his.

"Do you know how much I love you?"

"I have a pretty good idea, but I like hearing you tell me."

Instead of reaffirming his love, Jonah grabbed his cell phone and punched in a number. What on earth? Katy grumbled at him and reached for the phone. He chuckled and held it out of reach, high above his head.

"Mayor Wilson. Just to let you know—I made it past the front porch, and I have just put a ring on your daughter's finger. What time should we arrive for that promised visit?"

CHAPTER TWENTY-SIX

A whirlwind followed the phone call to Katy's father. After a few seconds of awkward silence, her father extended his congratulations and asked them to come for dinner. From the moment Mayor Wilson welcomed him into his home, Jonah felt nothing but warmth and acceptance. Was this the same man who had tormented him for the past three years? The dictatorial tyrant who had considered him a 'hoodlum and an imbecile' had miraculously disappeared.

Before they left the foyer, Katy's mother noticed the ring glistening on her daughter's finger. Examining the jewel from all angles, Mrs. Wilson held Katy's hand toward her husband. The large stone put on a show of color as it caught the lights from the chandelier. The smaller stones made a sparkling halo around the large diamond.

The mayor grabbed Katy's outstretched hand and issued a low whistle. "Wow, Jonah. This must've set you back a pretty penny."

The joy bubbling on the inside surfaced with a teasing grin. Jonah would enjoy setting her father straight—a perfect opportunity to introduce his "Yankee" relatives.

"Though your daughter is well worth the value, the ring didn't cost me a penny. The stones were a gift from my grandmother. They were in a ring worn by her mother, my great-grandmother. Uncle Melvin, who manages a jewelry store in New York City, designed the setting after I described my future bride."

Jonah winked at Katy and pulled her under his arm. "My mother's family have been in the precious stones business for over a hundred years."

"Really?" Katy's mother tilted her head as if not quite convinced "Well, it doesn't matter where the ring came from. Both the stones and setting are exquisite."

At the gong of the grandfather clock, Mrs. Wilson herded them toward the dining room. "Let's continue this conversation over dinner."

When no one paused to say grace, Jonah decided now would be an opportunity to insert his faith. He smothered a chuckle when he recalled using a similar tactic on Katy. "Do you mind if I say a prayer before we continue?"

Two sets of eyes gazed at him while Katy turned a begging-to-understand look toward her mother. "Of course, Jonah. If that's what will make you feel more at home."

Jonah thanked Mrs. Wilson with a smile before bowing his head. "Heavenly Father, thank you for this food and for the peace and acceptance around this table. Thank you for Katy's parents and their blessing on our engagement. Give us wisdom and direction as we look toward our future together. In the name of your Son, Jesus. Amen."

Not a sound was heard until Katy's mother cleared her throat. "Thank you, Jonah. That was lovely."

Mrs. Wilson shifted uncomfortably before turning her attention toward the head of the table. "Conor, will you begin serving before the food gets cold."

During the meal of grilled petite filets, creamed new potatoes, and glazed carrots, the women discussed a June wedding. Jonah didn't pay much attention until he realized Katy had grown silent. He looked across the table and studied her reaction. With her head bowed, she fiddled with her napkin.

Her mother continued a lengthy list of lofty ideas without the first input from her daughter. She sounded like a wedding planner had been consulted, and everything had been set in concrete. The hurtful look on Katy's face tempted him to interfere, but he knew better than to come between a mother and her daughter. *God, show my Katy how to deal with her controlling mother.*

"Mother, please. Jonah and I discussed this in the car on the way over. We want a simple service followed by an unpretentious reception." Jonah noticed the deflated look on Mrs. Wilson's face.

Coming to his wife's rescue, Katy's father cleared his throat and put down his fork. "Now, Princess, as I am mayor of the town, our friends will expect the event of the season. We only have one daughter. You have to let us give you that wedding you've planned since you were a little girl."

Her mother puckered her lips as if she might cry before reaching for Katy's hand. "Please, Katy. We must have the service in our church with a reception at the Country Club. That way all our friends can see our beautiful daughter married to the man of her dreams."

Katy looked at him and groaned. "Help me out here, Jonah."

Jonah wanted to blast the woman for trying to manipulate her daughter, but something warned him to hold his tongue. As for the ceremony, he didn't care one way or the other. He'd learned the night of the gala that with Katy by his side, he could endure almost anything.

Knowing she waited for him to intervene, Jonah debated his options—interfere or disappoint his sweetheart. Perhaps she would eventually forgive him, but he didn't expect anything good to come from his interference. Instead of trying to make her understand, he shrugged his shoulders and tossed her a sympathetic smile.

Jonah winced in pain when his fiancée kicked him under the table. He chewed his lower lip to keep from yelling and rubbed his aching shin. Without a hint of remorse, she pinned him with an angry glare and mumbled under her breath. "Looks like I'm on my own here."

Returning her attention to her mother, Katy stated her case without another look toward Jonah. "I will agree to your suggestions, Mother, with one stipulation. I will not pick out china and silver. In fact, I don't plan to register at all. The only wedding gifts we will accept are contributions toward the scholarship foundation we plan to set up for our neighborhood graduates."

While Jonah inwardly applauded Katy's bravery, her parents looked ready to protest. She stopped them with her hand. "Jonah and I talked about this before I agreed to marry him. I'm not sure why he isn't backing me up now, but there will be no compromise on the subject of gifts."

Katy's father patted her other hand, attempting to soothe her ruffled feathers. "It's okay, Princess. That's a fine idea. You probably already have all the pretty things you'll ever need anyhow."

The smile Katy gave her father warmed Jonah's heart. He wanted a little girl to smile at him like that—a miniature Katy to push on that swing in the backyard. Jonah's dreams faded when he noticed the disapproving frown again aimed his direction. He sure hoped making up was as fun as he'd heard. Jonah scratched his head and wondered how long the mother of his future child would keep him in the doghouse.

Before Jonah could intervene, Katy's father stood, pointed a finger at him and gestured toward the door. For a minute, he felt as if he'd been summoned to the principal's office.

"I'm fairly certain we can trust the ladies with this wedding talk. Let's retire to my office and discuss that list of clients."

Jonah followed his future father-in-law into a large office and took a seat across from the executive desk. Mayor Wilson removed a legal-sized envelope from a folder and passed it to him. Jonah slid his index finger along the top. He gingerly removed a single piece of paper and unfolded it. The paper held so few names, Jonah thought he had missed something. Rubbing his eyes, he scanned the list again and turned it over to check the back. The name Conor Wilson glared at him from the top.

A bit confused, Jonah swallowed the lump building in his throat and stared at the mayor. The smug look failed to clarify the situation. "Sir?"

Mayor Wilson's chair squeaked as he sat back against the soft cushion. In contrast, Jonah squirmed in what felt like a hot seat. "I understand your concerns. It's true we didn't have a good working relationship while you served on the force. But you are marrying my daughter and that makes all the difference in the world. The least I can do is give you a chance to prove yourself capable of taking care of her."

The man got that right. Jonah had despised every occasion that threw him in the man's path. While he searched for an appropriate reply, the old bulldozer broke the silence in full force.

"I'm giving you three months to show me what you know about financial management. At the beginning of the year, you will be trusted with a small portion of my portfolio. If I'm satisfied with the way you handle that, you won't need to solicit any other names on that list. You will have full management of my finances, along with serving as my personal accountant. The generous salary will provide more than enough income. Don't disappoint me, Son."

The mayor slammed a few papers on his desk as if finalizing the deal. Was this another attempt to control him? Jonah almost choked at the picture running through his mind—a large thumb smashing him to smithereens. "Sir, I'm flattered, but do you really consider this a good idea? My whole purpose in consulting was to have more time for pro bono work."

"That won't be a problem. If you get overwhelmed, just hire a few accountant types to work with you."

The mayor made it sound so easy, brushing off Jonah's concerns as if they were lint on his jacket. Jonah puckered his face and let his finger rest on his chin. Was he capable of working with a man he'd gone out of his way to avoid? "You've made a generous offer, sir, and I'm grateful, but I need to pray about this with Katy. Could you give me a week to decide?"

Katy acted withdrawn after they left her parents' home. Jonah knew what had her miffed, but he waited for her response.

"Wipe that smug look off your face. You know what's wrong. Why didn't you support me when my mother tried to railroad me with her grandiose ideas? We talked about a simple wedding with a limited number of guests."

Jonah reached across the console for her hand which she quickly pulled away. "Don't be mad, honey. I may be wrong, but I didn't want to start out by ganging up on your mother. She means well, and personally I don't care either way. I just want to marry the hottest chick in North Carolina."

Katy's doubtful look didn't compensate for the smile she tried to hide when she brushed her hand across her face. "What happened to we're in this together?"

"I figured your family, your problem. When we visit my folks, I'll be the one fielding the questions."

"That's not fair. Your family has no problems."

"You want to bet? Wait until you meet my brother Charles. If you think my mother's a stickler for rules, you are in for an awakening."

Katy released a breath and relaxed against the seat. "You really don't care if my mother turns our wedding into the social event of the year?"

"No, I don't, and I'll tell you why. Your parents have a certain standard to maintain. I saw that when we attended the gala, and your father demanded I play the part. They represent this town, and because you're their daughter, we are obligated to cooperate. Peace within the family is more important to me than a few hours of discomfort."

Laughter bubbled from Katy. "Fair enough. I don't care either. In fact, I sort of expected a big glamorous wedding, but I didn't know if you'd approve. That just confirms our need to communicate better. I based my assumptions on the way you complained before the gala. Unfortunately, we had little opportunity to discuss that amazing night."

Jonah glanced across the car. "After I got over your father's demands, that evening was incredible. I felt like a prince, escorting the most beautiful woman I'd ever seen. As we swirled around the dance floor, I wondered how I had managed to be so lucky."

After the closing words of his graduation ceremony, Jonah pushed through the crowd to find Katy and his parents. She squealed when she spotted him and jumped into his arms. "Wow, Jonah. Aren't you handsome in your cap and gown? Congratulations!" She moved back to make way for his parents.

"We're so proud of you, Son. With all you've been through, you still graduated with honors."

Jonah recognized the pride in his father's eyes. His mother was too emotional to express herself verbally, but the hug she gave him said it all. "Thank you, Mom. You're the best. I couldn't have done this without your support and prayers."

He held the diploma high in the air before he grabbed Katy and lifted her off her feet. She slid down his chest until her lips met his.

Tickets were at a premium, and Jonah had been disappointed when he failed to secure enough for Katy's parents. The Wilsons brushed off his apology by inviting his family to a luncheon following the ceremony. Neither he nor Katy relished the idea of their parents under the same roof. Before they left the car, they held hands while Jonah prayed for a peaceful meeting of the Hatfields and McCoys. Or was it the Democrats and Republicans? As he followed Katy through the front door, Jonah wondered if his jittery nerves would allow him to even enjoy the meal.

The introductions were made with tentative smiles amid an unnerving, forced politeness. Jonah paced about the foyer wishing they would move beyond the polite conversation to something more meaningful like the reason for the invitation—the marriage of their son and daughter.

Jonah's eyes collided with hers when he recognized Katy's nervous laugh. Snuggling beside her, he whispered in her ear. "Are you ready for another Civil War?"

Katy poked him in the side and giggled. "I worry more about your parents than mine."

"Really? I thought just the opposite. I know how my parents will react, but your parents are unpredictable."

Katy gave a defensive huff. "Don't worry about my parents. They know how to act in polite company."

Jonah caught himself before he spewed laughter into the room. "Well, since neither of us has to worry about the other's parents, we can relax and enjoy the afternoon."

Katy elbowed him again, smiled and they followed their parents into the dining room. Wonders never ceased. They were both surprised when the luncheon proceeded without the first battle. Not even a scrimmage. Nothing but an enjoyable meal filled the pleasant afternoon.

Lest he compromise Joe's undercover position, Jonah rented his own small apartment near Katy. He put down a deposit to secure a six-month lease. The efficiency had basic furnishings with little floor space. Knowing he'd have to change his ways, Jonah made a run to the grocery store and carried home two bags of cleaning supplies along with a bucket and mop. His mother hadn't tolerated his tendency to trash a place, and Katy would be no different. He might as well spend the next few months in training.

Instead of having to move his office after the wedding, Katy insisted he set up an office in the library of her home— the home they would share. Her idea made sense. In addition, it would give him an opportunity to observe the day-to-day operation of her interaction with the residents.

As a surprise, Katy removed her old desk and purchased a larger one for him. She would use the drop leaf cabinet in the corner for her own limited paperwork. No argument would change her mind.

Jonah had struggled with the mayor's proposal. After moving his books and computer into his new office, he asked Katy to join him on the sofa in the living room—their favorite place for serious conversation. They spent the rest of the afternoon discussing her father's offer. "I'm not sure I can move from being an 'imbecile' to a trusted advisor. What do you think?"

"I think my father wouldn't have made the offer if he didn't trust you. Besides, if you fail, we'll know God has something else in mind."

Ending the discussion with prayer, they both agreed Jonah would accept the initial challenge. Jonah picked up the phone to make an appointment before he changed his mind.

A few days later, Jonah stood outside the mayor's office. His mind drifted back to his police officer days. He had dreaded every summons to this very office. At least he looked better now. Jonah straightened the lapel of his dark suit and waited for the receptionist.

When the door opened, Jonah put on a brave front and walked into the room. At the mayor's invitation, he took the seat across from the man destined to become his new boss. "Sir, Katy and I appreciate your generous offer. After we prayed and talked about it, we came to an agreement. I will accept your proposal with one stipulation."

His future father-in-law raised an eyebrow. He tapped his pencil against the desk, waiting for Jonah to begin.

"If either of us is uncomfortable at the end of the trial period, we may rescind the offer without causing division within the family." In other words, you won't blow your top, Jonah added silently.

Mayor Wilson studied Jonah for a moment. A thin smile creased his lips. Jonah knew the man understood. "Fair enough. I like that you're thinking ahead, and that you didn't accept my proposal without considering the family. Family means everything. That's why I made the offer in the first place. And thank you for discussing this with my daughter. That's a good practice to remember. Women like to be included in our decisions."

Jonah chose not to remind the man that his main concern had been obtaining God's approval. His future in-laws would have to be fed one dose of faith at a time. On his way out, Jonah stopped by Mrs. Garret's desk and asked her to block off two hours on January second for an extensive meeting with his new boss.

"By the way, Jonah," she said, "I understand congratulations are in order."

"Thank you, ma'am." Jonah gave the woman a sheepish smile before he confessed. "It has to be a miracle."

The woman laughed as she recorded the appointment on her computer calendar. As for working with Mayor Wilson, Jonah would accept the challenge and see what happened. If the plan didn't work, he'd trust God to point him in a different direction.

CHAPTER TWENTY-SEVEN

On Christmas Eve, they went to church with Katy's parents and planned to spend the next two nights in their spacious home. Katy wanted Jonah to experience every moment of her family's holiday traditions.

Upon their return from the late service, her parents took their coats at the front door. Mrs. Wilson motioned toward the luggage Jonah had dropped just inside the door. "I had the guest room prepared for the two of you. It's at the head of the stairs on your right if you want to run the luggage up, Jonah."

Jonah raised an eyebrow at Katy who looked as if she might faint. "I-I-I'll sleep in my old room, Mother. We don't plan to share the same bed until after the wedding," Katy stammered.

"Really? Oh, well, fiddle-de-dee. I just assumed."

Her mother fidgeted uncomfortably and checked every corner of the room to keep from looking at them. She acted relieved when her husband inserted himself into the conversation. "That's a fine idea, Katy. I just have to wait a few months longer for grandchildren." The man laughed and grabbed his daughter in a warm hug.

Despite the most comfortable mattress he'd ever slept on, Jonah tossed and tumbled throughout the night. A vision of Katy on a similar mattress down the hall set him on fire. Every time he jerked from another romantic dream, his mind drifted closer to the gutter. Jonah tightened his fists and pounded the triple soft mattress topper. God give me strength. Even if he had to escape to the island, he was determined to remain sexually pure until after their wedding in June.

Around four o'clock, he checked the time on his cell phone for what he hoped was the last. What seemed like mere moments later, he was awakened by a soft tap on the door. "Jonah, are you awake?"

Jonah jerked the covers over his boxer-clad body as the door opened and Katy slipped into the room. "What are you doing, Katy?"

The girl with the bed head yawned and stretched like a sleepy cat. He groaned under his breath. She had on the cutest red flannels covered with jumping, red-nosed reindeer. His pupils dilated, and he grew uncomfortable as she tweaked the toe that had somehow escaped the sheet.

"Wake up, sleepy head. I have an early gift I want you to open."

One look at her pretty face sent flaming darts into his heart. "Katy, you need to get out of here now."

Katy ignored him with a brush of her hand until she noticed his bare chest. "I can see you neglected to bring pajamas!"

A nervous laugh escaped her lips before she tossed him the gift. "Here, open your present."

Instead of rushing to open the gift and sending her out of the room, Jonah admired the creatively wrapped package. The paper displayed hearts of all sizes with gold and red ribbons garnishing the top.

When Katy became impatient and reached over to help, Jonah couldn't resist. He pulled her across his sheet-clad body and released the unspent passion that had been building the last few hours. At her soft moan, he deepened the kiss and pulled her closer.

Jonah knew he was doomed until he felt Katy struggling against his hold. With quick movements, she disentangled herself and jumped off the bed. Several shades of red made their way across her face—a red remarkably like the now crushed package.

"I'm sorry, Katy, but do you realize how appealing you are first thing in the morning?"

Katy slapped his hand when he reached for her. "Behave and open the present."

Jonah wasted no more time. Taking the lid off the box, he found a pair of pj's identical to her own. He turned questioning eyes her way.

"It's a tradition at our house." She grinned. "We wear matching pajamas while opening presents and even during morning brunch. No one dresses until just before dinner. Welcome to the Wilson family, darling."

As Jonah reached for her again, Katy backed away. "Nope. Get dressed while I think about kissing you downstairs under the mistletoe and in the presence of my parents." With a flirty smile, Katy disappeared beyond the closed door.

Jonah gazed at the huge stack of presents contending for space under the oversized Christmas tree. When he saw Mrs. Wilson struggling with a tray, he left his spot and took it from her. "Where do you want this?"

At her instructions, he set it on the coffee table. "Would you like a cup of wassail, Jonah? If you prefer, I have eggnog, hot chocolate, or coffee in the kitchen. Help yourself while I get the tray of cookies."

Throughout the extended gift opening, Jonah consumed a cup of each of the delicious beverages along with more cookies than he could count. Each person had a stack of opened gifts before they finished. His wardrobe had tripled in a single morning. Classy shirts and ties competed with designer khakis, jeans, and tab-collar shirts.

A large box contained the most expensive suit he'd ever owned. Though grateful, he didn't know what to say. The lone gift he had purchased for each person seemed painfully inadequate.

When he opened a flat cardboard box and realized it contained a new laptop, Jonah gestured at the mound of presents. "I'm sorry, but I can't accept all this. It's too much."

His future father-in-law placed his hand on Jonah's shoulder. "Jonah. We have always overindulged Katy, but now we also have a son to buy for. Please don't deny us this pleasure."

Katy looked teary eyed as she moved closer and snuggled into his chest. He kissed the top of her head before responding to her father. "Sir, I understand. But since you have given me everything this year, what will you do about next Christmas?"

Her parents laughed at Jonah's attempt at humor. He and Katy would have a long talk and clarify a few guidelines for future gift giving. If her parents insisted on spending tons of money, they would have to donate his portion to charity.

The day after Christmas, Jonah and Katy left Trenton and headed east on I-40. As they crossed the bridge onto the island, Katy remembered her last visit. A single tear trickled from the corner of her eye.

Jonah reached for her hand. "That was a painful day for both of us. Forgive me, but I felt like a worthless cripple trapped in a wheelchair."

Jonah called his parents to let them know he and Katy had arrived. They were on their way from the church, excited to see them. Katy looked confused when he put her bags back in the car. "Don't tell me you're rejecting me again?"

Jonah laughed before he grabbed his single bag, put the other arm around her and walked up the sidewalk. "Since my brother is also coming, there's no room in my parents' inn. You'll love where I've arranged for you to stay, but we'll talk about it later. Right now, I want to snuggle on the deck with a cup of hot chocolate."

"Won't we be cold outside?"

"Don't worry. I have my ways."

Katy tickled him until he dropped his bag and captured her hands. He pulled her close and headed for the deck. Grabbing a thick blanket from a wicker basket on his way out the door, Jonah helped her into an oversized lounger with bright turquoise cushions. After adjusting the back, he stuffed the cozy blanket around her. "Think pleasant thoughts while I make our hot drinks."

Katy shifted on the cushions and thought how easily she might fall asleep. Resisting the urge, she let her eyes take in the surroundings. Last summer's colorful blossoms had been replaced with ornamental cabbages or remnants of pansies. The furniture was missing from the lower deck. Only a few ripples disturbed the current in the waterway. The water mirrored the trees on the distant shore. Even in the dregs of winter, an indescribable peace surrounded her.

Jonah returned carrying two huge mugs with steam rising from the top. She held up the turquoise and black cup he handed her. Katy smiled when she read the caption splashed across the outline of a bear. "Love Bears All."

Neither of them had escaped the turmoil of the past few months, but they had endured with God's unfailing love. Katy turned the mug around for Jonah to see. "Thank you for both the drink and the reminder."

Katy pulled back the blanket and made room for Jonah. She wiggled into a comfortable position and watched his expression as he looked about him. "It's not quite as pleasant as the last time you came, but I still love being here—especially with you."

"Even without the summer flowers, this is a peaceful place. I'm sorry my fear of rejection ruined the last visit for both of us."

"It's okay. We both needed God more than we needed each other. He brought good from what we thought was a disaster. I am so thankful."

Katy and Jonah enjoyed the peaceful setting in silence until they heard the garage door opening. A few minutes later, Jonah's father walked out on the deck.

"Katy, Jonah, it's good to see you. I'm sorry we weren't here when you arrived, but we had unfinished business at the office. Deborah will be with us shortly. She's changing into something more comfortable. How was your trip?"

Katy started to pull back the quilt so they could greet Jonah's father, but he stopped them with his outstretched hand. "You stay comfortable and finish your drink. There will be plenty of time for proper hugs."

Considering how much she liked the man, she smiled. "As for the trip, I always enjoy being with your son. Thank you for inviting me to your family celebration."

"You are family, Katy, and I want to be the first to welcome you. I like that sparkling diamond on your finger. Congratulations!"

Katy worked her way out of the lounger and took Jonah's empty cup. After placing them on the table, she opened her arms to the older version of the man she loved. Reverend Abbott had accepted her from their first encounter in the hospital. "Thank you, sir. I'm looking forward to becoming your daughter-in-law."

Jonah's mother joined them wearing stylish slacks and a red sweater covered in snowflakes. Katy accepted her brief hug and stepped out of the way for Jonah to greet his mother.

"Katy, I'm so glad you and Jonah arrived safely. Sorry for my delay in greeting you."

"Thank you, Mrs. Abbott. I assure you I've been welcomed graciously. Where did you find that beautiful sweater? It's festive without being the least bit ugly."

Katy bit her tongue hoping the woman got her joke. She didn't relax until she saw a hesitant smile lifting the edge of her lips. "Thank you, I think."

Deborah chuckled briefly. "I found the sweater at a little shop here on the island. As you've probably noticed, we don't have much of a commercial district. But the few shops we do have are an adventure. Perhaps we can plan a girls' shopping day. And please, you must call us Mom and Dad."

Deborah reached for Katy's hand. "Let me see that ring. It arrived after I left for work the morning Jonah drove to Raleigh."

Examining Katy's ringed finger, she continued. "The setting is perfect for you. You can't imagine how thrilled I am to finally be getting a daughter."

Deborah turned toward her son. "Jonah, did you call your uncle to thank him? You have to be pleased with the setting."

Jonah grinned at his mother. "Yes, Mama, I called him on the way back to Raleigh. Thank you for the reminder even though it wasn't necessary."

His mother hit him playfully and gave him another hug. "I can't help being a mother. Don't deprive me."

The woman turned her attention back to Katy. "I regret that we don't have room for you to stay here, but when the twins moved out a few years ago, I turned their bedroom into a home office. Charles will be occupying our only guest room."

After she noticed the time on her watch, Deborah looked about, not addressing anyone in particular. "Charles probably won't arrive until later this evening."

The woman smoothed an invisible wrinkle from her slacks. "If Chad would only come home, our family would be complete. I can't wait to tease the twins about their little brother beating them to the altar."

At her reference to the wedding, Jonah's mother remembered her guest. "Did Jonah tell you where you'll be staying, Katy?"

Katy's shoulders drooped. Where was the acceptance she hoped for? The rambling speech that followed only left Katy more bewildered.

Jonah moved next to her and took her hand. She glared at him. Did he think he could placate her with a sheepish smile? She deepened her frown. "No, he didn't. But he promised to make reservations for me."

His father moved to her other side. "Don't worry about a thing, Katy. Our dinner guests will be here soon, and you should get to know them. They have invited you as their houseguest for as long as you're here. Make yourself at home and continue whatever you guys were up to before we came home. We don't lack for chairs in case that lounger becomes too crowded." The man with the teasing smile winked at her.

Katy didn't take the bait, but she did reclaim her seat. If not for the need to respond, she would have covered her head with the quilt. "Thank you, I'm quite comfortable where I am, but I'm not comfortable going home with perfect strangers."

"Not to worry, Katy. Jonah will explain everything."

Rev. Abbott ducked inside the house as if anxious to avoid conflict.

"Jonah Abbott, what have you done?"

"I'm sorry, honey, but this is an old island with few accommodations. The nicer hotels are on the mainland. My parents and I thought you would be more comfortable with our friends, the Caines. Their house looks more like a luxury resort, right on the ocean. On the days I didn't have therapy, I worked out with Alex in his state-of-the-art gym and indoor pool. The man may be an icon to the public, but he and Sarah have become trusted friends. Please say you don't mind."

"If that's what you want, but I'd have been happy to sleep on the sofa in your parents' living room. You know I don't need luxury."

"I know, but I want you to get to know Alex and Sarah. They're a little older than us, but they're special. Can you believe they have two sets of twins? Their story will amaze you."

Though the names Alex and Sarah Caine sounded familiar, she didn't know them and didn't appreciate Jonah throwing her at them. She puckered her lips and turned her body away from him. Her pout was interrupted by Jonah's mother who acted clueless to Katy's concerns. "The Caines will arrive soon. You guys relax while I put together a salad."

"I should help."

When Katy started to untangle herself from Jonah, her future mother-in-law patted her on the shoulder. "That's not necessary. Just keep snuggling with my son. It does this mother's heart good to see him so happy."

Katy looked at Jonah. "Your parents are sweet, and I would prefer staying here with your family."

Jonah placed a passionate kiss on her lips and raised his eyebrows up and down. "Just think. When we visit over the summer, we will be husband and wife. I can't wait to share the guest room with you."

CHAPTER TWENTY-EIGHT

Jonah and Katy stood to greet Alex and Sarah Caine when they arrived with their four children. One of the boys ran up to Jonah, bouncing with excitement.

"Guess what we did yesterday?"

Jonah massaged his chin and pretended to guess. "Let me see. Is it possible that you went on a fishing expedition?"

Jonathan grinned. "Your daddy took us out on the boat. He caught a whole cooler full of big fish." The boy looked down as his excitement faded. "But I only caught one."

As Jonathan regained his confidence, he continued his excited fish tale. "Pastor Abbott said that was good for the first try, though."

Jonah gave the boy a fist bump. "I agree with him. How about you, David?"

A smile spread across the quieter boy's face. "I caught three. Only one was big enough to keep, but Daddy took a picture before we threw them back."

Jonah returned his attention to Katy. He wanted to see her reaction when Alex and Sarah finally caught up with the boys. Her mouth dropped open in surprise when she recognized Alex as the popular writer, Stephen Jacobs. "Katy, let me introduce you to our friends, Sarah and Alex Caine. They were a lifeline for me after the shooting."

Katy stumbled over her words as she reached a hand toward them. Each parent had a little girl hiding behind them. "I didn't realize you lived on Shell Island. I've read many of your books, Mr. Jacobs, I mean, Mr. Caine." She paused and moistened her lips. "Isn't using a pen name a bit confusing?"

Alex smiled comfortably while trying to pry Elizabeth off his leg. He took Katy's outstretched hand. "Yes, but the alternative isn't how I care to spend my life. The island has become my refuge and when I cross the bridge, I get to be the real me, Alex Caine. There's freedom here without hovering fans or photographers. You aren't going to become one of those groupies, are you?"

Alex's teasing put Katy at ease. Instead of shaking Sarah's hand, she peeked around her and tweaked Hannah's chin. The child giggled and pushed her away. "When Jonah said you had two sets of twins, I couldn't imagine. How do you tell them apart?"

Sarah responded after a futile attempt to pull her daughter forward. "Since both sets are identical, you can't just look at them and know. Sometimes, I must wait for their personality to surface. Alex is better with the girls than I am, but as you can see, even Jonah has figured out the boys."

Katy gave him one of her endearing smiles before returning her attention to their guests. "I'm anxious to hear more of your story. Unfortunately, I missed the interview you did on the morning show. How do you ever find time to write, Mr. Caine?"

"Alex and Sarah, please. There are no formalities here on the island. Our boys are David and Jonathan, and the girls are Elizabeth and Hannah. Since you are to be our houseguest, I hope you'll soon tell them apart."

Alex motioned for the boys to shake Katy's hand. "As for having time to write. Sarah and the children have become my priority. Over the busy summer, I didn't write more than a few chapters, but as soon as the boys were back in school, I made up for lost time."

Katy glanced around nervously. "Thank you for inviting me to stay with you, Sarah. I hope I'm not intruding on your privacy."

"Never. We enjoy sharing our home with friends and family. Alex's family just left this morning after celebrating

Christmas with us. My mother is still here, but she retreats to her cottage next door when the children become too much."

Sarah laughed and relaxed against the table. "With you living alone, Katy, I'm more concerned about your reaction to our busy household. At times, the chaos becomes a bit much even for me—especially in bad weather when I can't escape to the beach."

The conversation moved inside when his mother invited everyone to take a seat around the dining table. Jonah watched Katy's reaction to the plastic tablecloth covered with newspaper. His mother's specialty, a Low Country Boil, took the place of a centerpiece as the food spread down the center of the table. The traditional feast of shrimp, sausage, and veggies was cooked to perfection.

After his father said grace, Deborah passed the garden salad, coleslaw, and hushpuppies from a small table within easy reach. His father served sweet tea to the adults while Jonah passed glasses of milk to the boys. The little girls giggled at him when he pretended to hide their sippy cups behind his back.

When only empty corn cobs and shrimp shells remained, Jonah stretched back in his chair and rubbed his stomach. He grinned at the children and watched for their reaction as he grunted playfully. "I do believe I made a pig of myself. Oink, Oink!"

They didn't disappoint, and neither did the adults. Giggles and guffaws erupted up and down the table. Katy hit him on the shoulder. "Behave yourself, Jonah. What happened to my civilized fiancé?"

Jonah laughed and pulled her close. He whispered into her ear. "We could soon be gathered around this table with our own children."

Jonah squeezed Katy to emphasize his point, but his heart sank when he noticed tears gathering in her eyes. Knowing he would have to wait to ask about her reaction, he rubbed her shoulder and pulled her to her feet.

After his mother refused their help in the kitchen, Jonah and Katy helped the little girls into their jackets and took them outside. Alex and the boys weren't far behind.

The attentive father walked down the steps to the lower deck so the boys could explore near the water line. Jonah turned a chair so he could watch Katy entertain the little girls. She sat in the swing with a child under each arm. The children giggled and tried to hide beneath the shared quilt.

With her foot, Katy gently kept the swing in motion while reading from a book his mother had found for her. Jonah stretched his legs and relaxed to the sound of her calming voice. With his full belly, his eyes drifted to half-mast. Amid thoughts that Katy would make a wonderful mother, he remembered her reaction at the dinner table. They hadn't discussed the subject of children, but considering her background, he assumed she'd want at least two or three. His body tingled at the thought of Katy heavy with his child.

"I wonder what has put that satisfied smile on your face, Jonah. Was it the delicious meal or that pretty woman reading to my girls?" So engrossed in his thoughts, Jonah hadn't noticed Alex's return. After he'd been caught yearning for Katy, he shrugged—the only response he could manage.

Around eight o'clock, the Caines gathered their children and prepared to leave. "I know it's bedtime for the children, but I need a little time with Katy. I'll bring her over in about an hour if that's okay."

Alex's eyes sparkled accompanied by a knowing grin. "Since our house can be a bit chaotic at this hour, that will work for us. Take all the time you need."

After they left, Jonah rejoined Katy on the swing and took both her hands. "Something bothered you earlier when I mentioned our future children. I know we haven't talked about this, but do you want children?"

The tears came back like a flood. Katy's voice grew hoarse and shaky. "More than anything, I dream of having your children. But after complications following the abortion, the doctor warned of the possibility that I might not be able to carry a child to full term. Regardless of his pronouncement, I continue to hope and pray. Would you be too upset if we couldn't have children of our own?"

Jonah took her hands. "I'm not the least concerned. The first day we met, I imagined a woman pushing a little blonde-headed girl in the swing out behind your house. I can still see that miniature Katy, and I receive the vision as a word of hope from God. Whether she comes through your body or we adopt her, she will be ours. But don't give up, that little girl looked a lot like you."

Jonah's encouraging words stayed with Katy long into her first night in the Caine's welcoming guest room. He had been right about the accommodations. She would have paid a fortune to stay in anything similar. The suite had a large bedroom with a sitting area, along with an adjoining bathroom. Pale blues and grays traveled throughout the color scheme. She snuggled into linens of the finest cottons and awakened around nine o'clock, rested and refreshed.

After she showered and dressed, Katy wondered if anyone else was awake. Not a sound came from anywhere in the house. She followed the smell of coffee up the stairs. When Sarah saw her, she stood from her seat in the breakfast room and gave her a warm hug. "Good morning, Katy. I didn't expect to see you for a couple more hours. Jonah said you liked to sleep late. I hope the children didn't disturb you."

"Not at all. I suppose they get you up early."

"Unfortunately, the boys have always been early risers." Sarah handed her a cup of coffee and set a plate of warm muffins on the table. "With our housekeeper taking a much-needed break, I didn't realize how much I'd come to depend on her. Anna has become indispensable along with being a valued friend."

Katy admired the view while enjoying the quiet morning. "Where is everyone?"

"You just missed them. Since we have a rare warm day, Alex took the children for a walk on the beach. I know you're anxious to see Jonah, but I would love a few minutes of adult conversation before he arrives to take you away."

After Sarah's admission, the attractive woman tilted her head and smiled. "I think you were a surprise to Jonah's parents."

"You think?" Katy raised an eyebrow and grinned. She buttered her muffin and relaxed in the home of her new friends.

Katy didn't want to talk about Jonah's parents until she spent more time with them. Once she got over the disappointment of "no room in the inn," she'd accepted their genuine warmth. Yet, she sensed a reserve in his mother, and worried about Jonah's remark concerning his brother. At least their mutual interest in Jonah provided a conversation starter.

Changing the subject, Katy cleared her throat and smiled over her coffee cup. "Alex is amazing with the children. His affection seems unusual for a stepdad."

Sarah had a teasing grin. "I see you read the celebrity news?"

"Guilty. I didn't see the connection when Jonah mentioned your family, but now I recall reading about your marriage. Your story would fascinate anyone."

Sarah took a sip of her coffee. "I fell in love with Alex almost from the first day we met, but my first husband had been killed a few months before. I still loved the father of my children and felt guilty for even considering another man.

"Besides, I didn't believe Alex's reason for wanting to spend time with us. He claimed to need research for a book involving a family with children. If that had been the case, he would have disappeared shortly after I forced him to deliver the girls. But not Alex. He was the most stubborn, persistent man I'd ever encountered."

Love twinkled in the young mother's eyes when she talked about her husband. Katy sighed and thought of her own love for Jonah. Her dreamy mood was interrupted when Sarah picked up the carafe and warmed Katy's coffee.

Sarah scrunched her face and shook her head. "Unfortunately, my pride and guilt kept us apart for months.

It took a major crisis to bring me to my senses. Now, I don't understand why I waited so long."

"Alex should write a memoir about your lives. I know I would read it."

"You're not the first person who suggested the idea, but we prefer to keep our private lives separate from Stephen Jacobs. Perhaps when the children are older."

They continued to talk until Alex and the children returned from their walk. The boys almost bolted into Katy as they raced into the kitchen from the deck. They each held a treasure they had found on the beach.

Sarah pointed them back toward the door. "Sorry, boys, I know you're anxious to share your finds with Miss Katy, but you know the rules. Everything is kept outside until it's completely dry and no longer smells like a sewer."

The disappointed faces pulled Katy from her chair, and she followed them to the deck. "Show me your treasures, boys."

Katy walked down one level of the outside decking and watched the boys dip their shells in water and place them on the railing to dry. Her praise for the beautiful shells was interrupted by Jonah walking down the steps.

After a brief hug, he looked her over before checking his watch. "Look who's up and dressed at eleven o'clock in the morning."

"For your information, I've been up awhile. I even had coffee with Sarah."

Remembering the boys, she said, "Look what Jonathan and David found on the beach."

Jonah spent the next few minutes examining the shells and discussing the different species. After praising them for their knowledge of sea creatures, he returned his attention to Katy. "Sorry, boys, but Miss Katy and I need to leave. I promised my mother I'd bring her back soon. They want to celebrate Christmas with us."

Jonathan turned questioning eyes toward Jonah. "Why didn't you celebrate on Christmas day?"

Katy watched Jonah explain the reason for two celebrations. Warm fuzzies spread over her as she admired his patience with the children. *Please don't let me disappoint him.*

Back at his parents' home, Jonah's brother stood when they walked through the door. "This must be Katy. You don't know how pleased I am to finally meet the woman who has wreaked havoc on this family. My brother is so in love he doesn't know what to do with himself."

Katy smiled at the tease and reached out her hand. Charles ignored her hand and pulled her into a side hug. Jonah raised an eyebrow, surprised to see him breaking his self-imposed rule. As a minister he went to great lengths to avoid physical contact with members of the opposite sex. He must have given himself a special dispensation to welcome his future sister. Even the side hug was a stretch for his puritan brother.

"How is it that you are going to beat your older brothers to the altar, little bro?"

"If I had to wait for you and Chad, I'd be hobbling down the aisle with a cane." Jonah shoved him playfully and watched Katy greet his parents. His chest overflowed with pride in the woman he had chosen.

Before Jonah's mind drifted too far off course, his mother brought him back with a touch to his shoulder. "Katy, you and Jonah sit on the couch together. I know we are all anxious to catch up with Charles, but we need to open presents before lunch. We have all afternoon to talk."

Jonah watched Katy's expression when she noticed the few presents under the tree. "Did you get our presents from the car?"

"I did." To keep her from inflicting the Wilson family traditions on his parents and brother, Jonah had limited Katy to one gift per person. Regardless, she had insisted on purchasing something special for his parents to share. She even bought a gift for his missing brother, "just in case." If his parents had a dog, there would be an additional present under the tree.

As if pronouncing a blessing, his father glanced at each person. Jonah saw the love reflected on his face. After a few moments, he cleared his throat and picked up his Bible. "Today, we will celebrate one of the greatest gifts ever given—the birth of our Savior—the Light of Christ coming into the world."

On the heels of celebrating with her family, Jonah watched Katy's eyes fill with unshed tears. She had to see the difference. His attention returned to his father as he read the traditional story from the Gospel of Luke. "Let's pray together."

His father slipped to his knees and began his prayer with thanksgiving for the birth of the Savior. He then prayed for each family member, including his son Chad.

At the close of the prayer, his father stood and went to the Christmas tree. "As always, your mother and I prayed before we went Christmas shopping. I hope you will see our love behind the gift we chose for each of you."

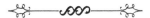

Katy held the leather Bible over her heart and smiled at Jonah's parents. "How did you know I wanted my own Bible? It even has my name engraved on the front like Jonah's. Thank you so much."

Touching him on the arm, she grinned. "I guess you'll be wanting yours back, huh?"

"No, keep it. I see how much you love reading my notes."

Though Katy would cherish the new Bible, she was relieved that Jonah would let her keep the one that had been her lifeline for months. The markings not only drew her to Jesus, but they gave her a spiritual connection to Jonah.

Katy mulled the difference in the way their families celebrated Christmas. Jonah had told her to not expect more than one gift, but she hadn't believed him until she saw the smattering of gifts under the small tree. In no time, the gifts had been unwrapped and the room had been cleared of discarded wrapping paper.

Deborah made her way into the kitchen and checked the food left on low simmer.

"How can we help?"

Each person was given a task, and they were soon seated around the dining table. The smell of a delicious feast drifted to her nose as Jonah reached for her hand. Instead of the casual meal of the night before, fine china and linens graced the table. Matching silver candelabras stood on each side of a fresh floral arrangement.

Katy touched a soft rose petal. "The arrangement is unique. Did it come from a florist on the island?"

Deborah's face lit up before she answered. "A florist on the mainland brings one every year without a card. They refuse to reveal the sender, but I suspect the arrangement comes from my missing son. I haven't purchased my own centerpiece since that first Christmas. Bouquets also arrive on my birthday and Mother's Day. I guess I'm the only member of this family in Chad's good graces."

Everyone laughed, but Katy saw the masked sadness on each face. But this wasn't the time to probe. Jonah squeezed her hand as if welcoming her into their pain. He loved his family, including the missing brother they all grieved.

Katy had trouble keeping up with the conversation as she filled her plate with ham, potatoes au gratin, green beans, and fruit salad. The brothers teased each other and their parents unmercifully. Instead of feeling disconnected, Katy had a strong sense of belonging. Her emotions swayed from weepy to incredible joy. She didn't quite know how to react.

"Okay, children. Game time."

With Deborah's announcement, everyone picked up their plate and headed to the sink. Katy stood back in amazement as Jonah took her plate and joined her brother in the kitchen. Their mother was putting away the leftovers.

"Let me help you with that."

"Thank you, Katy. I don't expect guests to work, but you are family. Would you mind bringing the serving dishes from the table?"

They worked together in the tight quarters while transferring the leftovers to plastic containers. The brothers entertained them with teasing and bumping in their haste to load the dishwasher. Katy grinned at the grown men, jostling each other like little boys.

When Katy looked out the window and thought of the little boys she and Jonah might have, the deep sadness returned. How she longed to hold a little boy of her own.

"You okay, Katy?" Deborah whispered as she handed her a napkin. Katy hadn't even realized she had tears running down her face. She sniffed and wiped her eyes.

"I'm sorry but watching those two acting like children brought back a painful memory. Forgive me for neglecting my duties. I'm fine."

Katy brushed off her mother-in-law's concern and returned to her task, but she doubted the sensitive woman would forget.

After a few rounds of Scattergories and Apples to Apples, Deborah stood with a basket in her hand. "Since this is Katy's first visit with us, I thought we might engage in a little activity to get to know one another better. Everyone take a question from the basket and answer as if you were a stranger to every other person here."

Katy wasn't sure she'd like this activity, but she reached her hand into the basket and picked a question. "If your question is number one, you go first."

After a moment, Deborah laughed. "And that would be me—caught in my own game. Here's my question: Tell us about the most painful time in your life."

Deborah blinked back tears. "I've had more than a few painful moments, but the year after Jonah was born probably tops the list. Though he was a beautiful baby, he wasn't the girl I had wanted. In addition, the doctor informed us that Jonah would be our last child."

Deborah gave Jonah an apologetic look. "Despite my being a Christian, I felt isolated from God and my newborn baby. Getting out of bed became a chore—just the smell of food nauseated me. Your father was so worried, he took me to a psychologist who confirmed the postpartum depression we suspected."

Putting her hand on her husband's shoulder, Deborah glanced at him with a warm smile. "Fortunately for my babies, their daddy took over their care. Overnight, your father became nanny, cook, and housekeeper. The depression lingered for several miserable months.

"One day, I saw Jonah crawling toward me, and my mothering instincts miraculously returned. I picked him up from the floor and cried. I begged his forgiveness. Instead of embracing me, he screamed and reached for his father. From that moment on, I had a reason to live. My babies needed me and so did my husband. I suppose that's why you and your dad are so close, Jonah."

Katy had been watching Jonah and Charles as their mother related her story. From their surprised looks, they were hearing it for the first time. When his mother started to sit down, Jonah pulled her into his arms. "I'm sorry you didn't get your wish, Mama, but Katy and I will do our best to provide you with a granddaughter."

Katy lowered her head after she noticed Jonah's teasing grin. She bit her lip to hide her inner pain. She had been relieved to see her card wasn't number one. Now, she was relieved that she didn't have to answer such a difficult question.

Charles stood and cleared his throat. "After that painful revelation, I am happy that number two will lighten our mood. What do you consider your favorite memory from your childhood? Let's see. We had so many special times, it's hard to pick just one. Personally, I never felt happier than those days we spent out on the water. Mother made us a picnic lunch and we left the dock before sunrise. We fished, waterskied and snorkeled until late in the afternoon when Dad pulled the boat up on a sandbar and built a fire out of driftwood. The smell of grilled fish drew us to the campfire. On the ride back to the dock, we fell asleep in the bottom of the boat. Thank you, Mom and Dad, for a wonderful childhood." Charles gave his parents a hug before he sat down.

Katy studied her question. "Wow. I'm not sure how to even answer this. The card says, 'Within the last year, what do you consider your best day?'

"I've thought of several, but the one that tops the list is the late afternoon when Jonah came to propose. Up until his knock on the door, the day had been one of my worst. I had just closed the door on a vile man from my past. Falling to my knees in defeat, I begged God to remove the man's filthy words from my memory. As I prayed, I remembered a verse of Scripture. 'Do not be afraid, for I have ransomed you. I have called you by name; you are mine." In the margin of Jonah's Bible, he had written, 'Katy is loved by you.'

"I wept tears of joy knowing how much God loved me. Even the disagreeable phone call from my mother didn't rob me of the joy. I had not heard from Jonah for several months, but when I opened the door this time and realized he had returned to me, I rushed into his arms. Before the hour ended, he had given me this beautiful ring."

Katy held up the ring and knew she had told the right story. Jonah put his arm around her and pulled her close. His mother had tears in her eyes and his father grinned as if she hadn't revealed anything new.

Charles clasped his hands in front of him and stretched before he sat back in the chair with a look of satisfaction. "Forgive me, Katy, but I need to apologize. When Jonah described your profession, I'm afraid I misjudged you. I now see how much you depend on God. You and my little brother are perfect together. Though you don't need it, you have my blessing."

Charles stood and pulled her away from Jonah. He gave her a rare frontal hug and smirked at his brother. "If you aren't good to this woman, I might steal her from you."

"You don't have a chance in the world, brother," Jonah grinned at Charles before standing to read his question, "Who is your hero?"

Katy wasn't surprised at the question nor his answer. Jonah talked about his father and again apologized to his family for his withdrawal when he needed them most. Reverend Abbott ended the sharing with his own question, "What do you like most about your family?"

"This time has been wonderful. I like that our family is gradually coming back together, plus we are growing in numbers." He sent a wink her way.

Jonah made a small airplane out of his card and flew it toward his brother. "So, Charles, when will you bring home an addition to our family?"

Katy turned questioning eyes toward Jonah while everyone else laughed. "My brother won't get within ten feet of a pretty woman. He insists his actions are based on the need to maintain his reputation as a pastor, but I suspect he's afraid to commit."

Charles winced before he threw the missile back. "One day God is going to give me a beautiful woman like Katy, and I will surprise you all."

"Forgive me if I don't hold my breath. Just saying." Jonah tossed the airplane back.

After a light supper, Jonah's father ended the day with a time of prayer. On the way back to the Caines, Katy tried to remember each detail. The conversations, the games, the prayers, all gave her a glimpse into the lives of her new family. If she ever had any doubts, she would remind herself of this incredible day.

CHAPTER TWENTY-NINE

Jonah and Katy established an easy routine during their daylight hours. Early each morning, he left his small apartment and traveled the few blocks to Katy's house. Sometimes he drove his refurbished Mustang, but more often he biked. Using a spare key, he opened the side door into the kitchen and started a pot of coffee.

After a few sips of the strong brew, Jonah walked out to the sunroom—his favorite spot in Katy's house. Two comfortable chairs with footrests filled one side of the room. The round table between held a variety of books, Bibles, and journals. Though they were rarely there at the same time, the room had become a sanctuary for both—a place to seek the Lord.

After an hour of quiet time, Jonah moved to the office and studied online. When Katy popped her head in the door, he dropped everything. That first kiss of the day always curled his toes. Her fresh shower scent stirred his senses and made him want to linger in her arms. But not Katy. She had a busy schedule outlined for the day and she rarely strayed far from her plans.

"Enough, Jonah," she giggled and pushed him away.

Jonah exaggerated his best frown and poked out his lower lip. "Busy Katy, no time to play?"

Jonah stole a few more kisses while they sauntered toward the kitchen. He rummaged through the refrigerator to come up with the ingredients for a quick meal. Sometimes he made French toast or Belgium waffles, but Katy preferred his veggie omelet. He had taken over preparing breakfast while Katy planned their dinner meal, usually putting something into the slow cooker.

Following breakfast, Katy took her turn in the sunroom while Jonah rebooted his computer. Instead of online biblical studies, he scrolled through the mayor's investments. If Katy's father wanted an aggressive investor, he should look elsewhere. Jonah's approach had always leaned toward conservative, even in money matters. His theory was to guard the assets by diversification.

After the first month of the challenge, Jonah had groaned at the scant increase which wasn't enough to convince anyone, especially his overbearing future father-in-law. During breakfast one morning, he asked Katy to pray with him about her father's portfolio. Her prayer pinpointed the problem. "Father, free Jonah from fear of defeat. Show him how to relax and trust you with the outcome."

From that morning on, Jonah scrolled through the numbers with confidence. Leaving the results to God, he refrained from checking his progress until the close of the challenge. When he ran the figures at the end of the trial, he rubbed his eyes. Not trusting himself, he ran them again and grinned at the outcome. A seventeen percent increase in today's market should impress anyone.

After scanning the printout, Mayor Wilson jumped to his feet and ran around his desk. He pulled Jonah into a tight hug. "Wow, Jonah! I knew I'd eventually find something good about you. Welcome aboard, Son!"

Jonah wiggled away from the hold and raised his chin. "I appreciate the confidence you have in me, sir. I'll do my best not to disappoint, but I need to remind you that my priorities will always be to Katy and the work in our neighborhood."

"I would expect no less. Katy's mother and I plan to support you there as well."

Jonah thrust his fist toward the ceiling as he left the office. He couldn't wait to share his good news. Checking his watch, he realized Katy's class had already started. He slammed his briefcase against his leg before he remembered his friend Joe.

Punching in the number for speed dial, Jonah paced the sidewalk. "Hey, Joe. Are you free for lunch?"

Joe walked into their favorite pizza joint with a wide grin. They fist bumped before placing their order at the counter. After filling their cups at the beverage bar, they chose the familiar table with an unobstructed view of the street. Old habits die hard.

"What's happening, man?"

Joe's eyes twinkled. "You miss us, bro, that's what's happening."

Jonah responded by shooting his straw cover at him. "I guess I do, but not enough to change my mind. My future with Katy means everything. Yet, I do miss being out on the streets. Her remedy for excessive energy has been to take prayer walks through the neighborhood. I haven't abandoned you guys; I'm just using a different strategy."

"Well, I for one appreciate your prayers."

Jonah studied his friend. "Do I detect an interest in spiritual matters?"

"Hanging out with Cora, I have no choice. The woman is a fireball." Joe hesitated before he winked at Jonah. "In more ways than one."

The guys chuckled as their knuckles met in an explosion. "Besides wanting to catch up, I'd like for you to be my best man at the wedding. What do you think?"

"What about your brother?"

"I'm close to my brothers, but I consider you my best friend. For three years, we worked almost twenty-four/seven as a single unit, and I still value your friendship."

"I understand, and I'm honored that you asked. So, what's the date for this big event?"

Jonah's energy increased as he made his way back to the car, anxious to tell Katy the news. Not only would they have a steady income, but she could put a check by his first entry on the groom's to-do list—the best man had said yes.

Katy had just dismissed her class when Jonah pulled his car into the driveway. After the women left, she rushed into the kitchen and met him with open arms.

Jonah nuzzled her neck. "From that greeting, I'd say you had a successful meeting."

"And you would be right. Since Cora and I started this class four months ago, we have placed six women in jobs. Desiree took the afternoon off and shared her experience with the women. She's my biggest success so far. The girl has been promoted twice within six months."

"I'm sure she encouraged the other women. Did you take them to the attic?"

Jonah liked to tease Katy about the fire hazard on the upper level. More clothes seemed to arrive than leave. One look at the feminine space was all he needed to know he didn't belong. Katy laughed at his unfounded complaints.

"So, when are you going to tell me about your meeting with my father? From your good mood, I'm fairly sure I already know."

Over dinner, Jonah gave her the details and then told her about his lunch with Joe. They laughed at his friend's reaction to Cora. "Those two are perfect for each other."

Before he could respond, Katy jumped up and began stacking the dishes. "We have the whole evening to ourselves. Let's hurry so we can have a cup of tea by the fire."

Jonah took the cups and sat them on the table. He put his arm around her and gently guided her head to his chest. Her nearness never failed to set his heart galloping like a racehorse. He kissed the top of her head and released a long sigh.

An angry word almost escaped when the doorbell disturbed their romantic evening. "That better be important," Jonah huffed as he untangled himself from Katy and stomped to the door.

Jaylen, one of their boys, almost fell into Jonah when he opened the door. "Take it easy, man. What's going on?"

The young man leaned against the doorframe, out of breath. "They're killing each other."

"Who? Calm down and tell me what's going on."

"We were all hanging outside the 7-Eleven and these mean White guys showed up with guns and knives. They said they were going to kill every 'N****r' in town!"

Jonah's shoulders tightened and his pulse pounded in his neck. The thing he feared most had come to his community. Hands shaking, he pulled the boy inside. Jaylen looked to him for answers, yet he had never felt more helpless.

"Your friend got hurt, Mr. Jonah."

"You mean Joe Riley?"

The boy nodded and sniffed into his jacket sleeve. "When the cops showed up and tried to break it up, the crowd turned on them. The White guys were calling them 'N****r-lovers' and the Black guys were shouting 'Black Lives Matter.' You've got to stop them."

Jonah didn't know what he could do, but he felt an urgency to go—at least to check on Joe.

"Tell me about Officer Riley. Is he okay?"

"No, sir, he got hit by flying glass. Before the ambulance took him away, he grabbed my arm and asked me to find you."

Jonah turned around and saw Katy staring wide-eyed in the doorway. All color had drained from her face. "Jonah, please don't go. If they remember you were a police officer, they'll kill you."

"I'm sorry, honey. I don't like it, but I need to go. You stay here and pray. This fight will be won by prayer."

Jonah didn't know where the words came from or the confidence that infused him, but he followed Jaylen as the boy retraced his steps. On his way, he called Joe's cell phone.

"What's going on, Joe?"

"Don't worry about me. Go see if you can talk some sense into those crazy kids."

"Not until I find out what's going on with you, man."

Jonah heard a muffled voice in the background. "Nothing worth making such a big deal over—I just got in the way of a flying bottle. The nurse is trying to take my phone so she can clean and bandage the cut on my arm. I'll be back out there as soon as they let me go."

"You stay put. I'll see what I can do."

Jonah stuffed his phone back in his pocket as they neared the crowd. Rocks and bottles flew in all directions. With the order to stand down, the police had backed away and watched helplessly from a distance. Jonah grabbed Jaylen's arm to keep him from going farther.

The two gangs were in a heated battle—shouting racial epithets and raising fists in defiance. Fortunately, Jonah didn't see any of the weapons Jaylen had reported.

Raking his fingers through his hair, Jonah felt his confidence slipping. *Pray.* Without an alternative, he fell to his knees and cried out to God for peace. *Lord, have mercy.* No other prayer came to mind.

After a few minutes, he heard a familiar voice shouting above the fray. His old nemesis, Alfonzo, had his hands raised toward heaven. The young man shouted at the top of his lungs. Instead of the expected profanities, the man was crying out to God.

"God, in the name of Jesus Christ, stop this violence. Deliver these people from the chains of bitterness, anger, and unforgiveness. Change their hearts; change their minds; change them deep down inside. Take away their hearts of stone and give them hearts of flesh. Bring peace to our community. Free them, God, from the chains that have gripped them for years. Free them to love their brothers and sisters no matter their color."

Had he heard right? Jonah hit himself on the side of the head to clear his ears. The evil man who had ratted on him and caused him nothing but grief had the gall to pray like a saint. Jonah's hands tightened into a fist. He wanted to jerk the man off his high horse and take him down.

I have called you to forgive.

Jonah wilted under the voice of conviction. He had no argument against truth. Again, he had mimicked his namesake with his anger at those God had called him to help. Jonah had no choice. Putting his face into the blacktop, he wept and prayed for God to give him grace to forgive. As the weight of guilt lifted, the Holy Spirit tuned his senses.

Go to Alfonzo—two are better than one. Jonah rebelled

at such a death warrant. He might as well be wearing a bullseye. The first person to recognize him as a former cop would kill him. With the urgency of the situation and the command so clear, Jonah stood on shaky legs. He pushed his way through the angry mob.

Reaching upward, he grasped his former enemy's hand. When Alfonzo recognized him, he whispered to Jonah. "Forgive me, brother."

With those three words, Jonah knew God had changed the man. He squeezed Alfonzo's hand. "Forgive me, brother."

Neither of them had to elaborate. They knew the history between them and the history of their ancestors. Perhaps the forgiveness would extend far into the past. Jonah wasn't sure what God intended, but because he had been forgiven— he must forgive others.

The crowd stilled and looked toward the two with joined hands—one Black, one White. Alfonzo's commanding voice broke the silence. "This man is no longer my enemy. He is my brother, because we belong to the same father, God Almighty. Only God can straighten out this mess. I beg you to go home and let him change you. Pray for his peace to fill your hearts."

Jonah's mouth hung open. The gangs fell back—dazed. Without another word, they scrambled in every direction. Alfonzo lowered their joined hands and grabbed Jonah so tight he struggled to breathe.

In that powerful hug, Jonah discovered something about himself, and he didn't like what he saw. He had dealt with the man for three years. They had talked over pizza and met in dark alleys to exchange information, yet he knew little about Alfonzo as a person. He had not even noticed how the man towered over him or the strength he felt in his massive arms. How could he call himself a Christian and not see Alfonzo as someone for whom Christ died?

Alfonzo broke the spell when he released Jonah and extended his hand. "How about we catch up over a few slices of pizza? I have a story to tell you that will knock your socks off."

Jonah chuckled as he took a few deep breaths. "That's some hold you got, man."

Alfonzo pointed the way and took off toward the Pizza Inn. Jonah rushed to match the man's long stride. God had given Jonah another chance, but this time he would be on the receiving end.

On the way to the restaurant Jonah's phone rang. Katy. He had forgotten to call her. "Honey, everything's fine. I'm going to grab a bite to eat with an old friend. You go on to bed, and we'll talk in the morning."

Once they were seated, Alfonzo said, "I heard you were marrying that woman in the white house."

"Yes, in June."

"You are a blessed man. I'm sorry for the pain I caused both of you."

Jonah looked intently at the changed man across from him. "My flesh wants to give you what-for when I consider our history, but my spirit calls for forgiveness."

"I know. Some of those same guys I ratted on got me hooked on coke. I had to sell to maintain my habit. They were out to destroy me, but I had something a lot of young men do not have. I had a praying mother. She prayed so loud, I heard her even in my drunken slumber. Mama saw something in me that I didn't see in myself. She encouraged me to stay in school and make good grades, but the effort seemed too great. Why work so hard when high school dropouts drove around in fancy cars?

"One night, I couldn't get enough drugs to ease the pain. Each dose yielded wilder hallucinations. I shook so hard I barely got the needle in my arm. The dark alley closed around me, and I knew I'd taken too much. I crumbled into a ball and waited for death to put me out of my misery. But all I saw was the disappointment and sorrow on my mama's face. Her prayers came back to me, and with the little strength I had left, I reached out to God. Your friend found me a few minutes later."

The young man's eyes brightened as he looked at Jonah "I'm surprised Miss Katy didn't tell you, but she got me into a Christian rehab program. Those three months changed me forever."

Jonah didn't know how to respond. He rubbed the back of his head. "Wow, man, I thought we experienced a miracle when the gangs dispersed, but your story tops everything. I'm humbled, brother." He paused to control his emotions before he embarrassed himself in a victory dance. "Besides praying down heaven on a mob, what else are you up to?"

Alfonzo sat up straighter in the booth. "I passed my GED and started classes at the community college. Miss Katy helped me get a job at the Winn Dixie. I'm just taking basic courses until I know what God wants me to do."

He brushed his hand across his short hair. "I hope Miss Katy knows how much I appreciate what she's done for me. You are one lucky man, Mr. Jonah."

"Don't I know it."

Jonah left the restaurant with an extra bounce to his step. He whistled the song by Jesus Culture, "One Thing Remains." The words were so true. No matter how far we stray, God's love never gives up on us.

Not long into their breakfast the next morning, Jonah realized Katy wasn't surprised with Alfonzo's actions. "Alfonzo almost died last fall. Joe called me from the emergency room. I picked up his mother and brought her to the hospital. Since you and I weren't talking at the time, I didn't realize you knew him. You hadn't mentioned him in the investigation, and I didn't see the connection. But his miraculous change renewed my faith in what we are trying to do here. Sometimes, we need a good dose of encouragement, and Alfonzo is a perfect example."

CHAPTER THIRTY

Bees buzzed around the thermometer outside the sunroom. As the days grew warmer, the flowers spread a profusion of color and fragrance over the garden. Katy looked out at the colorful display and thought about her upcoming wedding. Just the thought awakened her desire for the man she loved.

Katy and Jonah had established a routine so cordial it resembled a dance. Every day presented new opportunities along with challenging moments. Despite their contrasting styles—Jonah's casual approach and her strict regimen—they managed to work together.

They handled disagreements and problems with prayer and love. Often, during the day, they stopped what they were doing and fell into each other's arms. When the passionate kisses became too heated, either one or the other would come to their senses. Katy longed for the day when the passion police would no longer be required.

At Jonah's invitation, Alfonzo shared his story at Bible study. The boys sat on the edge of their seats and leaned forward, anxious to hear every word. The young man warned them of the dangers of drugs, alcohol, and gangs. "Bad company corrupts good character," he quoted from the apostle Paul. With tears running down his face, Alfonzo pleaded with the kids. "Haven't we seen the results of hatred and unforgiveness? I beg you to take a different path—the way of love instead of hate, forgiveness instead of bitter grudges."

Some young people took his challenge seriously. They began praying for the skin heads who bullied them at school. Long discussions ensued as they debated ways to bring about reconciliation. The girls suggested cookies and brownies while the boys thought one-on-one meetings would be better.

Katy wasn't certain which method worked best, but after a few weeks, two young White boys arrived. Her heart nearly stopped beating as she envisioned them bringing out guns and mowing them all down. She looked at Jonah and motioned for him to intervene. Katy wanted to scream at him when he shook his head. Couldn't he at least find out what their visitors were up to?

But Jonah no longer worked that way. His lips were moving in silent prayer as he waited on the sidelines. Despite her doubt and fear, Katy watched a miracle unfold. The newcomers hung close to the gate until a couple of guys walked over. After a bit of teasing and fist bumps, they were encouraged to grab a plate. By the next week, the White boys had doubled in number. Regardless of what came next, Katy had learned another lesson in trusting God.

At the end of May, Katy cleaned out the extra closet in her bedroom to make room for Jonah's clothes. She would spend the last week before their wedding with her parents while Jonah's parents stayed with him at the house.

Katy moaned at the stacks of gently used clothes, shoes, and accessories and picked up the phone. "Hey, Cora, I need my matron of honor."

"What's up?"

"Could you come by after work? I'm cleaning out my closets, and I'm overwhelmed. Our 'store' will be running over by the time I take my discards to the attic."

"All those extra outfits making you feel guilty?" Cora laughed to lighten the sting.

"Don't be mean. I almost puked when I found over a hundred pairs of shoes and three leather jackets. Just come help me."

The task took most of the evening, but Katy breathed easier when she stood in the door of their bedroom. She danced through the room and opened the closet doors. The new minimalist look appealed to her. A blanket of warmth spread from head to toe as she thought of the person who would soon share the clean space.

The next morning, she packed a small suitcase to take to her parents'. She would miss Jonah, but she wanted to spend the last week before her wedding with the two people who had always been there for her. His parents and brother would arrive early in the week. Almost every day, her mother had activities planned for the wedding party.

"I'm glad you're here, Katy. Your dad and I were just saying how little we had seen of you since your engagement. I hope you're prepared for a busy week."

Cora and Desiree had to take time from work to participate. Her mother had pursed her lips when Katy announced her matron of honor. "Why, Katy, she's almost as old as I am, and, and ... she works at a chicken plant." Realizing how she must sound, her mother stopped her complaints.

"I know she's not what you expected, but I've never had a better friend. Besides, she'll match the best man," Katy teased while her mother threw up her hands in surrender.

"I don't want to fight, but your ideas can be so frustrating."

"Wait 'til you meet her. She's funny and smart. You can't help but like her."

"You should have chosen at least one of your cousins. If not for Jonah's brother, the whole wedding party would be Black."

When Katy had thought about choosing a maid of honor, she failed to find the first person from her past who qualified. Her rebellious high school friends had scattered shortly after graduation. As far as her angry college comrades, she never heard from them unless they wanted her to appear at some hearing promoting abortion or women's rights. Until she became a Christian, she never understood the value of close friendships. Now she had several, but most came from her own neighborhood.

Katy brushed off her mother's objections and proudly introduced her friends to her mother's cronies at the bridal shower. Cora, with the help of Desiree and Sierra, gave the bridal luncheon at her church's social hall. Despite her mother's distaste, Katy had never laughed so much. Her friends knew how to have a good time without trying to impress or hide behind masks.

"Relax, Mother, and have fun. The mother of the bride shouldn't act so stiff." Katy put her arm around her and gave a tight squeeze.

A moment later, Cora plopped down in the seat next to her mother. "Mrs. Wilson, I would like to tell you what a blessing Katy has been to me. She came to my rescue when I needed her most. Thank you for raising such a wonderful daughter."

Cora knew the right things to say as she praised Katy's work and talked about the different neighborhood programs. Though her mother stiffened when Cora first reached for her, she soon relaxed and returned the warm hug. "My daughter tells me you have become a good friend to her as well."

Unlike Katy's mother, Jonah's mother didn't hesitate as she moved about the room with ease. Regardless of their social standing, their style of clothes, or the color of their skin, she greeted each person as if they were special guests. All the doubts Katy had harbored about her future mother-in-law faded as she opened Deborah's gift. The sexy short nightgown came with a note. "Just a little something to make my son smile." She and Cora had battled over the idea of gifts, but Cora won when she insisted the alluring lingerie would bring fun and laughter.

On the June morning of her wedding, Katy awakened with the music from the processional. "Joyful, Joyful, We Adore Thee" overflowing her spirit. She went to the window and looked out on a beautiful day. Hearing birdsong, she cracked the window to turn up the volume. Her heart sang along as she dressed and floated down the stairs for breakfast with her parents.

Her father met her at the bottom of the stairs with a kiss. "My Katy is getting married. I can't believe I'm giving you to that hoodlum."

Katy hit him playfully. "Well, at least you didn't call him an imbecile."

"After last month's accounting report, I've changed my mind. In fact, I'll have to consider a more appropriate name. Jonah no longer fits the title."

"He never deserved the title, and you know it. I knew you'd come to your senses." Katy snuggled under his arm as they walked toward the breakfast room together.

After the light meal, Katy and her mother met her bridesmaids and Cora at a salon where they relaxed for pedicures and manicures. Katy spent the next hour at the hair and makeup stations. For once, she felt as if she deserved her father's pet name—princess.

An hour before the ceremony, her mother helped her into her Vera Wang gown. The off-shoulder lace straps complemented the lace and beading of the fitted bodice. Swirled with the same design, the silk chiffon skirt draped to the floor in soft folds—ending with a long, detachable train. Katy and her mother stood before the full-length mirror in her mother's bedroom with moisture glazing their eyes.

Katy's father met her in the foyer and walked her out to the curb. "What happened to my little princess?" He kissed her on the nose and helped her into the white horse-drawn carriage. She rode alone with her thoughts to the large church a few blocks from her childhood home.

As she passed the familiar houses, she remembered her idyllic childhood—the spoiled little girl, the rebellious teen, the angry college student, the girl who had everything, yet longed for something more. She caught a tear with her tissue before it smeared her makeup.

Jonah had ushered her into another world. That day on the island turned into a blessing. Though she thought he had rejected her, her boast of not needing any man to make her happy became a reality.

By the time Jonah came to reclaim her, she had learned to depend on God alone. God had changed her into a woman of worth—for his kingdom and for her future husband. The scars from her past were healed, the voices that cried "unclean" were silenced. Katy could walk down the aisle into the arms of her husband as a redeemed bride, clean and pure.

Katy looked up when she heard the driver's sharp command. "Whoa!" The carriage had arrived at the front of the church five minutes before the ceremony. Her misty-eyed father reached for her hand. As they climbed the steps to the sanctuary, he squeezed her and whispered. "You're beautiful, Princess."

They waited outside the double doors while Jonah's brother seated their mothers and the wedding party processed to the sound of "Trumpet Voluntary in D."

Jonah ran his hand down the front of his tuxedo and grinned at his three friends. Joe, Charles, and Jeremy stood next to him on the right side of the altar. To control his nervous energy, Jonah gazed across the room at the wedding guests. He had a glimpse of heaven—a place where every tribe, nation, and tongue would gather around God's throne. If the music had not suddenly changed, he would have danced for joy.

Desiree and Sierra led the procession of Katy's attendants. Jonah grinned when he thought of Sierra's tendency to make exaggerated bows after she had entertained the youth with one of her funny quips. Jonah elbowed Joe when the matron of honor stepped into the aisle.

Her long gold dress shimmered in the candlelight. Cora's eyes sparkled when she looked at Joe. "You're next, bro."

"I know." The older undercover cop had it bad.

A short symphony of bells sounded, and the guests stood and turned their heads. Jonathan and David Caine marched down the aisle carrying intertwined circles of brass rings between them. From each of the lower rings hung ribbons with his and Katy's wedding bands. The top circle had a white silk dove extended in the center. Smothered snickers were heard above the music when the boys swung their cargo to make the bird fly. Jonah chuckled when he remembered Katy's hopes for the symbol. "The dove will swing gracefully in the top circle to represent our union with the Holy Spirit."

More laughter ensued when Hannah and Elizabeth followed their brothers dropping rose petals at intervals while giggling and waving at Jonah and his father. The little cuties stole the show from their brothers.

When the music changed to "Ode to Joy," the wedding planner straightened Katy's train and motioned them forward. Instead of rushing down the aisle, she stood inside the open doors and gazed across the room. Lilies, white bows, candelabra, and magnolias complemented the stained-glass windows, rich mahogany pews, and altar rail. The sun shining through the front window cast rays of light on the brass cross hanging from the ceiling.

With one step over the threshold, she saw a tall handsome man wearing a black tux. Jonah had a mysterious aura about him. She knew the moment he caught a glimpse of her. The expression of love shining from his eyes said it all.

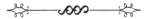

As the music changed, Jonah moved to the center of the aisle. He watched expectantly for the first glimpse of the woman who filled his heart. Moments later, a vision in white stepped through the double doors. Katy's sparkling eyes traveled over hundreds of guests before they found his. Just a glimpse of her smiling face weakened his knees. Her brilliant white wedding dress reminded him of her fear of being unworthy. Of all the men she could have chosen, she had picked him. He didn't deserve her, but during one of the lowest points of his life, God moved her into his world.

Katy's father brought him back to the present with a touch to his arm. "You be good to her, Son, or I'll come after you."

"I'll do my best, Dad." Jonah grinned as he emphasized the name and watched the mayor's expression change from shock to pleasure.

Katy took his hand, and they climbed the steps together. The service was deeply meaningful. Following the opening liturgy, Charles read the powerful words from Colossians.

> Since God chose you to be the holy people he loves, you must clothe yourselves with tenderhearted mercy, kindness, humility, gentleness, and patience. Make allowance for each other's faults and forgive anyone who offends you. Remember, the Lord forgave you, so you must forgive others. Above all, clothe yourselves with love, which binds us all together in perfect harmony. And let the peace that comes from Christ rule in your hearts. For as members of one body you are called to live in peace. And always be thankful. Let the message about Christ, in all its richness, fill your lives. Teach and counsel each other with all the wisdom he gives. Sing psalms and hymns and spiritual songs to God with thankful hearts. And whatever you do or say, do it as a representative of the Lord Jesus, giving thanks through him to God the Father.

After the reading, Charles left the lectern and placed his hand over their joined hands. He prayed over them. "Thank you for calling Jonah and Katy into your story. Together, they are stepping into the work of your kingdom. As you draw them closer together, may they become one with you. Show them how to encourage one another. More than anything, may they be surrounded with your overflowing love."

During the homily, the pastor of the African Methodist Church challenged them from Matthew 16 to take up their cross and follow Jesus. By the end of Reverend Peyton's words, tears dripped from Jonah's chin. Katy dabbed at her eyes to keep from streaking her makeup.

During the exchange of rings and vows, Jonah visualized two hearts becoming one. He held Katy's hand tighter as the Wilson's pastor pronounced them husband and wife. The couple knelt before his father to receive communion—their first act as husband and wife. Following the prayers, a soloist sang the "Our Father." A strong presence of the Holy Spirit filled the church.

When Jonah heard the words "You may now kiss your bride," they stood together. He moved closer and gently lifted Katy's chin. At the touch of her lips, a surge of passionate emotion swept over them. Jonah envisioned the two of them wrapped in a cocoon of love. Words of worship and praise spilled from them as they left the church, singing "For you shall go out with joy and be led forth in peace; the mountains and the hills shall break forth before you."

God could use anyone, but, in his mercy and grace, he had united Jonah and Katy to minister love and reconciliation in the town of Trenton, North Carolina.

Jonah moved about the lengthy reception in a daze, longing to be alone with his bride. When they finally said their goodbyes, they ran to the white carriage through a sea of bubbles and streamers. Jonah refused to wait another minute—he pulled Katy across his lap. "Well, Mrs. Abbott, we're finally alone."

Katy touched his face with her gloved hand and gave him a slow lingering kiss. "I know. The day was surreal—like something out of a fairy tale."

Jonah nuzzled her neck and chuckled. "Not sure about the fairy tale, but I can't wait to get you to the hotel and make you completely mine."

The lengthy kiss left them both breathless as they took the hotel elevator to their room on the fifth floor. After Jonah tipped the hotel attendant and waited for him to leave, he picked Katy up and carried her across the threshold. Waves of love passed between them as she slid down his body and looked into his eyes. Jonah didn't miss the mischievous twinkle. "Guess what, Jonah?"

"I'm about to explode here, and you want to play guessing games?"

Katy giggled and tweaked his nose. No teasing would quench the fire burning inside him. "Don't be brash, Jonah. I only wanted to point out something that we both have longed for—we can finally say goodbye to the passion police."

Jonah threw his head back in unrestrained laughter. "Under the circumstances, it's a good thing."

After many years of waiting, Jonah could freely love the woman God had chosen for him. Katy took his hand and led him further into the room. "Let me show you how much I love you, Jonah Abbott."

And she did.

ABOUT THE AUTHOR

Claudette Renalds has had a varied career—from college to the Pentagon to housewife and mother to Director of Children's Ministry. Several of her short stories and devotionals were included in anthologies published by Capital Christian Writers' Fellowship. Her debut novel, By the Sea, was nominated for the 2020 Selah Awards. Her first historical romance, Journey to Hope, was published in 2020. Jonah's War, her third novel, is a sequel to By the Sea. She and her husband, Charles, live in Haymarket, Virginia.

DISCUSSION QUESTIONS

1. What major events became game changers for Jonah?
2. What motivated Jonah at different points in the story?
3. What caused Jonah to withdraw from his parents? Have you ever felt justified in withholding information from your parents?
4. If you were asked to give a title to chapter eleven, what would it be?
5. Read the Scripture references found in chapter eleven. Discuss the points Jonah makes for abstinence.
6. In the story, what did Katy learn about sexual purity? How did her thinking change?
7. Do you think it realistic to expect a person to save their bodies for marriage? Why?
8. What struck you about Jonah's actions toward the different characters he met throughout the story? How did his attitude change regarding the drug pushers? Those of a different race or culture?
9. How did Jonah's career choices change throughout the story? What motivated those changes? Do you think he will succeed?
10. Did Katy's career change? How? What motivated her?
11. Which character in the story did you most often identify with?
12. List some of the obstacles Jonah and Katy faced in their commitment to one another.
13. Do you think a relationship with someone so different will last? Why or why not?

14. Describe how each family celebrated Christmas. Which description more resembles your family's celebration?
15. What surprised you in the story? What disappointed you? What convicted you?
16. What personal battles are you currently fighting? Are you willing to obey God regardless of the circumstances?
17. Read Ephesians 6:10–18. How might your battles change if you fought them using the apostle Paul's instructions?
18. Write an honest prayer to God. Tell him how you feel about the issues facing our world today. Ask him to give you eyes to see others as he sees them. You might be surprised at what he shows you.

SCRIPTURE REFERENCES

CHAPTER SIX:
Joshua 1:5—He is with us!
Micah 6:6-8—He requires us to do justly, love mercy and walk humbly.
Psalm 139:13-16—We are fearfully and wonderfully made.
1Thessalonians 4:3-5—Avoid sexual immorality.
1 Corinthians 6:19- Our bodies are temples of the Holy Spirit.
1 John 1:9 (King James Version)—God forgives!
2 Corinthians 5:17—We are new creations in Him.

CHAPTER SEVEN:
Ephesians 3:16-17—Christ gives us strength to believe in His forgiveness and love.
John 1:1—He was there from the beginning.

CHAPTER EIGHT:
John 4—Story of the Samaritan woman.
John 4:29 (Message)—He knew her even before she met him.
John 4:13-14—Living Water!
Psalm 51:10-12—Create in me a clean heart.
1 Samuel 11 and 12—Story of David and Bathsheba.

CHAPTER ELEVEN:
Genesis 2:25—Naked but not ashamed!
Proverbs 18:22—Advice to young men: Find a good wife!
Matthew 5:32—Jesus speaks against divorce and adultery.
Mark 10:9 (New American Standard Bible)—Wedding Vows.
Hebrews 13:4—Remain faithful in your marriage.
1 Corinthians 6:18—Flee from sexual immorality.

1 Corinthians 6:19-20—Honor God with your body.
1 John 1:7 (King James Version)—Walk in the Light.
1 Thessalonians 4:3-5—Control your passion.

CHAPTER FOURTEEN:
Matthew 5:4—Blessed are those who mourn.

CHAPTER FIFTEEN:
John 10:11—He laid down is life for us!
Matthew 18:12-14—He is the Good Shepherd who searches for the lost sheep.

CHAPTER TWENTY:
Jeremiah 29:11—God has a plan for you.
Jeremiah 29:13—He wants us to seek him with our whole hearts.

CHAPTER TWENTY-ONE
Jeremiah 29:11—God wants the best for us.

CHAPTER TWENTY-TWO:
Matthew 5:14-16—Jesus calls us the light of the world.

CHAPTER TWENTY-THREE:
Matthew 6:14-15—We must forgive to receive God's forgiveness.

CHAPTER TWENTY-FOUR:
Jonah 1-4—The biblical Jonah's story.
Acts 18:1-3—Paul makes tents with Aquila and Priscilla.
Jeremiah 29:11—God's plans are the best!

CHAPTER TWENTY-FIVE:
Isaiah 43:1—We belong to Him.

CHAPTER TWENTY-EIGHT:
Luke 2:1-20—The Christmas Story.

CHAPTER THIRTY:
1 Corinthians 15:33—Bad company corrupts!
Colossians 3:12-17—You are chosen by God.
Matthew 16:24-25—Take up your cross and follow Him.
Isaiah 55:12 (New King James Version)—We shall go out with JOY!

CPSIA information can be obtained
at www.ICGtesting.com
Printed in the USA
LVHW020258240522
719520LV00010B/1095